LUCKY SIGNALLER

LUCKY SIGNALLER

Michael Hancock

The Book Guild Ltd
Sussex, England

The Book Guild Ltd.
25 High Street,
Lewes, Sussex

First published 1998

Set in Times
Typesetting by
Acorn Bookwork, Salisbury, Wiltshire

Printed in Great Britain by
Bookcraft (Bath) Ltd, Avon

A catalogue record for this book is
available from the British Library

ISBN 1 85776 326 2

CONTENTS

FOR MY GRANDCHILDREN

Many people regret, when it is too late, that they did not seek from their parents or grandparents, or others of their more elderly friends and relations, details of their activities in years gone by. I recently compiled, from the researches of others, a family tree going back many generations. This merely gives names and dates. How much more interesting it would be to know what sort of people they were and what they did apart from being born, getting married, giving birth to the next generation and dying. With this in mind, and pressed myself by younger friends, Tony and Penny Andrews, I have written this personal story which may interest my grandchildren and future generations.

I have never succeeded in keeping a diary and so the whole of this is written from memory. There are therefore bound to be some errors but I do not think that they are significant. Necessarily I have left out much that is dull and, in common with most autobiographers, have probably also omitted some less creditable episodes!

The book may amuse some of my contemporaries. If, however, it should come into the hands of any young man contemplating an army life in the future, he must remember that the conditions of his service will be very different. But I am sure that it can be just as much fun and as worthwhile.

FOREWORD

Admiral of the Fleet The Lord Hill-Norton GCB

Michael Hancock has written a most interesting and informative account of his life, which has so far covered about 80 years of peace and war, and for half of which he was in the army. He writes in a clear and succinct style, with an economy of language and a dry wit, which makes for an easy and entertaining read.

What follows is not a history of the war, nor even of his part in it, but an interesting thread in the tapestry of soldiering in peace and war, by a man of great integrity and zeal, who overcame a number of serious difficulties to rise to the rank of general officer.

He started this present endeavour for the benefit of his family, a most worthwhile objective, and in chapter 2 we quickly learn what an unusually large, diverse and extended family it is. Throughout his many and widely spread appointments all over the world, it seems that wherever he was sent to serve there was to be found an aunt or a cousin or a sister either of his own or of his wife's. Coming as I do from an exceptionally small family, this seems very much to be envied, and the detail will be of lasting interest to all those who come after the two of them.

He had what, for him, must have been a most frustrating war. We read in the first dozen chapters, of his many changes of job, starting something up here and moving to there, from 1939 to 1942, but never getting to the sharp end, where he, like all of us, naturally wanted to be. Indeed, his only real spell of fighting was in Tunisia where he and his signallers made a most important contribution. Quite often, these many changes contributed to his remarkable record of good luck: men he relieved went off and almost at once got killed; operations for which he had prepared were delayed and by the time they came off turned into disasters, but by then he had been posted away. His description of the muddle which all arms suffered in the first year of the war, brings to vivid life what his generation and mine can even now remember so well, though they seldom find a place in more formal histories.

In what are really asides to the main narrative, we are taken into the arcane (and to a sailor almost incomprehensible) area of army brevet promotions; to the impact on the size of your married quarter of whether you are in a staff or command appointment; to over payment 'by fact' or 'by accident'. We are given a first-rate account of some of the serious difficulties for the army in the years leading up to the independence and partition of the Indian subcontinent; and the wise words of General Auchinleck on the always awkward and controversial exercise by the military of 'Aid to the Civil Power'. Later, his story covers the withdrawal of France from the military structure of NATO, and the consequent move of its headquarters to Belgium. We also learn some of the problems in Far East Command when, first, it became a unified commander-in-chief's appointment, and 10 years later when the whole Command was withdrawn. Hancock was privileged to play a part in all these seminal events and his account brings them vividly to life.

Running through great military landmarks such as these, and his increasingly important part in them, we learn a great deal of the man. He was skilled in several non-military activities; a glider pilot, an aircraft pilot, a skier, a sailor of boats, a golfer, all related with modesty. He was without doubt and as his title asserts, lucky; and was so in things both great and small: the Customs were conveniently absent when he returned to the country with grog or silk stockings; after nearly being invalided out of the army he recovered completely from TB to reach general's rank; he was made a brevet lieutenant-colonel just before this system was abolished; he walked away from his flying accidents when they might have killed him, he might well have drowned or been severely injured on half a dozen occasions before he was 10 years old. Above all, but of a different sort of luck altogether, he married a charming wife (whom I have had the privilege of knowing for many years) and with whom he celebrated their golden wedding several years ago; and they are blessed with loving children and grandchildren.

Throughout his army service Hancock was privileged and fortunate to work for a succession of most distinguished senior officers, and this stood him in good stead in his own progress from one posting and one rank to another. The jocular tag 'it's not what you know but who you know' applied in the army of his day, and stood him in good stead more than once.

His stated objective in starting this work was to bring to life the bare bones of his place in his family tree, for the interest and information of his descendants. I can assert with confidence that his account fills the bill admirably, and I commend it to you, who are about to start reading it.

HILL-NORTON
October 1997

HANCOCK

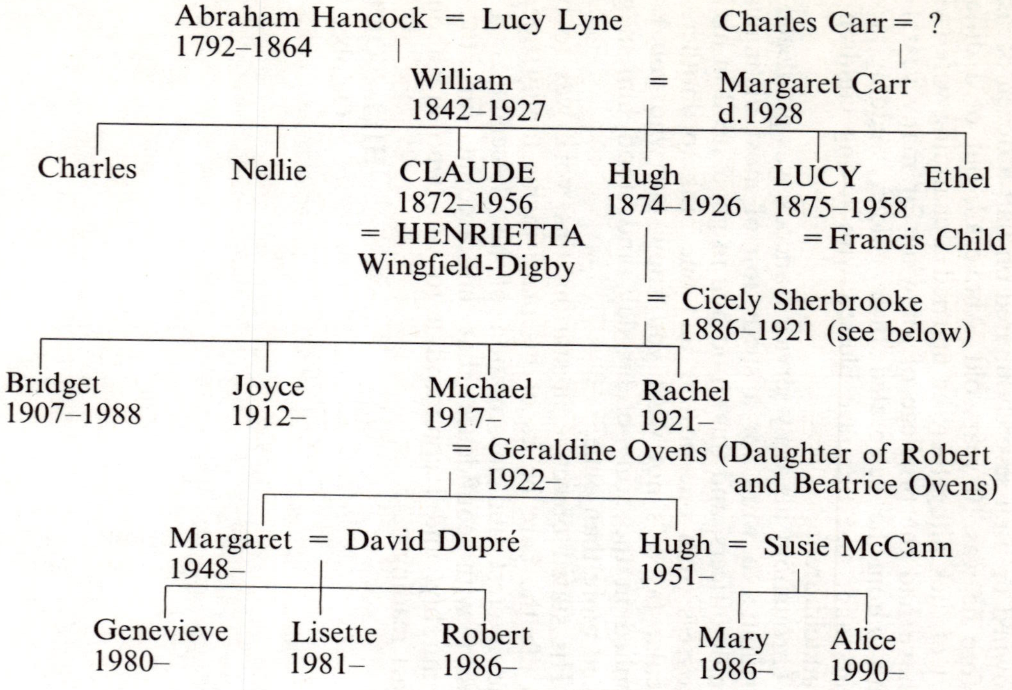
Abraham Hancock = Lucy Lyne
1792–1864
Charles Carr = ?
William
1842–1927
=
Margaret Carr
d.1928
Charles
Nellie
CLAUDE
1872–1956
= HENRIETTA
Wingfield-Digby
Hugh
1874–1926
LUCY
1875–1958
= Francis Child
Ethel
= Cicely Sherbrooke
1886–1921 (see below)
Bridget
1907–1988
Joyce
1912–
Michael
1917–
Rachel
1921–
= Geraldine Ovens (Daughter of Robert
1922–
and Beatrice Ovens)
Margaret = David Dupré
1948–
Hugh = Susie McCann
1951–
Genevieve
1980–
Lisette
1981–
Robert
1986–
Mary
1986–
Alice
1990–

SHERBROOKE

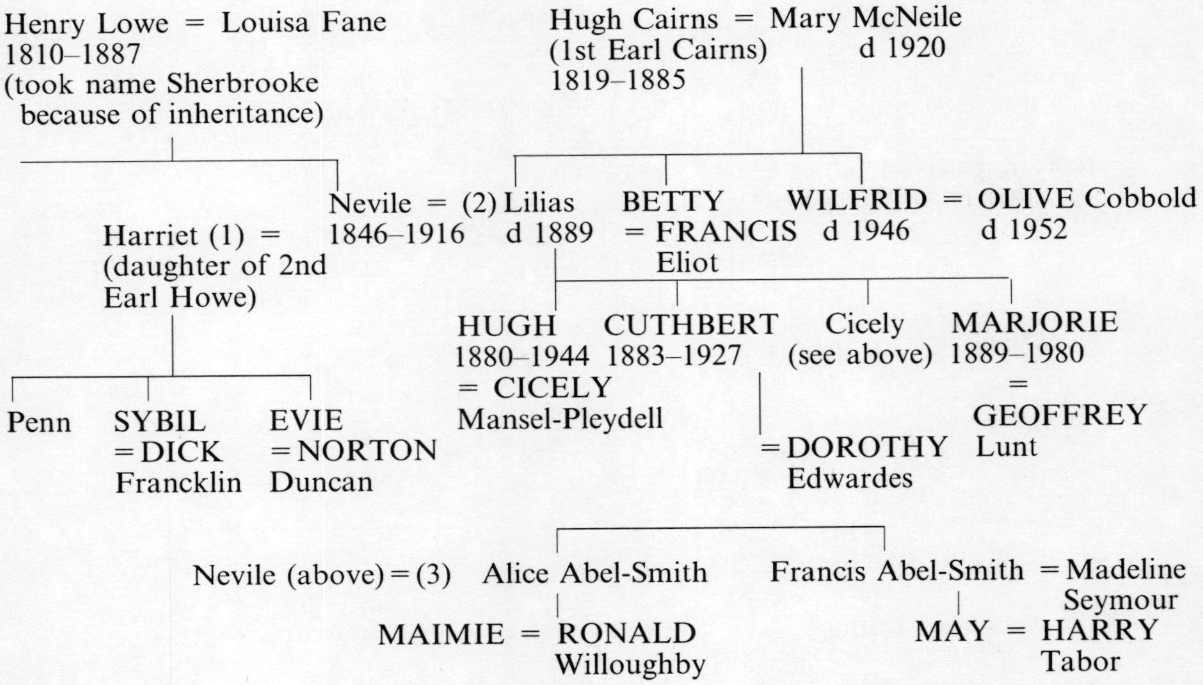

AUNT and UNCLES (Chapter 2) are in BLOCKS

PROLOGUE

At the age of 3 I was sailing a small boat on the end of a string in the 'River' Bourne at Bournemouth, where, at a width of perhaps 12 or 15 feet, it flowed through the formal gardens between the Square and the Pier. When I turned to pull the boat upstream, the gentle current took me by surprise and I fell in. This was hardly life-threatening and my nurse, Edith Chapman, got me out with all speed.

Four years later my father took my elder sisters, Bridget, 16, and Joyce, 12, and me in our bull-nosed Morris for a picnic on the Dorset coast at Chapman's Pool: the coincidence of the name Chapman I found confusing. After tea we children walked down to the sea and on the way back we got into a bog. I sank up to my thighs and might well have gone further. Joyce had her work cut out to avoid a similar fate but Bridget somehow or other managed to get to me and, lying on one or two firmer grass patches, succeeded in extricating me.

When I was 9 and only just beginning to swim, Bridget and I were bathing near Southbourne when I got out of my depth on a slight outgoing tide. Again Bridget rescued me.

The next year I was staying north of Dundee with a family called Agnew for the Easter holidays. Their son, Quentin, and I were playing in their disused outhouses and then climbed on the roof of one of them. I sat in the top of a big square chimney, built of brick with a solid stone top, and was careless enough to slip into it. The chimney tapered as it went down and I was stuck with my hips wedged cornerwise. I shouted to Quentin to get help and it seemed a long time before I could persuade him that I really was in trouble. For some time after that I waited impatiently, with dusk approaching, until I discovered that the brickwork was rotten. I thought that all I had to do was to kick it to pieces and climb down: but I had not allowed for the solidity and weight of the square stone top. I overbalanced and rolled down the sloping roof and then fell another 10 feet on to cobblestones below, complete with the unbroken stone chimney top. The rescue party arrived just as this happened. I was astonishingly lucky to have no more than scratches on my face and a headache. When a week later I fell into a duck pond, my long-suffering hostess could stand no more and my visit was terminated prematurely.

Newly commissioned from the Shop (Royal Military Academy Woolwich) I attended the usual 18-month Q Course (Qualifying Course for Royal Signals) at Catterick Camp. One of a series of old cars, mostly costing around £5, that I then had was an Austin 7 which had no body other than front seats and a bonnet. One evening another YO (young officer), Charles Golden, who had an MG Midget, and I decided to race by timing laps around a square of roads in the camp. I took one corner too late and turned over through a three-quarter turn, pivoting when upside down on the radiator cap, the steering wheel and my head. Luckily I suffered no material injury and the car was still drivable.

Whilst at Catterick another YO, Tony Deane-Drummond, persuaded David Gibson and me to take up gliding. In those days only single-seater machines were available and so one had to learn solo but the additional risks from this were offset by the slow flying speed, normally between 20 and 30 knots. In the early stages I broke a wing in two but otherwise came to no harm.

As result of these incidents, and others, I had probably developed an unjustified faith in my own indestructibility. Certainly I seemed to have had more than my share of good fortune. Moreover it will be seen that I had much good luck for the rest of my career in the army. Hence the title of this book. Nevertheless I believe that to some extent luck comes to the person who is ready to take a chance and I am wholly opposed to the advice which used to be widespread, 'Never volunteer'. Napoleon always asked if a general were lucky, no doubt meaning was he lucky in battle. I think that an officer is unlikely to become a general unless he has more than his share of luck of all kinds.

1

FAMILY

My paternal grandparents, Canon William Hancock and Margaret Carr, were married in 1869. William's paternal ancestors all came from around the Devon and Cornwall border but his father, Abraham, acquired in the 1820s a property in Ropley, Hampshire: The Grove. When he died in 1864 William inherited it at the age of 22 but, as he was then, I presume, in the process of becoming a parson, he cannot have lived there for long. However he did not sell The Grove until around 1908 and I remember being told by an uncle that he had sold it to an admiral who had a daughter with tuberculosis. As result the admiral had built on a large enclosed balcony where she could get plenty of fresh air even in poor weather. In 1957 I was travelling in a train from Waterloo to Ash Vale, which is on the line to Alton, and, because I had to be in uniform, was in the unwonted comfort of first class. The only other person in my compartment was a lady in her 60s and we got talking in a casual way until I discovered that she was going on from Alton to Ropley. I asked if she knew The Grove and found that she was the admiral's daughter.

My grandmother was the daughter of Charles Carr of Cramlington Hall, north of Newcastle, and her ancestors all seem to have come from Northumberland or thereabouts. She and William had 7 children, of whom my father, Hugh, was the fourth, born in 1874. Four years later William became vicar of Halifax and in 1888 moved on to be vicar of Knaresborough, where he remained for the next 32 years, retiring at the age of 78 in 1920.

One gets an idea of the size of establishment maintained by a parson with a good living in those days by visiting the present council offices in Knaresborough, which used to be the vicarage. Cousins 10 years or more older than I, who remember our grandparents well, told me that William was jolly, generous and a spendthrift. Certainly his children inherited little or nothing, although The Grove, a 10 or more bedroomed Queen Anne house with a considerable estate, must have been sold well. Margaret is reputed to have been much more serious but I have a portrait of her in her 20s in which she appears to be a most attractive and charming girl. My only recollection of them is at a luncheon party when I was about 5. My grandfather was distinctly stout and, in a pause in the conversation, I said, 'Grandfather, why do you wear a pillow?'. Grandfather was hugely amused but grandmother was not.

My father went to school at Rossall and thence to Cambridge and into the church. He met my mother when he was 24 and she was 12 and decided then and there to wait for her to grow up. They were married 8 years later.

My mother's father, Nevile Sherbrooke, born in 1846, second son in a Nottinghamshire family, was commissioned into the 43rd Foot and later entered the church. He was the minister at Portman Chapel, London, and later rector of Clifton, Bristol. He married in 1871 Lady Alice, only child of the 2nd Earl Howe, by whom he had 3 children; she died in 1875 at the birth of their third child. His uncle, Robert Lowe, Viscount Sherbrooke, was Gladstone's Chancellor of the Exchequer, which may be how he met his second wife, Lilias, daughter of the 1st Earl Cairns, who was twice Disraeli's Lord Chancellor. They were married in 1878. She had 4 children, of whom my mother, Cicely, was the third, born in 1886. Lilias died in 1889 at the birth of her last child. Nevile then married Alice Abel-Smith, whose family were connected with Smith's Bank. A local paper at the time of the third marriage commented that the first was for beauty, the second for duty and the third for booty!

My parents were married in early January 1907 and my

eldest sister, Bridget, was born in late October. My father became rector of Welbourn in Lincolnshire in 1908 and in due course they moved into the new 'small' rectory, only 8 bedrooms. My next sister, Joyce, was born there in 1912. By the end of that year, my father decided that it was his duty to go as a missionary to Japan and in January 1913 the whole family set off by sea from Liverpool, calling at Malta, Port Said, Colombo, Penang, Singapore, Hong Kong and Shanghai, finally arriving at Kobe in Japan. They settled into their new home in Hiroshima on 24 March.

Bridget had been ill on the voyage out and made no proper recovery. Finally it was decided that, for her sake, the family would have to return to England and they left Kobe in September. Although I believe little was known of the disease in those days, it appears with hindsight that she had meningitis, which to some extent incapacitated her throughout her life.

My father's next job was to be rector of Furneaux Pelham in Hertfordshire, and in 1915 he became vicar of St Paul's Church, Bournemouth. As a boy he had had scarlet fever, which was a more serious illness than it is now considered to be and as a result he had not been accepted for the Royal Navy. For the same reason he was not accepted as an army chaplain in 1914. I was born in St Paul's vicarage in July 1917. By that stage in the war the authorities were no longer so strict about health in accepting volunteers and in September my father left for France, becoming chaplain to the 8th Battalion, the Yorkshire Regiment. In November the battalion was moved from the western front to the Italian front. In April 1918 my father went down with tuberculosis and was invalided home.

Having apparently recovered, my father became rector of Leadenham in Lincolnshire in 1919 but he had a relapse in 1920. Switzerland was then considered to be the best place to convalesce after tuberculosis and my parents went to Davos in that autumn. Meanwhile we 3 children, with my nurse, Edith Chapman, the daughter of the village carpenter in Leadenham, went to stay with our grandmother, our mother's stepmother, Alice Sherbrooke, in a large house near the cliffs at Bournemouth, The Red Court. My parents returned in April 1921 to collect us from The Red Court and we all went to live in Switzerland at Chateau D'Oex. On 17 November my mother died giving birth to twins, one of which, a boy, was stillborn: the other was my sister Rachel. We stayed on in Chateau D'Oex until the following spring, when my father decided that he was well enough to resume work and we went back to Leadenham, where the living had been held open for him.

During the next winter he was ill again and had to give up Leadenham. We then rented a small semi-detached house in Westbourne, a suburb of Bournemouth, and only about a mile from The Red Court. I attended a kindergarten immediately next door. In early 1924, my father bought a house on the edge of what was then an isolated village some miles from Poole, Broadstone. He seemed to keep very well while we were there, doing some carpentry, keeping bees and occasionally playing a little mild family tennis. I attended another kindergarten, run by a retired naval captain.

The chief event of that year for me was being taken to the Great Exhibition at Wembley. My father particularly took me to see a very realistic demonstration with models of the Royal Navy's raid on Zeebrugge. I imagine that his particular interest in this item stemmed from his inability to get into the navy. Rather later I was not accepted by either the navy or the air force because I am mildly colour-blind.

In early 1925 my father tried once more to resume work and took on the very small parish of Shalden, near Alton in Hampshire. In May I was sent to a preparatory school, Pembroke Lodge, Southbourne, near Bournemouth. After my time there it moved to Fordingbridge and was renamed Sandle Manor. My cousin and near twin, John Sherbrooke, whose father was in the army serving in India, had gone there 2 terms earlier just after his 7th birthday. My father felt well enough in that summer term to play in the Fathers v Sons cricket match (scoring a duck!) but was ill again in November. He went into a nursing home in Bournemouth and we children spent Christmas with our grandmother, who had by then moved into a smaller house, Sunnington. A month or so later my father bought a house on the cliffs at Southbourne less than half a mile from Pembroke Lodge. He moved into this house on the basis of being permanently in bed.

I got scarlet fever at the end of the Easter term and had to go into an isolation hospital, where I caught chickenpox. After that I had already missed half the summer term and it was decided that I should stay at home and miss the rest of it.

During the next term, my father died, on 17 November 1926, exactly 5 years after my mother.

2

AUNTS AND UNCLES

My elder sisters, Bridget and Joyce, and I stayed on in Southbourne and an aunt, Maimie Sherbrooke, came to live with us and look after us. Her mother, our step-grandmother, was only 4 miles away in Bournemouth and there was a close liaison between the 2 households, particularly as our youngest sister, Rachel, was living with her. Bridget, who was 19 when our father died, nobly stayed on at home, helping to run the household and doing the cooking. Joyce went to school in Bournemouth, staying with friends near the school from Monday to Friday and coming home for weekends. I continued to board at my prep school and, as was common practice in those days, was only allowed home for a Sunday twice in each term.

Pembroke Lodge was, I believe, a good prep school and it had the advantage that Mr Meakin, the headmaster and owner, was well off and able to subsidise the school when he saw fit. He provided occasional picnic days in the New Forest by coach and other outings. When it froze enough to flood a lawn for skating, he provided enough skates for the whole of the senior part of the school. There was a great emphasis on games, particularly cricket, and as I was bad at all the games, cricket, soccer, rugger and athletics, I did not enjoy them. But my first 3 years at Marlborough were worse. I think that in both cases the fault was mine, largely because I found it very difficult to make friends. Only in my last 2 years at Marlborough did I begin to develop the self-confidence to enjoy a reasonable part of the time. Altogether my schooldays were far from 'the best days of my life' and I shall recall no more of them.

For parts of my holidays I was nearly always sent to stay with various of my many relations. Why this was I now find it difficult to understand; my own home with my own family, however limited the financial resources, would have been preferable. I was sent for a month one summer holidays to a holiday home for boys whose parents were in places too distant for them to go home and this to me was worse than going to a new school and having little to do but play games badly. Going to stay with relations was much better than that. It meant that I had to learn to fit in with all sorts of households in all sorts of income brackets and this gave me a wide experience of different kinds of family life. I probably developed a measure of adaptability and tolerance. It was very good of them to put up with such a visitor and I must have been a great nuisance. I was lucky to have so many welcoming relations, some of whom I will describe in order to show their variety.

My mother's half-sisters by my grandfather's first marriage, Evie and Sybil, were 2 very different people. Evie was married to a very devout low church parson with the strictest views on conduct, particularly on Sundays. Ordinary playing cards were always forbidden: they were the devil's picture books. On weekdays picture cards, such as for happy families, were permitted. One must not use a bicycle, still less a car, on a Sunday because it gave more work to policemen but an exception could be made if it were the only practicable way of getting to church. They had 6 children, of whom the youngest was Lionel, a boy of my own age who was as much irked by these rules as I was. The 4 eldest, 2 boys and 2 girls, all became missionaries: China, the Arctic, India and at home.

Sybil, on the other hand, lived a comfortable, rural life in Nottinghamshire with a retired husband who was very keen on horse racing. He kept volumes of records, from which he devised various betting systems: they kept him occupied but I don't imagine that they were profitable.

HANCOCK

Abraham Hancock = Lucy Lyne   Charles Carr = ?
1792–1864

William = Margaret Carr
1842–1927   d.1928

Charles   Nellie   CLAUDE 1872–1956 = HENRIETTA Wingfield-Digby   Hugh 1874–1926   LUCY 1875–1958 = Francis Child   Ethel

Hugh = Cicely Sherbrooke
1886–1921 (see below)

Bridget 1907–1988   Joyce 1912–   Michael 1917–   Rachel 1921–

Michael = Geraldine Ovens (Daughter of Robert and Beatrice Ovens)
1922–

Margaret 1948– = David Dupré   Hugh 1951– = Susie McCann

Genevieve 1980–   Lisette 1981–   Robert 1986–   Mary 1986–   Alice 1990–

SHERBROOKE

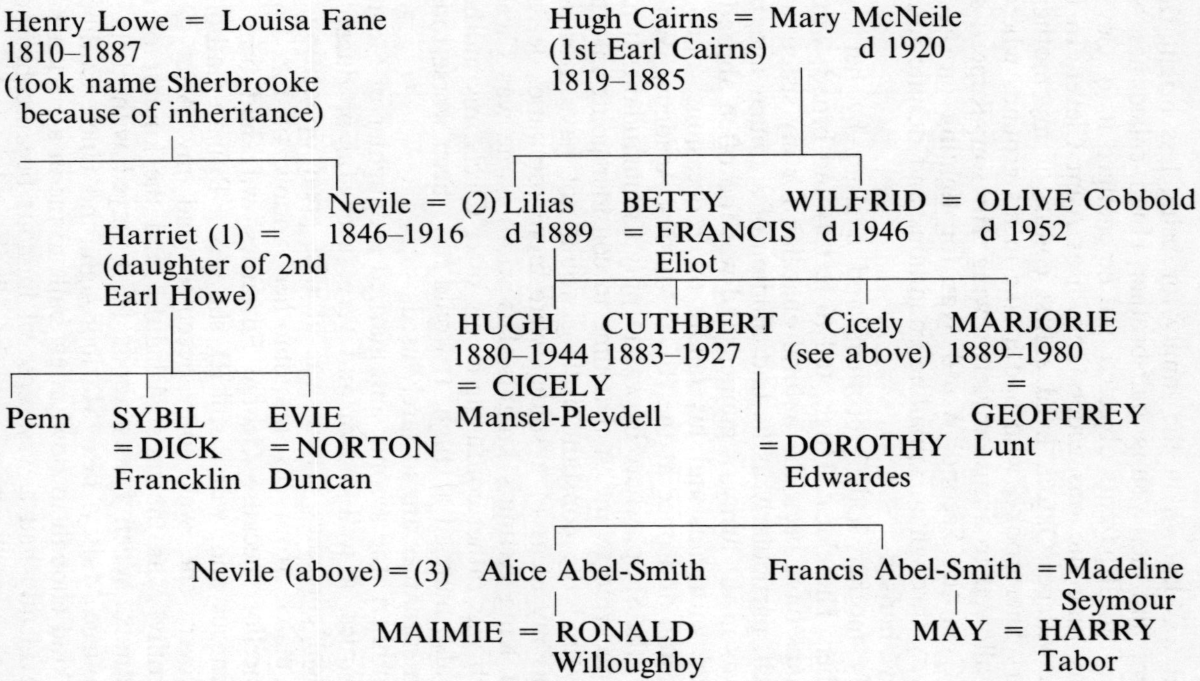

AUNT and UNCLES (Chapter 2) are in BLOCKS

Sybil was known in the family for being less bright than others and her young half-brother Hugh called her 'old stupid' until parents objected and he changed it to 'clever'; in my time she was widely known as Aunt Clever. In the same village, Oxton, lived a first cousin of my mother's. Henry Sherbrooke, who had a lake in his grounds where I was allowed to amuse myself rowing. His son, Rupert, got a VC in the Second World War for fighting an Arctic convoy through in appalling conditions and despite losing an eye himself.

My mother had 2 brothers and a sister by her own mother. The eldest, Hugh, tall (6 feet 4) and broad, would perhaps have been the natural guardian for my sisters and myself, particularly as he had children of a similar age, but he was in the army, a gunner, and was too often abroad. I stayed with him and his family on 2 occasions, once in Kingston and once at the Royal Military Academy, Woolwich, the Shop, where he was Deputy Commandant. It had not occurred to me at that time to consider going into the army and the constant drilling would not have attracted me as my ideas of a soldier were more romantic: derived from King Arthur's knights. His wife's name was Cicely, which was rather confusing as his sister Cicely, my mother, had also married a Hugh. It would have been worse today when surnames are so rarely used.

Cuthbert, the second son, married a daughter of George Edwardes, a well-known and very successful producer of musical comedies. There was at first great opposition to this match from his grandmother, widow of the Lord Chancellor, because George Edwardes' wife had been in the chorus and, worse still (!), she was a Roman Catholic. However, she was soon accepted and my Aunt Dot (Dorothy) was the most delightful and the kindest of all my aunts. When I was about 11, I stayed with them at Ogbourne Maisey, near Marlborough, and Uncle Cuthbert was kind enough to bowl a few balls to me in a cricket net. He evidently had a wry sense of humour because he soon excused himself, saying that he felt ill and had the same complaint as my mother had died of: she had died in childbirth. He died only a few days later – of drink. I, and my son after me, had many happy days with Aunt Dot when at school at Marlborough.

The youngest of this part of the family was Marjorie, who married a parson, Geoffrey Lunt. I stayed with them when he had a parish in Sheffield and again in Portsea, a part of Portsmouth, where Geoffrey had a number of churches and 12 curates. It was a job which normally led to further preferment and he went on to be Bishop of Ripon and then Salisbury. He was a large man with a large round head and a large round body; when I read a quotation in Wavell's *Other Men's Flowers* from a poem by Raymond Asquith which started, 'The sun like a bishop's bottom, round and rosy and hot', I knew exactly what it meant. They were very kind to me as a boy and later when I was at Catterick and they at Ripon. Marge, as she was usually known, was apt, in all innocence, to put her foot in it but Geoff was adept at retrieving the situation. When at the Palace at Ripon they had about 20 young people to stay for a weekend's study, she made them welcome, apologising for them having to share rooms and saying that she hoped that they were all sleeping with the person they wanted to. Geoffrey much enjoyed an occasion when he was staying in a small country inn, where the Boots had been suitably briefed what to say when he woke the bishop in the morning; he knocked and announced 'It's the Lord, m'boy!'

Maimie, the only child of my grandfather's third marriage, was the only one unmarried when my father died. Although she was 8 years younger, my mother appears to have had a much closer rapport with her than any other of her siblings. When my parents went to Japan in 1913, for my father to be a missionary, my mother wrote 20 long letters to her half-sister, Maimie, eg after leaving Colombo, 'I said to Hugh directly I saw this lady, "See if she is not a missionary". . . . Her hair was coming down and of course her petticoat was shewing!! This is only for you because without any doubt she was better than I could ever hope to be! But why oh why need their petticoats shew!'

Maimie continued to be close to my father and to help him with the problems of moving house at the times when he was ill. So it was natural that this very sympathetic aunt should take over the upbringing of our family when my father died. Sad to relate, I doubt whether we ever said thank you; certainly I just took it for granted.

My most exotic holiday at this time was travelling to Switzerland in the summer of 1929 to spend a month in a hotel in Grindelwald, the Schönegg, with my great-aunt Kathleen Eliot, my mother's mother's sister, and her husband, Uncle Francis. As was unusual in those days, she insisted that everyone should call her by the christian name that she preferred to use, Betty. Francis was a parson, in, I suppose, his 60s, who had the delightful job of Archdeacon of Gibraltar. This meant that he was concerned with all the Church of England churches around the north Mediterranean coast from Gibraltar to Malta and that he had direct responsibility for the English church in Beaulieu in the south of France. There were at that time many English who spent the winter months in the pleasant winter climate of the French Riviera and so he looked after his own parish from about November to April. He normally went to England for the next 2 or 3 months, taking a locum job in Switzerland between July and September and then visiting some of his archdeaconry. He had been a keen mountaineer, being one of the earlier people to climb the Eiger in the 1890s. It must have been as much of a shock for the headmaster of my prep school, Mr Meakin, as for me when we came face to face staying in the same hotel, the Schönegg in Grindelwald!

Two holidays I spent with my father's brother, Uncle Claude Hancock, and Aunt Etta (short for Henrietta Maria). They had brought up 6 children in a village near Worcester and could not have been kinder hosts although clearly very limited financially: no domestic help, no electricity or gas, all water to be pumped by hand. They kept about 700 chickens. I very much enjoyed these visits.

At another time I stayed with my great-uncle Wilfrid and great-aunt Olive Cairns. He was the third son of the Lord Chancellor but had inherited the title as his 2 elder brothers had died childless. Uncle Wilfrid, who was an invalid, needing sticks to walk very slowly, had an electric bath chair, a rarity in those days, and the chauffeur allowed me to drive it to the front door on one occasion: it would do about 25 m.p.h. They had a specially designed car, a Minerva, with extra leg room for my uncle's comfort and a boot in which to carry the chair. This enabled them not only to visit friends but also to make an annual visit to Germany to take the waters. Their butler, Evan Tomkins, who, unusually in those days, was always called by his Christian name, had a son of my age and when we were about 10 or 12 we played together, roaming over a considerable estate with little restriction. The principal game that I remember was played with bows and arrows which we cut and made ourselves and then shot at each other, perhaps from a reasonably safe distance. Then we discovered that if one put a nail into the head of a bamboo arrow it would fly further and more accurately. We both survived unhurt!

During a later visit I decided to take a photograph of a swan on their lake and, having difficulty in getting close enough, I rigged up my camera on a tripod on the bank with a string and a weight on the trigger and a stone under the weight. To this stone I then attached a long string which, with a rowing boat, I led out on to the lake and attached to a float. I then tried to chase the swan in front of the camera whilst I pulled the string. The swan won. It tripped over the string and took a photograph of me in the boat.

In 1930 there were changes. In the summer term Aunt Maimie married Lieutenant-Commander Ronald Willoughby (RN retired) and I got a foundation scholarship for Marlborough. Only sons of clergy were allowed to enter for these scholarships and there were 14 of them each year; so this was not the distinction it sounds. Nevertheless it was worth £50 a year out of fees, which for all sons of clergy were reduced from £150 to £135.

As result of my aunt's marriage, our house at Southbourne was sold and the Willoughbys bought a house in Guildford. Bridget went off to various occupations. Joyce, aged 18, was unofficially engaged to a third cousin once removed, Francis Fane, who was then farming with his brother Harry in the Northern Transvaal. She, and I for my holidays, were based with the Willoughbys. Rachel continued in Bournemouth but during the next summer our grandmother died and she was added to the Willoughby household.

In August 1931 Joyce and Francis were married from Beaumanor Park, in Leicestershire, the home of our late step-grandmother's widowed sister-in-law, which shows how this extensive family kept in close touch and were always willing to help. It was a marvellous house for such an occasion: I found I had to share a bedroom with a cousin because there were only 28 bedrooms!

Towards the end of that holiday I was in Bournemouth at my late grandmother's house whilst her daughter, Aunt Maimie, cleared it up for disposal. I complicated her work by getting a severe attack of 'flu. I then went back for my fourth term at Marlborough. I spent the first 3 weeks of the Christmas holidays with the Eliots in Beaulieu and the last week with my father's sister and her husband, Lucy and Francis Child, in Bordighera, where he, a partially retired doctor, had taken a locum for the winter. I had stayed with them several times in England. Their youngest daughter Nonie (Oenone) was about my age and, in earlier years, we had both had clockwork Hornby railways which when amalgamated made a fine railway system. I remember this Bordighera visit chiefly for putting my foot in it at a meal. The conversation had turned on the Ten Commandments and I in all innocence said, 'What is adultery?' My uncle and his three daughters sat in stunned silence. Eventually Aunt Lucy said, 'Your uncle will explain to you afterwards': a task which he clearly did not relish.

When I got back to London, I was put into a hospital for observation as result of the 'flu I had had earlier, thereby missing the start of the next term. It was decided that I should miss that term altogether and in March 1932 I was despatched to live with more remote cousins, the Tabors, who lived in the country a few miles out of Wolverhampton. Harry Tabor had lost a job with Tarmac due to the slump. Of average height, he was dark and good-looking, with a frequent smile and a nice sense of humour. His wife, May, was very large and moved slowly on a tennis court but she had a wicked underhand serve. There was current at that time a phrase of American origin, 'big boy', which was used in a polite context, and the Tabor sons got the habit of using it to their father. But he put his foot down when one of them called his mother 'big girl'.

From my point of view this was a very good move because they had 4 children, a girl and a boy older than me and 2 boys younger. They were very good to me and treated me as entirely one of the family. So for the next 2 or 3 years I had a settled home to go to for my holidays and there was no question of my being pushed off to stay elsewhere, apart from one holiday with my sister Joyce and her husband Francis when they were back from South Africa for 6 months.

3

WOOLWICH, CATTERICK, ALDERSHOT: 1936–40

Whilst with the Tabors the question of my future career was considered and I found that several of my many relations wanted to have a say in the matter. My own first choice was to go into the RAF but this seemed doubtful because I am somewhat colour-blind. So it was arranged that I should go to the Air Ministry for a preliminary medical examination, about a year before I could make a formal application. I was put through all sorts of tests and the last was on colour sight. The doctors were very sympathetic about it but were quite definite that there was no question of my being a pilot. They seemed almost as disappointed as I was, because I had passed all the other tests to their entire satisfaction, which was apparently not too common amongst preliminary applicants. Whilst in London for these tests, I took the opportunity to go to the Science Museum to see a demonstration of television, which, in I think 1934, was very new.

The Tabor's next suggestion was that I should work my way up in local engineering industry and in particular that I should join a firm in the Wolverhampton area where I could continue to live with them and travel daily by motorcycle. This had two attractions for a 16-year old: leaving school early and having a motorcycle! I looked no further ahead. I was interviewed by the boss of the firm concerned, Mr Reeves, who owned Revo, which made a number of electrical goods, including traffic lights, which Mr Reeves had been largely responsible for introducing in Britain.

Arrangements were almost completed for this plan when my official guardian, my uncle Hugh Sherbrooke, intervened. He thought that the army was the right place for me.

I then expressed my own view: I wanted to build bridges and the like, that is to be a civil engineer. Loughborough was thought to be the place to go to get a foot on that ladder but that would cost money, of which I had little. Uncle Hugh therefore suggested that I should go into the army with a view to joining the Royal Engineers, whose training included a degree at Cambridge. After 5 years commissioned service one would be permitted to resign and, in his opinion, one would then be sufficiently trained to become a civil engineer. I accepted this argument and, when I reached the appropriate age in January 1936, became a cadet at the Royal Military Academy, Woolwich, otherwise known as the Shop, which trained prospective officers for the Royal Artillery, the Royal Engineers and the Royal Signals.

This decision on my future was taken in the late summer of 1934 when I had just obtained my Higher School Certificate, with mathematics as my primary subject and physics as the principal subsidiary subject. At the beginning of the autumn term I therefore automatically entered the form known as the Mathematical Sixth. When a few weeks later my plans for the future were communicated to the school authorities, they immediately moved me to the 'Woolwich Form', where studies were directed solely at the examination for Woolwich, Sandhurst and Cranwell. I had nearly 4 more terms at Marlborough but it became quite obvious to me after a few weeks that I was going to have no difficulty in passing this relatively simple exam. Not being given to doing more work than seemed worthwhile, I spent more than a year in relative idleness. This should never have been allowed and I blame the school authorities for letting me get into idle habits.

One useful thing was achieved during this period. For the Easter holidays in 1935 my Uncle Hugh wisely arranged for me to stay with a French family. The father was a retired lawyer in his 70s and lived with his wife and 2 unmarried daughters in a tall terraced house in Boulogne. Only one of the daughters spoke some English and she was careful not to use it unless it was essential to elucidate some problem. Not unnaturally, at the age of 17 I was very bored, even to the extent that I hired a bicycle and rode to Dunkirk and back in the day, 90 miles. Living in such a family, however, was a good way to learn colloquial French except that, for the second 2 weeks that I was there, another English boy was there too and, as his French was much worse than mine, we inevitably spoke too much English when on our own.

In the autumn term of 1935, I passed in to Woolwich 3rd, but during my first term there dropped to 35th, because I had got out of the habit of working. The system of choice of arm on leaving Woolwich 18 months later depended on one's placing, number one having a free choice and so on down the order according to the vacancies available. There were about 20 RE vacancies which would usually be taken up by the first 25 or so in the order, whilst the 8 R Signals vacancies would often not be taken up until near the bottom of the list of 85 cadets. It was usual for a few of those high in the list to opt for RA, but as RA required around 57 of the cadets they usually had to accept most of those near the bottom. Thus, on my first term showing, it seemed unlikely that I would get an RE vacancy. I did not like the idea of not having a free choice and so I had to get down to serious work with the handicap of my first term's marks: one was marked for every activity throughout the three 5 or 6 month terms, making a glorious possible total of 10,000 marks. At the end I achieved 9th place and therefore had a free choice, but I had by then considered the alternatives.

I was drawn to Royal Signals by the fact that I had always had an interest in wireless, having built my first crystal set at the age of about 10 and progressed to valve sets at 14 or 15; and because I had spent 3 years in the

Signal Section of the OTC under the guidance of a master with exceptional enthusiasm for everything he did, Arthur Pepin. He had been a naval signaller in World War One and so enthused this section that, of my contemporaries within a couple of years either way, no less than 5 progressed through Royal Signals to become major-generals, as well as several brigadiers and colonels. A further factor in my decision was the information from a Signals officer at the Shop, Jack Hardy, that, unlike Gunners and Sappers, a Signals subaltern would, in India, normally have a fairly independent job and that it was possible to maintain 6 polo ponies on one's pay. I was commissioned into Royal Signals.

One of the activities at Woolwich which I particularly enjoyed was riding. I had never been on a horse before; but this seemed to be no disadvantage as those who had done so usually rode in quite a different style from what was taught there and had to unlearn before relearning. The riding instructors, warrant officers and sergeants, were renowned for their picturesque language. I had at one time developed a bad habit of leaning too far forward and, riding a mare called Vinny who compounded my problem by pecking on landing after a jump, I went over her head and landed on rather hard ground. I was somewhat dazed but recovered enough to hear the instructor say, 'Mister 'ancock sir, if you goes on riding like that, you'll end up in a mon—ast—ery'.

We had some weeks' holiday between leaving the Shop and joining at Catterick. I went in my £10 Austin 7 to stay with cousins, the Meath-Bakers at Hasfield, a small village 8 or 10 miles from Gloucester. I had spent one or two holidays there before and, on one occasion, my host, Francis Meath-Baker, had initiated me into the mysteries of cement mixing in an effort to narrow the stream running into his small lake, so that the water would run faster and trout might be induced to spawn. I rather think it didn't work.

On another previous visit my hostess, Susan, was playing a leading part in the organization of a pageant. Such events, the depiction of historical events without much attention to accuracy, were very popular in the '30s and were often on a large scale. By way of advertising it, about half-a-dozen of us agreed to ride, a few days before the event, from Cheltenham to Gloucester dressed in our pageant clothes. I appeared as a beefeater and I am fairly confident that beefeaters do not ride horses. Their clothing is not designed for this activity and I was very sore after it.

Susan's father-in-law had died a few years earlier and Susan had had to make the funeral arrangements. Although their garden adjoined the churchyard and we normally went to church by the direct route, it appeared that, if a coffin were taken that way, the route would, by law, become a public right of way. So it had to be carried down the drive and along the road, about a quarter of a mile further. The undertaker told Susan that she ought to order a lead-lined coffin, which would be a good deal more expensive than a plain wooden one: otherwise the bearers would notice the difference. After some debate and in great secrecy, it was arranged with the gardener that some old lead pipes would be put in the coffin. Perhaps the amount of lead was too great because, when the bearers lifted the coffin, one said, 'This is mighty 'eavy for such a small man'. The gardener, who was another bearer, replied promptly, 'Lead-lined coffins does weigh 'eavy!'

For this visit in 1937, my youngest sister, Rachel, was staying there too. The family and guests were due, a few days later, to drive to near Newquay in Cornwall to stay in caravans or tents. I had arrived in the £10 Austin 7, but one hot day in Gloucester I had great difficulty starting it because the magneto would only generate enough electricity for a spark if turning over really fast. So, as I had done before, I pushed the car in an empty side road and then put it into 2nd gear. The engine fired and I reached in to pull the gear lever into neutral but accidentally knocked it into top. The car leaped forward with me half in and half out. It crossed a main road at a T-junction and I just managed to stop it as it ran over a bicycle parked on the far side. It came to a halt a foot short of the large plate-glass shop window. By the time I had reimbursed the cyclist and soothed the shopkeeper, I had decided that I must find a more reliable vehicle. I went there and then to a breaker's yard and sold him the Austin for £5 and bought from him a 2-seater open Clyno for £6.

Rachel and I went to Newquay in this Clyno but had trouble with a leaking radiator. Putting in a proprietary concoction ('Neverleak' or 'Stopit'?) lasted only a very few miles. In Porlock oatmeal was advised but worked only until we went up Porlock Hill, then 1 in 4. The car would only just get up it, even with Rachel walking. The water boiled and burst the radiator again. In Lynmouth I was advised to use white of egg, but even this addition to the car's breakfast only lasted until we neared the top of Linton Hill. After these delays we had to stay the night in Barnstaple. From then on the radiator never leaked again, even driving from Cornwall to Catterick.

All RE subalterns on first commissioning took a degree at Cambridge in mechanical science in 2 years instead of the usual 3, as it was assumed that they had learned enough at Woolwich to be able to forgo the extra year. Royal Signals normally sent to Cambridge only one out of each half-year entry and he was sent 3 years later, it being thought preferable to complete the 18-months Royal Signals Qualifying Course (Q Course) first, followed by about 18 months' regimental duty. So all 8 of us for Royal Signals from the Shop reported to the School of Signals at Catterick at the end of August 1937.

There were about 6 other students on this course. One had been to Cambridge first instead of to the Shop and others came from the armies of South Africa, Egypt, Iraq and Siam. Our work was mainly academic but there was a good mixture of outdoor activities such as learning to signal with lamps and even morse flags: well out-of-date methods even then. Cable laying was much more practical and we spent a good deal of time on that. Laying with a 6-horse team had only a few years before been superseded by laying from a 3-ton lorry with a mechanical layer which spewed the cable on to or over a hedge. We learned the theory of radio communication and a good deal about the sets then in use in the field. One of the more useful things that most of us learned was not in the curriculum: the repair and maintenance of motor cars. Few of us could afford to run a car and get it serviced and so we went to scrap dealers, where it was possible to get a runner for £5 to £10, and then carried out the essential work ourselves.

Motorcycle riding caused both hilarity and grief. One of the Egyptians, Captain El Rafi, who was older than the rest of us, in his 30s, fell off frequently. We helped him on again and as he surged forward, he would look round at us with a beaming smile and say, 'Alright, my friends! I go! I go!' and promptly fall again. Our Canadian, Buster Stethem, who had transferred after being at the Royal Military College in Kingston, Ontario, to the British Army, was a large and heavy man who came off his machine, getting painfully tangled with the back wheel. He sent a cable to his parents: 'Matrimonial prospects halved'. The reply was, 'Half a loaf is better than no bread.' I happened to hear 3 years later, when visiting Kingston, that his father was in hospital there and I went to see him and learned that Buster was married and had children. Colonel Stethem, the father, had been in command of a prisoner-of-war camp in the foothills of the Rockies. When some prisoners had escaped up into the mountains, he, although in his mid-60s, had insisted that it was his duty to lead the search party, as result of which he was now seriously ill and, sadly, died not much later.

On arrival at Catterick each of us was interviewed by the Commandant of the School, who discussed our personal finances, which, in addition to one's pay, then about £15 a month, ranged from nothing up to about £10 a month. I had £5 a month extra and so I was told that I could quite well afford to hunt. This was possible because the local hunt allowed us to come out on very generous terms and because army horses were available: indeed the Q Course still included a riding course to supplement that at the Shop. Nevertheless, although I thoroughly enjoyed riding both at the Shop and at Catterick, I blotted my copybook with the brigadier by saying that I felt my first priority within the funds available was to run some sort of car. Some months later I was glad that I had taken this line because I was persuaded, along with a fellow YO (young officer) David Gibson, by Tony Deane-Drummond, who was in the course 6 months ahead of us, to take up gliding. Incidentally, all 3 of us had been in the Marlborough College OTC Signal Section together. Gliding was an economical sport because it was subsidised by the government and because a very large proportion of the work of running the club was carried out by volunteers who gave generously of their time.

Tony Deane-Drummond progressed rapidly and earned the highest qualification, a Silver C certificate. For this one was required, during 3 separate flights, to remain in the air for 5 hours, to reach a given height (which was I think 1,000 metres), and to fly for a distance of 50 kilometres. I achieved the 5 hours but not the other two. Tony took it up again after the war, winning international competitions and representing Britain.

The last item of our course was learning to drive 3-ton lorries. In January and February 1939 the weather was bitter and we spent days driving 1922-model vehicles, with no more protection than a small rectangle of glass in front of the driver, over the moors and in the snow.

We were told that our next appointments would be at Aldershot, Tidworth, Canterbury or Tien-Sin in China and we were asked to say which we would prefer. I asked for China, Canterbury or Tidworth in that order and so I was posted to Aldershot. I was, however, glad to learn at the same time that I had been selected to go to Cambridge in the autumn of 1940. After so many near starts that had come to nothing, I did not really believe that the war would happen and so I looked forward to an enjoyable couple of years at Cambridge. Thus at the end of March I joined 1st Divisional Signals at Aldershot and was given the job of OC K Section in 3 Company.

There was at that time a curious system of brevet promotion. A senior major could be promoted to brevet lieutenant-colonel. This meant that from the date of such promotion he took his seniority as a lieutenant-colonel in the army; but it had no effect on his seniority within his own corps or regiment. He continued to do a major's job and was paid as a major but he dressed as a lieutenant-colonel and it was understood that he would be promoted to colonel within, I think, 4 years. This produced interesting anomalies. My commanding officer was Lieutenant-Colonel Harris, holding his rank normally, but his second-in-command was Brevet-Lieutenant-Colonel Nalder. On a Friday afternoon it was customary to hold a regimental parade at the conclusion of which Nalder marched the regiment past Harris, his regimental senior. But on Sunday there was a garrison church parade and here Nalder took command, being senior to Harris in army seniority.

I was very underemployed initially because K Section, which existed to provide communications for 2nd Infantry Brigade, consisted only of myself, my sergeant and 4 No. 1 wireless sets with their associated gear. In those days the sections serving infantry brigades, as well as those serving artillery brigades (which were no more than regiments in fact and were later renamed accordingly), lived and trained as part of their divisional signals, only joining the headquarters they served for a few short exercises each year. My company commander was Peter Blake, a delightful and rather easygoing officer. He was responsible for the training of the 3 infantry brigade signal sections. By about the end of April enough men on the reserve had been called up to serve with the Colours to enable me to have a full section of about 35 men: an excellent and experienced lot they were.

The one major exercise that summer to test command and control required the full deployment of the HQs of 1st and 2nd Divisions and their 6 brigades, 1st, 2nd and 3rd and

4th, 5th and 6th respectively, together with their two divisional signals. My brigadier, Hudson, who had earned a VC in the First World War, was pleasant to deal with and tolerant of the ignorance of his newly joined signal officer. There was a highly competent brigade-major, who was a captain, and a charming but less talented and rather elderly staff-captain, who was a major. An RASC officer joined the HQ for exercises, as I did. During the 1939 exercise we had our offices in a pub and one morning I was sitting in a rather dark corner of a room, the only other occupant being Hudson, when there stormed in unannounced the divisional commander, Alexander (later Field Marshal Lord Alexander of Tunis). He did not notice me and proceeded to say in no uncertain terms exactly what he thought of Hudson. Until then it had never occurred to me that a brigadier, who to a second-lieutenant was only one step short of the Almighty, could be subjected to such treatment.

The editor of the Royal Signals magazine, *The Wire*, was at that time a retired lieutenant-colonel named Yule, obviously referred to as Loggy. He had persuaded me to write a short article for *The Wire* on gliding. As result of getting to know him, he further induced me to do a job in connection with some intelligence work. He told me that a certain German, who was a keen and competent yachtsman, had been entering in his Dragon in various regattas but had also been seen sailing in the vicinity of Scapa Flow. Our authorities wanted to know more about him. It was suggested that I should try to get to know him, leading him to believe that I was rather too fond of drink and somewhat in debt (I wasn't flattered to be cast for this part!).

As result Roy Tayler, a friend from Catterick days, and I went to Gosport to pick up a 14-foot International dinghy that I had just bought, taking with us also a Folbot, a folding, sailing canoe. We packed our gear in the canoe and towed it behind the dinghy. After a pleasant sail across to Ryde on the Isle of Wight on a Friday evening, we anchored off Ryde pier and slept on lilos in the dinghy.

Next morning there was a strong wind and it was rough. However, we set off for Cowes and noticed that sizeable yachts which had started out before us had run for shelter. Our dinghy was almost completely open and shipped a lot of water. So Roy bailed and I sailed. After about 4 hours' exhausting work we made it into Cowes for the beginning of Cowes week. It is interesting that in those days life jackets were not normally worn for small-boat sailing: indeed we did not own any and it never occurred to us to get them.

We managed to stay at the same hotel in Cowes as our German quarry and hoped for an opportunity to make his acquaintance. No suitable chance occurred but we found that he was due to take part in a Dragon race on the Tuesday from Cowes and another on the Thursday starting from Southsea. So we sailed over to Southsea on Tuesday, planning to intercept him on his way to Southsea on Wednesday. Roy's leave was up and so I had to manage as best I could on my own.

On Wednesday morning there was a good breeze and Spithead was choppy but I managed to sail about a mile offshore in the folding canoe. I passed a passenger ferry where those leaning over the side were clearly voicing the opinion that I ought to know better than to go out in such a frail craft in that weather. They were not to know that I intended to do an 'accidental' capsize at a moment when this German would have to pick me up. I was fortunate to spot his sail approaching quite soon. I thought I had timed it perfectly, letting go the main sheet, reaching for it and thus 'accidentally' capsizing near enough for him to have to rescue me, yet far enough away for the reason not to be obvious. He put about to come to me but a large motor yacht in the vicinity saw what had happened and sent a dinghy with an outboard which got to me first. Like the ferry passengers, they told me that I was mad to have ventured out in that weather, a criticism which I reluctantly had to endure without telling them that I could quite well have sailed on if I had wanted to.

I got in touch with every likely hotel in Portsmouth and Southsea to find out where my German quarry was staying, without success. After dark I was able to deduce from the light on board that he was sleeping in his Dragon. So I telephoned Loggy Yule and he told me to abandon it for the moment but suggested that I should attend the Clyde races in September, when I would be able to introduce myself to this German as the chap he had tried to rescue. But the war had started by then. I wonder whether this man's visit to Scapa Flow was connected with the sinking by a German submarine of a battleship there.

It was early in August that I returned to Aldershot to find that I had been posted back to Catterick to teach militia cadets. These were those from the first intakes of conscripts selected for officer training. They had not yet arrived and so, with war seeming imminent, it was thought that I might as well use my time training about 10 officers' daughters in the use of the very latest cipher machine. These girls had been subjected to no form of security check. It was later decided that the very existence of this machine, let alone how it worked, should be classified 'most secret'. Very strange!

Hitler invaded Poland early on a Friday morning and general mobilisation was ordered that day. On Saturday and Sunday many hundreds of reservists started to report to the Royal Signals Depot. I was told to help their adjutant and, while he coped with the resultant office work, I had to represent him on the square. Others organized tented camps on the moors. It was an exhausting couple of days and then I was told to go back to Aldershot because it was laid down in the mobilisation plan that those instructing at the School of Signals should form 151 OCTU (Officer Cadet Training Unit) Royal Signals in Mons Barracks, where I had spent the last 6 months.

As soon as possible after my arrival I tried to get transferred back to 1st Divisional Signals, even appealing for an interview with the Chief Signal Officer. I was ushered into an office shared by Colonel Fladgate, whom I had known

FIGHTING UNITS: No. 11

A ROYAL SIGNALS TRAINING UNIT — BY "MEL"

Just because the Royal Corps of Signals is not quite so intimately concerned with villainous saltpetre as some others, this does not make it any the less a battle-fighting unit. Even in these times, when signalling has gone a long way ahead from the flag-wagging and helio days, its most important work is done in a zone where things are apt to fly about and hit people. This unit, whose C.O. and officers "Mel" collected somewhere that has to be nameless, has, it will be observed, one officer who could almost be utilised as an aerial!

NEXT WEEK: No. — GROUP, R.A.F.

as CSO Aldershot Command and had now become CSO 1st Corps, and Colonel Bald, who had rejoined from the Reserve and was now CSO Aldershot Command. They were very civil and kind but said that the army was not going to repeat the mistake of 1914 of sending all the regulars to the front at the beginning. Robert Barlas, a friend from my Q Course, who had an artillery signal section in the same unit, had taken over my 2nd Brigade Signal Section: he was killed in the Dunkirk retreat. So I was lucky.

We spent the next month getting ready to accept a steady flow of cadets. The first three courses were for those regulars who were still part way through their Q Courses. The next two were those from Woolwich, plus a few from Sandhurst, who were not yet commissioned. Then came a succession of those straight from civilian life, a fascinating variety. Sixteen arrived weekly for three weeks out of four. As I was required to teach general army organization and administration, not the most enlivening of subjects particularly as I had almost no practical knowledge of it, in about four weeks to every one of these courses, they must have become as bored with it as I was.

After Christmas I was delighted to get transferred to teaching 'signal tactics', about which I knew even less, but it was at least potentially more interesting and involved some outdoor exercises. My masters in this group were Lieutenant-Colonel Stratton, an Oxford don, and Captain Ronnie Postill, a master at, and after the war headmaster of, Victoria College, Jersey.

Much more important to me personally was that, in January, I had planned to go to London one evening with some others to sup and dance. My prospective partner cried off at the last moment with a cold and I tried another girl, Kitty Yule, daughter of Loggy Yule. She was willing to come but only if she could bring one of the daughters of the family with whom she was staying, and she said she could procure another male escort to keep the numbers even. At the end of that evening I told Kitty that she had started something. The girl she brought was Geraldine (Gerry) Ovens. We went skating on Hawley Lake next day. We were married a year later.

One evening that spring, in the early hours of a Sunday morning, I was driving a carload back to Aldershot after a party in London. We were stopped by a motorcycle policeman for exceeding the 30-mph limit. He peered into the car and saw another subaltern and myself in front, with two girls and a third subaltern in the back. He waved us on, saying, 'I don't like to stop officers on duty'.

4

BREST, BELFAST, NEWMARKET, LISBURN, LONDON: 1940–41

After my first abortive attempt to escape from 151 OCTU I pulled various other strings but all to no avail. However, on Sunday, 9 June 1940, my luck turned. I came into breakfast in the mess and found myself sitting next to Brian Birkett, 18 months my senior and now Adjutant of 2 Corps Signals. His unit had returned through Dunkirk 10 days earlier and he told me that it was now re-equipping urgently for some further activity. He said that they were short of a subaltern for a wireless section and he agreed to do what he could to get me the job. There followed a fascinating couple of weeks.

On Monday morning I reported to the Commanding Officer and from him to the Company Commander concerned and was told to get hold of my section which consisted of 26 men and no equipment. On Tuesday a second line TA Corps Signals had laid out in a field all their equipment and vehicles for our unit to take over. The normal lists of what we were entitled to, Army Form G 1098, were not available and we helped ourselves as seemed appropriate. I had to collect four 15-cwt trucks with No. 9 wireless sets, one 3-ton lorry and an 8-cwt truck.

We spent the rest of that day, some of the night and all the next day fitting the sets and all their gear into the vehicles and making sure everything worked. The unit had had no leave since Dunkirk and were given 24 hours from Wednesday evening to Thursday evening. It was a London-based TA unit and so nearly all came from there.

Reassembling on Thursday evening, the whole unit drove off in convoy on Friday morning to Southampton, where we handed over our vehicles for loading into ships, while we went off to a transit camp. We were apparently intended to sail as soon as possible to Brest with our Corps Headquarters and, presumably with some formations under command, to bolster up the left of the French Army. At 10 pm that night another subaltern, Powis-Lybbe, and I were told that one of us was to embark urgently with his wireless section: we tossed for it and I won. I had to go and ring the War Office at once to get my instructions.

We set sail about 6 am on Saturday morning in a 6,000-ton cargo ship, just my section with its 6 vehicles. I set the men to checking once again that all our equipment worked and they soon discovered that we had the vehicles and equipment, including the personal kitbags, of the other wireless section.

As we were not due to reach Brest for about 24 hours, I decided to make use of the time for driving instruction in the hold. We had no more qualified drivers than there were vehicles and it seemed a chance to impart the rudiments of the job to a few more, in case of casualties. The captain, Mr Briggs, was concerned that the noise of vehicle engines might make it easier for the ship to be detected but he accepted that the small additional risk was worth taking.

During Saturday evening, we were told that we could not enter Brest because German aircraft had laid mines across the entrance; and so we went further down the coast to the area of the Iles de Glenan, anchoring to await mine clearance. We spent a glorious day there swimming round the ship.

Briggs, a merchant seaman who had been through the First World War, was fond of a drink and invited me to join him. His routine was beer from 11 am to 1145, then gin until lunch about 1215; high tea at 5 pm followed by beer and then whisky until bedtime. About 9 pm that Sunday evening, when we were into the whisky, a signal was delivered to him and I asked him whether it meant that we could go back to Brest but he said not, the signal was of no importance.

About 8 next morning I happened to meet the captain on my way to get a shower and he told me that there was still no news of the mines being cleared. I asked him whether last night's signal gave us no clues. He had forgotten about it and sent for a copy: it said, 'Mines clear. Proceed to Brest forthwith.' However, Briggs assured me that he had not got adequate charts of these waters and he would have had to wait for daylight anyway.

We entered the long estuary leading to Brest about 1 pm when I heard on the BBC news that France had finally surrendered. The French pilot had just come on board and when I told him this he found it impossible to believe. As we went in, there passed us, coming out, five ships: the first was laden to the lifeboats with tired-looking British soldiers, the second a little less overcrowded, and so on until the last appeared no more than normally full. When we finally got to the port area, I arranged to go ashore with the pilot to find out what was happening. I was halfway down the rope ladder when I heard a yell from the other side of our ship, plainly giving us some order which I could not hear. So I climbed back on board and, going straight up to the bridge, heard my captain shout to a British commander RN, on the bridge of a small vessel nearby, 'Did you say Belfast?' in tones of astonishment. The reply was 'Yes: Belfast and don't argue!'

This commander was evidently going round the harbour telling every vessel he could to get away, giving them a variety of British ports to go to so as to avoid too much confusion at any one. Briggs was not best pleased with our destination because he reckoned that he would have only one day's coal to spare and he had only small-scale charts of the Irish Sea. I learnt recently that it was on this same afternoon of Monday, 17 June, that, off St Nazaire, only a little further down the coast, the *Lancastria* was sunk with appalling loss of life.

On the Tuesday evening when we were somewhere off

the south-east corner of Ireland we saw, in the very calm sea, perhaps half a mile astern, an unmistakable periscope, and this was confirmed not long after by a patrolling aircraft of Coastal Command, which flashed down to us by lamp 'Submarine'. Briggs ordered full speed, which he reckoned at 13½ or possibly 14 knots. He said that a submarine might keep up with us on the surface but that no submerged submarine could do more than 11 knots. Fortunately the submarine commander was unaware that we had that morning broken the larger of our two guns and that, had he surfaced, he would have run little risk. I stood with Briggs on the bridge watching the periscope as the sun was setting and the moon rising on this perfect summer evening, which he spoilt by saying 'It was just such a night as this that I was torpedoed in the last war!'

All was well and we arrived off Belfast Lough next morning. Lacking the necessary information, we could not fly the right signals and so we were brought up short by a shot across our bows. In due course we came alongside and my vehicles were off-loaded. I reported to the Chief Signal Officer and we were provided with accommodation. I assumed that he would inform my parent unit that my section had returned and no doubt he tried to do so. Meanwhile I rang up Gerry Ovens and my sister, Joyce Fane, in Lincolnshire. 2 Corps Signals, wanting news of my section's whereabouts and getting nothing through official channels, rang Joyce, who was on their records as my next of kin, and thus learnt what had happened.

A few days later we were told to rejoin the unit and we crossed to Heysham and drove to Aldershot, delayed somewhat by having inadequate maps and all the signposts having been removed so as to confuse any German invader. In Aldershot we were told that the unit had gone to Cambridge. So I told the men, who all had homes within reach in London, that they could go home for the night if they wished, provided that every man was back by 0900 next day. I stayed the night at Gerry's home at Mytchett. In the morning they were all punctual and off we went to Cambridge. As result of asking there for the whereabouts of 2 Corps Signals we were suspected by undergraduates of being Germans in disguise but we eventually found the unit in Newmarket. It had been an eventful fortnight.

We remained in Newmarket for only another two or three weeks and then, having despatched a convoy of our vehicles, the unit set off by train in a northerly direction. We were not told where we were going but in due course a rumour ran down the train that we were on our way to Lisbon: rather puzzling as there had been no indication that Portugal was likely to enter the war. By the time that the train got to Stranraer, it was clear that we were going to Lisburn near Belfast. Our Corps HQ was renamed 6 Corps HQ and we became 6 Corps Signals, presumably with the object of leading the enemy to believe we had more troops available than we had.

Initially we lived in tents. Officers were sent to reconnoitre all possible institutions, halls etc. which might be requisitioned as accommodation for us. One subaltern found a large hall belonging to a Protestant organization which looked useful but it was immediately and mysteriously burned down. I found a convent which looked large enough to house about 400 soldiers and there were only 12 nuns living there. Within 24 hours, before the requisitioning papers had gone through, there were 50 nuns and, it was said, no possible room for soldiers.

I was told by my company commander to find out just what was the effective range of the No. 9 sets with which we were equipped. So I sent one detachment to the east coast, south of Belfast, whilst I took my sergeant and another detachment to Belleek, as far west as one could go without crossing the border. On arrival I made contact with the local Head Constable of the RUC (Royal Ulster Constabulary), who was most helpful in finding us a suitable site for our tests. As we were going to be there for several days, I agreed that my sergeant and I would help with the drilling of his newly recruited LDVs (Local

Defence Volunteers, later renamed the Home Guard). One day the Head Constable invited my sergeant and me to attend a party that evening at the police station in the next small town. It was a farewell party for the police sergeant in charge there. As arranged we set off about 9.30 pm in the Head Constable's car and he then mentioned that we would have to go briefly into the Republic and back to avoid a very long journey round the east side of the nearby lake. Eire being neutral, this was of course strictly against the rules, particularly in uniform. However, I accepted his assurance that there was no possibility of trouble resulting.

We were welcomed to the party where there were some 18 people, about half from the RUC, several from the Irish police, the Gardai, and three or four known members of the IRA. My Head Constable, as the senior police officer, was formally declared to be chairman for the evening. We sat on both sides of a long table with him at the end. Beer flowed very freely. Every now and again the chairman said, 'I call upon Constable X for his pleasure', whereupon the man indicated would rise to his feet and sing a song or play a tune on some instrument and do it most competently. About midnight the beer disappeared and was replaced by an equally liberal supply of whisky. An hour or so later, when the party had become less formal, I found myself sitting between the Head Constable and one of the IRA and I said to them both, 'I am new to Ireland and don't understand these things but please tell me what you [Head Constable] will do if you get a message now to arrest him [IRA]'. The answer was, 'I would tell him to get across the border but if he came back tomorrow I would shoot him'. This appeared to be accepted as entirely reasonable by the IRA man. The party finally adjourned about 2 am and we returned to Belleek without incident. I think that every man in that room had a loaded revolver concealed about him: I certainly had! It was a pleasant and instructive evening.

On 9 August I was posted to 1 HQ Signals, the unit providing communications for GHQ Home Forces, which was in St Paul's School, Hammersmith, as adjutant. This meant promotion from second-lieutenant to captain, a normal progression during the war: lieutenants were rare. The unit, more than 1,100 strong and located at various places in west London with its HQ in the old council offices on Hammersmith Broadway, was from the Supplementary Reserve recruited in Glasgow and to a large extent composed of employees of the General Post Office. The commanding officer, Lieutenant-Colonel Cummings, was delightful but perhaps rather too easygoing and, by wartime standards too old for the job, although there seemed to be no doubt that the unit under his command had performed most creditably in the few weeks leading up to the evacuation from Dunkirk.

Soon after I arrived, it occurred to me that gliders, of which I had had some experience, could well be adapted to war uses. When at Catterick, encouraged by the commandant, Brigadier Chenevix-Trench, I had been one of the founder members of the Royal Signals Gliding Club. As Chenevix-Trench was now signal officer-in-chief at GHQ, he seemed a likely person to sponsor the idea. With Cummings' permission, I wrote out a proposal, marked it 'SECRET' and sent it to him. He took up the idea quickly and then discovered that it was already in hand. He sent for me, told me this and that volunteers as glider pilots would shortly be called for. He added the order, 'You will not volunteer!'

In September Cummings was replaced by a highly competent but rather serious regular officer, Kenneth Thursby-Pelham. My sins quickly found me out. A new second-in-command had recently been posted to us, having been sacked from command elsewhere, and he had to share my office. I had a row of about seven trays in front of me and I was extremely busy. He could find nothing better to do than to pick up a paper from one of my trays, glance through it and usually put it back in the wrong tray. I happened to dine one evening with an officer in the Royal Signals postings branch and told him my woes. Two days later our new second-in-command was posted elsewhere. Cummings would have been quite happy with this but, before the second-in-command actually left, Thursby-Pelham had arrived and one of his first questions to me was did I know why the second-in-command had been posted just when there was a new commanding officer too. I took a deep breath and came clean. Thursby was very reasonable: he kept the second-in-command but arranged for him to share his office and gave him some work to do.

In August and September, what was subsequently called the Battle of Britain – the air war over south-east England – was building up to its climax on Sunday, 15 September. Meanwhile, we all had our work on the ground to get on with and this meant very long hours. To avoid getting too stale over a long period, all ranks were required to take one day off each week except in the most exceptional circumstances. So, whenever possible, I went to spend the day with Gerry and her family at Mytchett. It was on Sunday, 8 September, that, with the approval of her parents, Gerry took the plunge and agreed to marry me. We decided to announce it in the papers on her 18th birthday, Tuesday, 17 September, and, subject to my commanding officer's concurrence, to get married on 1 January 1941.

On 15 September, I again went to Mytchett for the day and had an even more than usually delayed return journey by train because of bomb damage. Little did I appreciate that the most significant air battle of the war had been going on overhead all day. The following Tuesday, the 17th, Gerry came to London and after lunch we chose a ring in the Goldsmiths and Silversmiths, now Garrards. We then got a taxi and, just as I was putting the ring on her finger, there was the all-too-familiar wail of the air raid siren.

I had that morning put into the CO's in-tray a copy of that day's *Times*, having marked our engagement. I was severely taken to task for announcing this without having first obtained his permission, apparently a peacetime custom of which he considered I should have been aware.

However, he accepted that it was a fait accompli and that his predecessor had known that an engagement was imminent.

The general rule up to 1939 had been that marriage allowance would not be paid to an officer until he was 30, or to an other rank until 26. Even if an officer accepted the financial implications and married earlier, it was generally frowned upon as unmarried subalterns were thought to be more readily available for duty. In some regiments the 30 age limit was a cast iron rule and anyone transgressing it was invited to transfer elsewhere. There is always an element of luck in a marriage and probably the element is larger if one is young. Married at 23, I can now, well after our golden wedding, say that I was very, very lucky.

We arranged to be married on 1 January 1941 and it was unlucky that, rather later, GHQ decided to move the main part of its headquarters from Hammersmith to premises off Whitehall on the same day. It was very good of Thursby-Pelham not to insist on us changing the day, as well as allowing a representative five officers from the unit to attend our wedding. He also accepted the absence of my assistant adjutant as my best man, David Gribbin, who had been in the Marlborough College OTC Signal Section with me.

Gerry's grandfather was a surgeon-major serving with the 5th Inniskilling Dragoon Guards in the Heavy Brigade in the Crimean War. Her father, Robert Ovens, one of numerous children, was born at Aldershot in 1868. In 1870, when the Royal Army Medical Corps was founded, her grandfather retired from the army rather than accept a transfer away from his regiment. The family went to live at the family home, a Georgian ex-rectory, Aughnagaddy House, outside Ramelton in County Donegal. Robert went to Sandhurst and was commissioned into the 80th, later the 2nd Battalion the South Staffordshire Regiment, in 1888. He served for a number of years in India and Burma. In 1910 he married Beatrice Clibborn. Her family also came from Ireland although she was brought up in London. Her

Captain R.M. Ovens.
Brigade-Major.
India.
1906.

mother was a Miss Walpole of the family of the then well-known department store which started in Dublin and later opened in London.

They were first stationed in Gibraltar, Robert being second-in-command of his battalion. He was promoted to command the 1st Battalion, the 38th, and went to South Africa where in 1913 their first daughter, Araminta (Minta), was born. The battalion returned to England in 1914. Robert Ovens served on the western front throughout the 1914-18 war and rose to command a brigade, being awarded a CMG. In 1919 he was stationed near Mansfield in Nottinghamshire, where their second daughter, Honora (Honor), was born. In the same year he retired and they went to live at Aughnagaddy. The following year he was invited to serve again, to command the troops in Ceylon (now Sri Lanka) on promotion to major-general, but being well settled declined. In 1922 their third daughter, Geraldine (Gerry) was born. In 1932 they decided to get a house in England in which to spend the winter months and in due course acquired Mytchett Heath, 3 miles out of Aldershot.

We were married at St Peter's, Frimley, in Surrey, on New Year's Day 1941. Gerry's mother had worked very hard to give us as near to a peacetime wedding as was possible. Her parents were also kind enough to lend us their car for our honeymoon. I had found a sympathetic chap in the office that issued the very limited petrol ration then available and he gave us enough to go to Devonshire and back.

We spent our first night at the George in Amesbury. It was a cold evening and before dinner we were glad to find a good fire in the lounge. Being wartime I was of course in uniform and the only other person besides us having a pre-dinner drink was a gunner lieutenant-colonel. We got talking and, in due course, we could not do other than invite him to join us for dinner. Part way through the meal he suddenly said, 'How long have you been married?' I looked at my watch and said, 'About 6 hours'. He was somewhat embarrassed and insisted on ordering a bottle of champagne, adding that he had been shot in the head in the last war and could not drink much. In fact he happily drank his share with the result that, when he had called for tomato sauce with the savoury and was hitting the bottle hard to get it out, he broke into song, 'O God our help in ages past. . . .' This was not conduct appropriate to our staid surroundings!

On return from our honeymoon in Westward Ho, we moved into a ground-floor flat in Castlenau Gardens, 3 streets to the south of Hammersmith Bridge. As London had been bombed regularly for several months, rents were low and we were fortunate to find a furnished flat with 3 rooms, kitchen and bathroom for 2 guineas a week. I spent half my working day in the Hammersmith office dealing with regimental administration and the other half 2 floors below the ground off Whitehall adjacent to the signal office for the new GHQ. Owing to the limitations of air-conditioning there were strict 'No smoking' rules in all the rooms of the signal office but when Winston Churchill wandered in, as he occasionally did late at night with a guest, I don't think anyone asked him to extinguish his cigar.

The first serious disciplinary case that I was concerned with as adjutant was that of a reservist subaltern in his 30s who, as signalmaster in charge of the GHQ signal office in the basement of St Paul's School, Hammersmith, was accused of being drunk on duty. The evidence against him was that, in an ill-lit corridor, he attempted to kiss the senior officer of the ATS (Auxiliary Territorial Service). It was unkindly said, with what justification I do not know, that one only had to look at the lady to know that he must have been drunk! The officer was placed in open arrest and confined to his room in the mess. It was my duty to deprive him of his revolver and I found that the poor chap was so depressed that I was very glad of a reason to take it away. In the end he escaped with a formal reprimand because he had lived in the East and had been in the habit of taking quinine to ward off malaria and had done so on this occasion. He got a doctor to give evidence that only a pint or so of beer could in these circumstances have been enough to make him drunk, a result which he might not have foreseen. He was then posted elsewhere.

In February Thursby-Pelham left, on promotion I think, and there was nearly a disaster. A farewell party was held in our mess on the 7th floor of Latimer Court in Hammersmith. It had an old-fashioned lift which, with a little ingenuity, one could hold on a floor ready for use by putting one's hand through the protecting cage and pulling the right lever. When Thursby was ready to leave, some helpful chap did this so that there would be a proper and undelayed send-off. But there were no lights in the passage because of the blackout and, when Thursby strode forward into the lift, it wasn't there. He was quick enough to seize part of the ironwork and just saved himself when his head was nearly at floor level.

He was replaced by Lionel Harris, an engineer from the Post Office, who in the 1950's became Sir Lionel Harris, Engineer-in-Chief of the Post Office, now British Telecommunications plc. He had been on the staff of the signal officer-in-chief Home Forces and therefore was already well aware of the functions of this large and complicated unit. He arrived having had no leave for a long time and soon went off for a week. He gave me his home telephone number in case of urgent need. It happened that the very next day some problem arose which really did need his decision. I rang and his wife answered. I asked to speak to him and his wife said, 'But I'm not expecting him until tomorrow'. Like a clot I said, 'That's odd: he left here yesterday!'

One night in March we were woken up by a more than usually loud bang and our bedroom windows were shattered. In the morning we found that it had been caused by a landmine exploding in the river to the north of us. Curiously it was our south-side windows that were broken, and ours were the only ones in the street to have gone.

About this time we were honoured by a visit to our underground signal office by the King, HM King George VI. Before going round the various sections, he came unaccompanied into the small office that I shared with the commanding officer, where we had rather complex wall diagrams of the principal military line communications throughout the United Kingdom and of the wireless back-up. The King, obviously well briefed, asked detailed questions. He discussed our resources and problems in a delightfully informal way and, incidentally, he spoke without a trace of the stammer with which he had some difficulty in public.

In early April, after 8 months in the job, a fairly normal period in wartime, I was posted to the School of Signals in Catterick.

5

CATTERICK, UNITED STATES, CANADA: 1941

A three-week course was being run at the School of Signals at Catterick with the object of bringing reserve officers up-to-date in both signal tactics, ie how to handle signal units in the field, and current signal equipment. The course was run by two officers, a major and a captain, and the pupils were generally rather elderly lieutenant-colonels and majors from the reserves. Everest Mozley had been the captain for some time and had dealt with the technical side but now he was promoted to major and took over tactics, whilst I was required to deal with the equipment. Mozley was an odd character, as can be deduced from the fact that, when he and his wife had their second child, the announcement, for which I feel sure he was entirely responsible, read, 'To Everest and Anthea Mozley - a mistake'. Fortunately the students on this course did not know that their instructors, who were much junior to them, were, very wrongly, required to write reports on them.

I lived in the mess initially whilst searching for accommodation and Gerry stayed with my aunt, my mother's sister Marjorie Lunt, and her husband, Geoffrey, who was Bishop of Ripon and thus only about 25 miles away. Gerry was not well at the time and this was soon diagnosed as thyroid. She went into hospital in York for what was then a major operation. In due course we moved into a room in a small cottage in Hudswell a few miles from Catterick Camp. The ceiling of our bedroom was so low that I, at 6 feet 6, could not stand upright anywhere in it.

After the excitements of the Blitz in London, Catterick and this course seemed very remote from any war, although, even there, one followed war events from newspapers and the BBC as far as possible. The major event that summer was the German invasion of Russia. This apparently made the Russians our friends, which was at first difficult to comprehend as they had been fighting our friends the Poles and the Finns.

In July I received a posting order to join a newly forming unit known as N Corps Signals. This unit was, though of course I did not know it then, intended to be part of a formation going to Singapore or Malaya to strengthen our defences there. In fact they were sent soon after the Japanese entered the war, and arrived in Singapore just in time to surrender as prisoners.

I was very lucky that, before I could join this unit, my posting was superseded by one to form part of a team of 18 officers of all arms being sent to the United States as observers on their manoeuvres in Louisiana. The objects of this team were to report to the British on the competence of the American Army and to put at the disposal of the Americans lessons from our own operational experience. With these aims, some arms sent those with recent active service and with considerable soldiering experience: in certain cases it meant temporary lieutenant-colonels reverting to major in order that all would appear to be on an equal footing. Royal Signals were very short of experienced officers because before the war they had formed less than 4 per cent of the army and now, with the number of formation headquarters which had had to be created, they were about 8 per cent of a much larger army. They managed to send one officer of some seniority, Ewbank, who had been one of the instructors on my Q Course, but they were really scraping the barrel in sending me aged 24 with no operational experience at all.

We landed at Halifax in Nova Scotia and travelled by train to Washington. We all wore civilian clothes and travelled on hastily granted passports as 'Mr '. In order to get the passports quickly, we had all been sent to one photographer in London and, as we were in uniform, we each borrowed the photographer's jacket in turn. Our passports were thus remarkably similar and we were each described as 'Government Official'. When we crossed the border into the United States the immigration official came into our coach and examined our passports against a list he brought with him. I noticed that on his form he wrote against each 'Army Officer' but he made no objection to our arrival.

We then spent a few days being briefed at the headquarters of the British Military Mission. We were given generous allowances and, in some cases, such as mine, acting paid promotion. Not surprisingly we were able to spend 2 or 3 enjoyable evenings in good restaurants free of rationing. The *Washington Times Herald*, echoed by the *Chicago Tribune*, headlined our arrival, 'YOUNG BRITISH OFFICERS OF MILITARY AGE EATING AND DRINKING IN THE NIGHT HAUNTS OF WASHINGTON AT THE EXPENSE OF LEND-LEASE'. This embarrassed both American and British authorities, particularly as it was factually correct: I have no doubt that our allowances came indirectly from Lend-Lease.

We were then despatched to spend a few days with our respective Arms Training Centres, Ewbank and I going to the School of the US Signal Corps at Fort Monmouth on the coast of New Jersey, about 40 miles from New York. At this time the US Army had for about 6 months embarked on a massive expansion programme and it was obviously a difficult problem for Signals, with the long technical training needed for many signals trades, to keep in step with the rest of the army. To some extent the shortage of instructors was solved by issuing the bulk of the instruction in writing and severely restricting the amount of personal tuition. I got the impression that this resulted in high qualifications for those who could learn by heart, with a majority not really understanding their subjects.

At that time the responsibilities of their Signal Corps

differed from ours in various ways. The point which struck us as so different as to be almost unworkable in the field was that the signals commander at any level of headquarters was responsible to the senior logistic staff officer and had no direct access to the commander or operational staff. This must have made it very difficult to plan ahead for the operational communications which would be wanted.

Their Corps was still training carrier pigeons, which had certainly played a valuable part in the 1914 war. In 1941 they were experimenting with getting pigeons to fly a triangular course: first to their food and then to their mates. The provision of training films for the whole army was also the responsibility of the US Signal Corps and to this end they had gathered together a large team of Walt Disney's artists. Ewbank and I spent a most interesting hour in their studios, not realising that we were being drawn from every angle! At the end we were presented with a sheaf of delightful cartoons, samples of which are at pages 53 and 54. They had been particularly entertained by our wearing shorts, which were then the standard hot-weather uniform of the British Army and quite unknown in the United States above the age of about 5.

We were not far from Deal, New Jersey, and, British persons being rare in the United States at the time, we were invited to attend an 'aquacade' there which was being staged to raise charitable funds for bomb relief in Deal, Kent. An aquacade proved to be a floodlit demonstration by a group of attractive girls, swimming in patterns before a considerable audience. This was before the United States had television but the proceedings were broadcast by radio on the coast-to-coast network in a programme sponsored by Bromo-Seltzer. At the end Ewbank and I were required to come on to a platform to be interviewed, whilst the bathing beauties were sitting on its edge in front of us. Fortunately Ewbank had been to Deal and could answer some of the questions. Then the interviewer announced that he 'would like to make small presentations to these

ANIMATION DEPT.
AUG 2 9 1941
DO YOU FEEL A DRAFT!

YOU KNOW V FOR VICTORY EH WHAT!
ANIMATION DEPT. AUG 29 1941

gentlemen'. After giving Ewbank a few shirts, he turned to me and, whilst very pointedly looking down at one of the girls, handed me a dressing gown with the remark, 'I hope you can make good use of that!'

We flew from New York to Little Rock, Arkansas, where we met the rest of our party of 18. We were all invited to dinner at the Little Rock Club, where we found that our hosts were nearly twice our number of general officers, which in American means brigadier-general, the equivalent of our brigadier, upwards.

Next day Ewbank and I joined the 50th Signal Battalion, whose job was to provide communications for Third Army. A month-long exercise started a day or two later, being a battle against Second Army. It was a most ambitious project as it is generally accepted that it is not practicable to run a continuous exercise between 2 sides, properly umpired, for more than a week or so. Moreover, conscription had been introduced only about 6 months earlier and here were more than half a million men with little or no military experience to be controlled, moved and supplied. It was quite a remarkable achievement that it worked at all and not surprising that after 10 days it was necessary to call a halt for a week and then start again.

During the break we were near the town of Shreveport in northern Louisiana and one evening I was invited to join a party attending a very large dance arranged specially at no notice. Not long after our arrival, the dance band leader noticed my unfamiliar uniform and came and asked my name and regiment. He played a roll on the drums and stopped the dancing; then he gave me a 5-minute write-up on the loudspeakers entirely from his imagination, including evacuation from Dunkirk, a place I had not visited since my bicycle ride there from Boulogne 6 years earlier. The band then played 'God Save the King' and he asked me to say a few words, a task which would have been quite beyond me, at this dry dance, had it not been that my hosts all seemed to have hip flasks charged with rum. When I had finished, they played our national anthem again.

At the end of the manoeuvres several of the observers were in New Orleans for a few days. Having time to spare, Alan Forward of the RASC and I arranged to have some flying lessons, an activity which was of course impossible in Britain at the time. When I came down from one flight I was immediately accosted by a newspaper reporter. He asked me whether I thought America ought to come into the war. I sensed that whatever I said was likely to be wrong and tried to avoid the question by replying that I thought America was doing a very useful job supplying munitions. Next day the *New Orleans Times Picayune* had a small headline 'British Major says America not required in war'.

On return to Washington we had to spend about 10 days being debriefed. In particular we each had to write one report for the British Military Mission on what we thought of the US Army and of our own arm in it; and another, more tactfully worded, for our own arm branch in the US Army HQ. Following submission of the latter, Ewbank and I were invited at short notice to come to meet representatives of the US Signal Corps to discuss what we had learned. On arrival we found to our dismay that they had assembled about 20 senior officers and we were asked to start the discussion by each talking for about a quarter of an hour. We were asked to speak frankly about any shortcomings, and we did. It was very encouraging that this led, not to resentment as it so easily might have, but to a worthwhile debate about organization, methods, equipment etc.

During this 10 days, I managed to fit in some flying lessons by having them from 6 to 7 am each day. My instructor had available 2 small aircraft in which he and I sat side by side. One plane had a 50-hp engine and the other 65. The latter was distinctly preferable as it allowed one to clear, with a reasonable margin, the telephone wires at the end of the grass field from which we operated. One morning the instructor said I must learn how to get out of a spin. He explained that an aircraft got into a spin as a result of too little speed and therefore stalling. To get out of it one must increase engine revs, put the stick forward to dive and put on rudder opposite to the direction of spin. He demonstrated and then put the aircraft into a spin again and told me to get out of it. I did all I had been told but rather too vigorously. As result of the sudden dive my knee hit and bent the throttle lever, which was full out, jamming it in that position. At the same time the instructor, who was not as tightly belted in as he should have been, rose suddenly in his seat and hit his head hard on a metal bar above it. He was dazed and I was not too sure what to do next. There was a notice on the dashboard: 'This aeroplane must never be allowed to exceed 130 mph'. The air speed indicator read 160 mph before the instructor recovered sufficiently to solve the problems.

In order to be allowed to fly alone and to qualify for a Student Pilot's Licence, the equivalent of a British A licence, I had to take a medical exam. One doctor was testing 7 or 8 persons at the same time for all medical aspects. I was lucky that, owing to an oversight, he missed out on giving me the colour-blindness test. So I have a somewhat out-of-date American flying licence.

Whilst I was enjoying life in a country still at peace, Gerry at home was having another operation. Having tonsils out is not normally serious but can be painful and it was her second operation in a few months.

In Washington the head of the Signals Branch in the British Military Mission, Colonel Harries (father of the present Bishop of Oxford), told me that he needed an extra officer on his staff and that he was going to ask AG 11, the posting branch for Royal Signals, to post me into the vacancy. I objected that I was a regular officer and that in the first 2 years of war I had been nowhere near any operational front. He said that is was so difficult to get people across the Atlantic that I would have to put up with it. As already mentioned, I happened to know well the relevant officer in our postings branch and I wrote to him by the next post, with a copy of my letter in the diplomatic bag to make as sure as possible of one of them reaching him in time to get this idea scotched. A day or 2 later Harries happened to mention to me that, if I were posted to Washington, I should realize that new arrivals could no longer get their wives to join them. He followed this up a bit later by telling me that the vacancy was for a captain and so I would have to revert to that rank. Fortunately, for whatever reason, I did not have to stay there.

We were next required to go to the training centres of our respective arms in Canada. Ewbank did not come with me as he had to return home for some other job. I arrived at the Canadian Signal Training Centre at Kingston, Ontario, on a Sunday evening, having had dinner on the train. My hosts in the mess plied me generously with drink and invited me to join a game of poker that was in progress. Not long afterwards the commandant called in the mess to welcome me, a very civil gesture. It was a few days later that I discovered that he had 2 pet abominations: drink and gambling!

I spent 3 weeks there, during which I was required amongst other things to address all ranks, some 400 of them: an ordeal as I could speak from so little experience. There was also located in Kingston the Canadian Defence College, the equivalent of our Imperial Defence College, and to my surprise I was asked to talk to them about the American Army and their manoeuvres. It seemed very odd that they were not already closely in touch.

There were 13 of the original 18 who assembled in Ottawa in mid-October with thick snow lying. We were first invited as a group to a general discussion with the Canadian Army's training staff, followed by lunch with the Minister for the army. In the afternoon we had more detailed discussions with the senior officers of our own Arm, followed in the evening by drinks with the governor-general, Lord Athlone, and Lady Athlone. This was interesting for me because, 10 years earlier their daughter, Lady May Cambridge, had married Colonel Henry Abel-Smith, brother of May Tabor, with whose family I had spent my school holidays for 2 or 3 years.

After a few days in Ottawa we left by train for Halifax and sailed in a ship which was part of a convoy taking Canadian troops to Britain. A fellow passenger was May Abel-Smith, with whom I and 2 others played bridge for most of the voyage. Whilst in the USA and Canada the 13 of us had naturally bought various items of clothing for our families in England, where it was rationed. Amongst other things we had between us some 400 pairs of silk stockings, items which were quite unobtainable in England – this was of course before the invention of nylons.

Having been so royally entertained in Ottawa, I think we had most of us begun to get an inflated idea of our own importance. We came down to earth with a bump. Arriving in Liverpool about midday on a Sunday, there were no facilities for unloading baggage and the Canadian OC Troops decreed that no one would go ashore until the next day. Our group had been away from home for more than 3 months and were not going to waste a day. We insisted on leaving the ship at once. Whilst OC Troops could not forbid this, he did his best by declining to give us any help with handling our baggage. So 13 majors by co-operative effort collected their considerable quantity of baggage from a hold and put it ashore, watched by many hundreds of idle Canadian soldiers. Our efforts not only got us home early but to our surprise avoided us having to pass through customs as they were not working on Sunday.

6

NORTHAMPTON, BOVINGTON, LONDON, LARGS, PERTH, COWES: 1941–42

On arrival in England in mid-November I was posted to 9th Armoured Divisional Signals in Northampton. I should perhaps explain that in Royal Signals at that time lieutenant-colonels' commands, ie the equivalent of regiments or battalions in other arms, were known as units and they took their names from the formation headquarters that they served. The terms 'regiment' and 'squadron' were adopted after the war and it was not until 1959 that a consistent numbering scheme was adopted for the whole Corps.

It was found soon after I arrived that this unit had one more major than its establishment allowed and so, by wartime rules, the junior temporary major had to revert to captain. It was uncertain for a few weeks whether Major Frampton or I were the junior and so we were both told to continue to wear major's badges. It was, I think, shortly before Christmas that Gerry was able to join me in Northampton, just in time for her to remove a major's insignia and sew on the three pips of a captain.

At about the same time my bank statement caught up with me and I found that, owing to some mismanagement, Cox's and King's, the army pay agents then, had not been told of my promotion to Major to go to America and had assumed that I had reverted to my substantive rank of lieutenant. So I had a considerable overdraft and it took quite a long time to get it sorted out. There was no hope of getting the interest on my involuntary overdraft refunded but, as I will recount in due course, I got it back somewhat unconventionally 5 years later.

Of rather more world-shaking importance than my pay, there occurred in early December the Japanese attack on Pearl Harbor and the entry of Japan and the United States into the war. Also in that month the Desert Army advanced rapidly across Cyrenaica and it seemed possible that, if we could launch a sufficient force quickly through Algeria into Tunisia, the whole of North Africa could be cleared of the Axis forces. Planning staffs were set up in London with this aim and Colonel Kenneth Thursby-Pelham, who had been my commanding officer in 1 HQ Signals, was appointed as chief signal officer of 116 Force, which was to do this job.

Meanwhile, having joined an armoured division, Frampton and I had been sent to Bovington on a 3-week course to learn something about armour and armoured communications. Frampton and I used to play chess each evening. Chatting on one occasion, he happened to mention that he had been living in a mess with ATS members. I said how strange it must seem: and in those days it was something quite new. He said he rather enjoyed it; it seemed like home with the old woman darning socks on the other side of the fire.

After 10 days I was extracted from the middle of a lecture one morning and sent to London to be Thursby-Pelham's SO2 (staff officer grade 2, a major). We were joined by Frank Stoneman as SO3 and we all had a very busy 2 or 3 weeks contributing the signals share of the plan. However, by late January 1942, the Desert Army had had to go into reverse when Rommel's German forces arrived to bolster the retreating Italians and so our plans had to be abandoned. Then 116 Force Planning Staff was sent to Largs, on the coast west of Glasgow, to amalgamate with another such outfit, 110 Force.

Gerry and I were invited to a wedding on my last day in London: Lance-Corporal the Earl of Harrington and Miss Grey. The connection was that I had spent 2 or 3 holidays in Gloucestershire with Susan Meath-Baker, a cousin of my mother's, and I had met Eileen Gray there. She was a ward in chancery, looked after by Susan. Both bride and groom were vastly rich and the very large reception was held at Claridge's. During the speech-making, all the guests were invited to return to Claridge's in the evening for a dance. Unfortunately I had to take the night train to Scotland.

It seemed probable that we were going to be in Largs for a few months and so both Thursby-Pelham and I wanted to get our wives there. Accommodation was scarce and we had little spare time to look for it but one Sunday afternoon we decided to go out searching together. All we could find was part of a house with 2 bedrooms which could just be called double, a very small living room, and use of kitchen and bathroom. We decided to share this: it proved to be a great mistake. Thursby and I saw too much of one another throughout a long working day and then walked home together to face one another at close quarters for what was left of the evening. Moreover, there were only three even reasonably comfortable chairs and so inevitably I had a hard one!

In early April a signal came into the office decreeing that 1st Guards Brigade, which until then had been a 'lower establishment brigade' (ie a small brigade headquarters and signal section with 3 battalions with limited manpower) was to become an independent brigade group. This meant that it would have a large enough brigade headquarters to act independently without any divisional headquarters and would comprise 4 battalions, a field regiment RA, a field company RE, and a full range of supporting services. As far as Signals were concerned it would have about 80 men under a major instead of 35 under a captain.

So I took this signal into Thursby and suggested that it was about time that I went back to regimental duty and this seemed a good opportunity. Not surprisingly he jumped at the opportunity but at once realized that this was rather rude and made polite noises about how sorry he would be to lose me!

The captain I was replacing left a few days before I arrived at the brigade HQ in a large house about a mile to the east of Perth. Late on a Saturday afternoon in April I drove up and it happened that the first person I met was the brigade major, Willy Pike, a grenadier. He gave me 3 bits of news: 1 of my 2 cipher corporals was under close arrest; the only remaining officer with the brigade signals, Second-Lieutenant Frank Menendez, had taken the unit out the previous day on a route march in order to teach them how to cross a river with the help of a rope, and 3 men had been drowned; and the following night I was to take the night train to London to start planning a special operation for which the brigadier wished to brief me.

Having discovered that the cipher corporal was under arrest only because close arrest was a habit in the Brigade of Guards when anyone was charged even with the most minor misdemeanour, I had him released because it was pointless and because we could not reasonably function without him. I then discussed the drowning with Menendez and my sergeant-major and decided that, for reasons of morale, it was necessary at once to do another and successful river crossing; this was fixed for the next afternoon and very full precautions were planned.

Next I went to see the Brigadier, Copland-Griffiths, Welsh Guards, who told me that the brigade group was to move to the Isle of Wight shortly, preparatory to a cross-Channel operation. Meanwhile there would be planning in London with Combined Operations HQ starting on the Monday. I then had a further session with Willy Pike, who told me to go to Richmond Terrace, off Whitehall, and get myself an office. Members of the brigade HQ staff would be there by Monday afternoon.

I did all that was possible to meet the principal NCOs and to acquire such information as I could about the brigade signals and its state of training, before taking them out on a 10-mile route march and river crossing on the Sunday afternoon. I was very relieved when we were all safely across the river. I then took the night train to London.

Security at Combined Operations HQ seemed lax that Monday morning. I stated who I was at the door but was not asked for any form of identification and I then acquired an office, a typewriter and stationery. When later on I contacted other members of the brigade staff, I also got clerical help. I learned that we would be spending that week in London planning, whilst the brigade group moved to the Isle of Wight. The intention was to seize the island of Alderney and hold it for a limited period with 3 objectives:

a. to go some way towards stilling the current public demand for a 'second front now';
b. to destroy the considerable installations with which the Germans controlled their Atlantic submarine fleet;
c. to stay long enough to persuade the Germans that this was really only a preliminary to an assault on France, thus attracting the German forces away from the Russian front (surely wildly optimistic?).

On one pleasant sunny morning I rose from the desk in my 4th-floor office to look out of the window, attracted by peals of girlish laughter. In the courtyard below was a naval officer surrounded by 6 or 8 Wrens (ladies of the Women's Royal Naval Service). I soon realized that the officer thus privileged was the Chief of Combined Operations, Vice-Admiral Lord Louis Mountbatten (as he then was).

The accommodation allotted to our 4 battalions was, roughly, at the 4 corners of the island. At the northern corner the battalion was on the east side of the River Medina, opposite to Cowes, where Brigade HQ was established. After dinner on my second night there I went back to my office in a new block of flats. About 9 pm an air raid started. Although I had been fairly used to them in London, a raid by 70 aircraft, as was afterwards estimated, on a small town like Cowes seemed a good deal more personal. When a bomb had fallen close enough for my 6th-floor office to sway back and forth by several feet, I decided that it was time for me to go and make sure that my radio communication to all battalions was working satisfactorily, as it seemed unlikely that all post office telephone lines would have remained intact. I spent the rest of the night sorting out various problems until, about an hour before dawn, there was a 2nd raid of similar proportions. When I went in search of breakfast in the brigade HQ mess, I found that several ceilings had come down but that all the rubbish had already been removed and an excellent cooked breakfast was being served as usual.

We were lucky to have had only 3 casualties in the whole brigade: our brigade post office. Before lunch that day several of us were chatting on what was left of the lawn in front of the mess, looking down into the crater of the bomb which had damaged the building, when someone sharper eyed than the rest said, 'Isn't that another bomb down there?' We evacuated the mess rather rapidly and lunch was delayed.

A new wireless set started to become available at this time, the No. 46 set, a small portable designed specially for ship-to-shore communications during an assault landing. I went to Ecko's factory to collect the first 24 of them, 12 for the use of my brigade signals and 12 for my naval opposite number, Lieutenant Peter Howes (who retired as a rear-admiral and then became secretary to the Lord Mayor of London). These sets had their frequencies crystal-controlled, which for a small portable was a great advance at that time, and they gave reliable voice communication over the sea for 5 miles or more. I was assured that they were completely waterproof.

Our first major rehearsal for landing in Alderney was at a beach some miles east of Cowes at dawn on a rainy morning. The 46 sets worked well for a time and then 1 or 2 of them ceased to function. We found water had got inside. I rang Ecko and they sent one of the designers down next day. He refused to believe that water could have got in and plunged a set into a bath full of water. There was a tell-tale stream of bubbles! He arranged for all 24 sets to be re-waterproofed, wholly effectively, in a very few days.

At the same time as the practical training for this operation was going on on the Isle of Wight, detailed planning continued in Combined Operations HQ in Whitehall. I had to make a number of journeys between Cowes and London and usually managed to spend the night at Mytchett, where Gerry was staying with her parents. The fact that our brigade was no longer in Scotland was of course secret and, as far as Gerry and her family were concerned, I was making visits to London for some planning from Perth. I normally wore service dress when visiting London and at Mytchett Gerry was kind enough to clean my buttons. It was unfortunate that she spotted sea spray on them, which resulted from my crossing from the island in an open RN craft. I had to admit my location and swear her to secrecy: no problem as she has always been better at keeping her mouth shut than I.

Shortly before we were due to embark for this operation it was cancelled. The first reason was that, as Alderney was heavily defended, a massive air bombardment was considered necessary before our assault and it was estimated that the RAF would lose 400 aircraft, which could not be afforded. It had been planned that we should have a parachute battalion under command and they would land in the way that was normal at that time, 20 men per aircraft jumping one after the other as quickly as was possible. In practice this meant at least 100 yards on the ground between each man and the next. Depending on the wind direction, aircraft might have drop their loads across the narrow width of the island, in which case each aircraft was bound to drop the first or the last few men in the sea, a reasonable further objection to our plan.

As we had assembled a large raiding force with the necessary shipping, it was decided that, instead, we would stage a major raid on the French coast in the Boulogne area. We embarked in our ships on the appointed day but it was too rough for such an operation and so we waited at anchor in the Spithead area. The Headquarters ship, in which Peter Howes and I were, was a flat-bottomed river gunboat and spending 3 days at anchor in rough weather was not comfortable. It was then decided that the tide would be wrong for our landing and that any material further delay was too much of a security risk for an operation which depended for its success on surprise. So the whole Brigade Group returned to Scotland and our place on the Isle of Wight was taken by the Canadians who later carried out their disastrous raid on Dieppe.

So we returned to routine training and exercises. For one such exercise our HQ was established for 1 night at Glamis Castle, as result of one of our liaison officers being related to Lord Strathmore. We were treated most hospitably, with the result that my batman, Whiteside, told me next morning, in an excited voice, with what truth I don't know, 'Did you know, sir, that you've been sleeping in the bed that Princess Margaret was born in?' I think that in his view that made me slightly royal!

Having been out somewhere, I returned to the HQ one morning to hear a continuous ringing of the alarm bell on our telephone exchange and to find that the exchange was unmanned. It transpired that the DAA&QMG (Deputy Assistant Adjutant and Quartermaster General, in other words the major responsible for administration) had had words with the exchange operator, who had been unable to get a reply from the chap he wanted. Although a Highlander, he had caught the Guards' disease of putting a soldier under close arrest for the most trivial reason and had ordered the operator, by telephone, to place himself under close arrest and report to the guardroom at once. This the operator had done.

Having remonstrated with the DAA&QMG and released the operator, I decided that, as this was not the first occasion on which a staff officer had been gratuitously offensive to an exchange operator, I would man the exchange myself for an hour or 2. It had a most salutary effect.

One Sunday afternoon the Roman Catholic padre of the Brigade and I played golf on the commonland course outside Perth. Apparently this was wrong on a Sunday: we should have played on the club course. We were in battledress, my companion with his dog collar on. We passed close to an elderly Scot and his wife taking a walk when the former said, loud enough to make sure we heard, 'He's no meenister!' Hearing this, my friend explained to me his understanding of the Scottish attitude to Sunday observance.

'An English traveller,' he said, 'stayed on Saturday night in a village inn in Scotland. Next morning he came downstairs with his golf clubs and asked the manager for advice about where to play. "You can't play golf here on Sunday" was the reply. So the traveller returned to his room and came back with a fishing rod only to be told "You can't fish here on Sunday". "Well, what can I do?" he asked. The manager said that he would arrange something. The traveller returned to his room and soon there was a knock on the door. In came a pretty young girl who, without a word, started to undress. Slightly surprised, the traveller turned to the window and started to whistle. As the girl immediately started to dress again, he said, "What's the matter now?" "Ye dinna think I'd sleep with a man who'd whistle on Sunday!"'

One Saturday morning in July the news came through that our Brigade Group was to be absorbed into a newly forming division with 2 other brigades, 11 and 36, and that the present commander of 11 Brigade, Vivien Evelegh, was to be promoted to command the new division, 78 Division. As Evelegh was junior to our brigadier, Copland-Griffiths, and as our Brigade Group was a much more important formation than an ordinary brigade, we felt that this was a slap in the face. At lunch that day in the Brigade HQ mess, Copland-Griffiths sat at the head of the table as usual and a dozen or so of us were down the 2 sides. Not one word was spoken by anyone throughout the meal.

7

STIRLING TO ALGIERS: 1942

78th Divisional Signals, formed in Stirling to serve the new 78th Division, was based on 43 (Wessex) Divisional Signals TA, which provided the RHQ and the 3 company HQs as well as the whole of No. 1 Company. No. 1 Company consisted of A Section, which provided radio communication to the 3 brigade HQs; B Section, which provided a signal office and radio links for rear divisional HQ; C Section, the cable section, was responsible for lines to brigade HQs; D section was for despatch riders, normally on motorcycles; and O section manned the main divisional HQ signal office. No. 2 Company served the Royal Artillery. No. 3 Company Commander was responsible for the 3 signal sections serving the 3 infantry brigades.

So my 1st Guards Brigade Group Signals (about 80 strong) was reduced to about 40 and became J Section in No. 3 Company in 78 Divisional Signals. I was replaced by Captain Paul Strange and became 2IC of the Divisional Signals, combined with OC 1 Company. There was a temporary hitch in my appointment because a wartime rule decreed that no one could be 2IC of a major unit unless he had had a recommendation for command. However, someone, I presume Brigadier Copland-Griffiths, was kind enough to sign the necessary document.

My commanding officer was J C Rau, an Australian who had started in the British Army in Royal Signals and had then left and gone back to Australia. Being on the reserve, he had rejoined when the war started. He was popular with the soldiers but his officers, for the most part, found him rather difficult. He wore a very large, black moustache, which tended to droop in the rain. During an exercise in Scotland, 2 small boys asked him whether they could swing on it: I wonder who put them up to it! His everyday language was quite unprintable. A normal greeting to the GSO1 of the division, asking for news, would be, 'Morning, cock. Got any f—ing griffin?' He knew that it had to be censored in the presence of ladies, with the result that, when he came to lunch with Gerry and me, he was almost silent.

There was much work to do to get this new unit shaken down together, culminating in taking part in a large exercise for the whole of 5 Corps, consisting of 78 Division and 4 Division. A strip of land in Scotland about 2 or 3 miles wide was designated as sea and represented the English Channel. The exercise was to form up the Corps in assembly areas to the north and then to 'embark', cross the 'Channel' and assault 'France' on the far side. Our vessels were of course imaginary but each group which would have occupied a ship was led across the 'Channel' by an umpire on a bicycle. A good deal of imagination was called for and it was further complicated by requiring us to assume that, for every actual hour which passed, 2 had gone by. The exercise was called 'DRYSHOD' and was the wettest I have ever attended.

We were told, around the end of August I think, that we were to start planning an operation, and Rau and I went to London to join a nucleus of the divisional headquarters staff in some offices opposite the Cumberland Hotel, near Marble Arch. One morning Rau glanced out of the window, seized my arm and said, 'Look, cock, look!' The occupant of a bathroom opposite was having difficulty opening the window and had climbed onto the window sill. When I looked there was a perfect female figure spread-eagled against the window for all the street to see!

The outline of the plan, which developed over the next few weeks, was that an American divisional headquarters, with under command 2 US combat teams (approximately equal to British brigades) and one British brigade, 11th, were to seize Algiers; 78 Divisional Signals were to provide the communications for this force. Although 78 Divisional Headquarters would take no part, they would be there as observers, getting ready to move eastwards some 400 miles into Tunisia. They would take 11 Brigade with them overland. Meanwhile 36 Brigade would have landed at Bougie (about halfway to Tunisia), with one battalion about 50 miles further east at Djedjelli. Ahead of this force, leading the advance into Tunisia would be a parachute battalion, followed by an armoured regimental group, to be known as Blade Force, based on 17/21 Lancers, commanded by Lieutenant-Colonel Dick Hull, of whom more anon. 78 Divisional Signals would move east with the Divisional Headquarters.

One of the problems facing 36 Brigade Signal Section was that the distance between Bougie, where Brigade HQ would be, and Djedjelli, where the forward battalion would land, was about 50 miles, whereas the wireless sets available (No. 11) had a reliable range of less than 10 miles. I therefore went to the War Office and asked, to their surprise, for 4 heliographs. I had remembered using them in the Marlborough College OTC Signal Section and finding that, with a bright summer sun, they were dazzling at 7 miles: it seemed likely that with an African sun they would provide reasonable communication at 50 miles. Unfortunately this was never put to the test because the sea was so rough that the forward battalion had to land with the rest of the brigade at Bone.

After planning started, Rau went back to Stirling to prepare the unit as far as was possible without breach of security. Only he, I and one clerk were allowed to know the details of the forthcoming operation, although the fact that we were going on some operation somewhere was more generally known. Over the next few weeks I travelled back and forth between Stirling and London about 5 times. During one of my visits to Stirling we had arranged for an appropriate army doctor to lecture to all ranks on the probable diseases to be met in a subtropical area and the precautions to be taken. With no pictures or other such aids, he gave such a graphic account of the horrors to be encountered that 2 soldiers fainted.

At this time armoured command vehicles (ACVs) were in use at the headquarters of armoured divisions and brigades. Each had room for about two staff officers and one or two wireless operators. They were specially built and normally housed a main wireless set to communicate with a lower or higher headquarters and a small set for communication with the other ACVs at the same headquarters. By this means it was possible to keep the headquarters in business on the move. It was now decided that an infantry division should be similarly equipped but with unarmoured vehicles: lorry command vehicles or LCVs. As these vehicles did not exist, we were issued with an appropriate number of 3-ton lorries and told to adapt them with the help of 1 or 2 engineering firms. They were converted to our own design in an astonishingly short time. There was one compartment for the sets and 2 operators and another for 2 staff officers with appropriate headsets and microphones. Realising that in quiet periods the staff would not be keen on manning both sets, I gave each staff position a switch with 3 positions: one to engage set A, one for set B, and one in the middle which allowed him to listen with one ear on A and one on B.

There was a great rush to complete the final detailed planning, that is to say, exactly what men and what vehicles and equipment went into each ship. I had to work this out with the help of the one clerk who was in the know. It took us from a Saturday morning to Tuesday evening with no more break than an occasional nap in a chair. We had to distribute about 350 men between 13 ships and prepare detailed orders for the senior rank of our unit on board each ship, who in some cases was no more than a lance-corporal. Those in personnel ships had to be told what MT ship their vehicles would be in, how and when they were to transfer to the MT ship, when they were to go ashore and where, and what their task was on landing. The orders had to be prepared about 4 weeks ahead of D-Day and were not allowed to be opened until the fleet had been at sea for a week, ie long after there was any possibility of asking questions. A further complication was that, for security reasons, frequencies and call signs were changed every 24 hours and we did not know for certain, except within 3 or 4 days, which would be D-Day.

After embarkation there was a practice landing on a beach on the west coast of Scotland and then ships assembled again off Gourock. I found that there had been a small amount of damage to equipment during this rehearsal and sought permission to go ashore to get spares, permission that, for security reasons, was granted only grudgingly. Many of the ships in the convoy had both British and Americans aboard and we had found, after embarking, that all ships were to be bound by the American rule that no alcohol would be available. So I returned from foraging for spares with a large box labelled 'WIRELESS PARTS – WITH CARE – THIS SIDE UP', which made a marked contribution towards solving the alcohol problem.

Shortly before we finally sailed, the army commander, Lieutenant-General Kenneth Anderson, visited all ships to speak to the troops. It was a drizzly afternoon and he was wearing a rather scruffy mackintosh. He was an unimpressive speaker and I'm afraid that his visit was not the tonic to morale that it was no doubt intended to be.

The convoy sailed south-west from the British Isles until we were in mid-Atlantic and then south, encountering very rough weather. One day I was duty officer and had, amongst other things, to inspect meals, which were sparsely attended. I had not seen my batman, Whiteside, for a day or 2 and thought he was still laid low. However, he appeared for this meal looking most unwell. I asked him if he were really better. He replied, 'No, sir, but I heard it was tripe for tea'!

My driver was travelling in an MT ship and he fared

worse in the storm. He was sick over the side and lost his false teeth. It was impossible to replace them for many weeks after we landed and he had to consume 'compo' rations without teeth. Fortunately Whiteside, who did the cooking for our small group, devised a way of pounding the hard biscuits to make a kind of porridge.

Eventually the personnel convoy turned north-east and passed through the Straits of Gibraltar during the night of 6/7 November. We continued on a course north of east as though making for Malta and then turned south towards Algiers just after dark on Saturday evening, 7 November. The personnel and MT convoys met about 2 miles north of Algiers around midnight. We could see the lights of Algiers, a most unusual sight for us coming from more than 3 years of blackout.

There were initial landings by Commandos soon after midnight and, later, leading units of our main force went ashore in a large bay about 10 miles west of Algiers. At the same time there was a lot of movement in small craft carrying men from personnel ships to vehicle-carrying ships, whence people would go ashore in their own vehicles. Around 3 or 4 am I embarked with a party of about 8 in a small craft and it was not until one got down to water level that one realized that it was distinctly rough. Reaching our MT ship, we found that our craft was rising and falling in relation to the ship by 4 or 5 feet. Each man had to balance on the gunwale, wearing his full kit, wait until the top of a rise, jump on to a rope ladder and go rapidly up a couple of steps to make sure that he did not leave a leg to be crushed between boat and ship.

The next job was to sort ourselves out to the particular ship's boat which carried our own vehicles and then to check the equipment in the vehicles and start the engines, which had not of course been run for a month. Our boat was lowered into the water about 6 am just as it was getting light. the RCNVR (Royal Canadian Naval Volunteer Reserve) sub-lieutenant in charge of my landing craft then turned to me and said, 'Where do you want to land?'

I had assumed he knew! However, I got out my map, not chart, and gazed at the coastline a mile or 2 away. I pointed to what appeared to be the eastern end of a large bay and said, 'I think it's over there'. Fortunately this proved to be right and the craft was beached on to hard sand, enabling us to drive ashore without incident. If this was typical of the arrangements for landing, it seems that we were very lucky not to be seriously opposed.

We went a few hundred yards inland, joining the advance element of the American Divisional HQ we served and opening radio communication to the main HQ afloat and to the HQs of the Brigades/Combat Teams ashore. A new series of convenient abbreviations had just been introduced: eg Sunray meant Commander, with Seagull, Acorn etc for the various staff branches. As we were serving both American and British headquarters, one commonly heard, 'Do you want an American seagull or a British one?'

Movement towards Algiers seemed ridiculously slow as there appeared to be no opposition. It was only much later we heard of the complicated political talks going on with the French authorities. By Monday night I had established a so-called advanced signal centre a short distance outside a village about 5 miles from Algiers. I found that our lighting facilities were rather limited and so I sent a soldier to the village to buy candles, which he did with no trouble. About 10 pm an American colonel warned me to double sentries as there was real danger of attack from this same village! I didn't take him too seriously.

The following morning we moved to a hilltop only 2 or 3 miles out of Algiers. By this time General Vivian Evelegh was getting impatient at the slow progress into Algiers. Until we could get into the town and start unloading at the port, we could not begin the long but increasingly urgent journey east to Tunisia. Meanwhile the Germans were already starting to bring troops from Sicily and Italy into northern Tunisia. Evelegh could not persuade the American Divisional Commander to move faster because the latter was himself tied by the American political authorities and their negotiations with Admiral Darlan who had, until 8 November, been a firm supporter of the French Vichy Government. Darlan was now sitting on the fence waiting to decide what had the best prospects for Darlan.

To try to discover what was the actual situation, Evelegh sent his ADC in a scout car down the road towards Algiers and was somewhat anxious when he had not returned a couple of hours later. It turned out that he had stopped at a French Army barracks, where he was ushered into the officers' mess and given an alcoholic welcome, which he could not opt out of without causing grave offence. He eventually returned and reported that the locals appeared to be friendly!

About 5 pm that evening 2 or 3 German bombers came over Algiers, presumably wanting to demonstrate to any wavering Frenchmen that the long arm of the Führer was still in business. They passed not far from our position and there happened to be a Bren gun on an anti-aircraft mounting near where I was standing. I fired at one of the aircraft and was delighted to be able to shout to someone, 'Look! There are sparks coming out of his tail', only to get the damping reply, 'It's his tracer coming back at us'.

Later that Tuesday night we entered Algiers and took over the German consulate as the British Divisional HQ. The Germans had evidently left in a hurry, their dirty lunch plates being still on the dining-room table. During the next 2 or 3 days our heavy vehicles came ashore and we were nearly ready to move east.

On Thursday evening Bertie Ashe, who commanded 3 Company, and I went into the town on one motorcycle to try to get a meal. Bertie and I were to see a lot of one another. He was a consulting engineer in the Territorial Army, with a wife and 2 children, a delightful man of around 35 who was highly competent at all he did. He never betrayed any irritation at being subordinate to a pip-squeak of 25.

We went into a restaurant where we were almost mobbed by hospitable Frenchmen who regarded any hesitation in accepting their drinks as an insult. We eventually escaped, having had only a liquid supper. Neither of us was fit to drive our motorcycle but I did so and a guardian angel protected us. My only recollection of that ride is that, when faced with a large grass-centred roundabout, I drove straight over the centre of it.

On reaching our HQ about 10 pm I was told that the general had just summoned an 'O' (Order) Group and that Rau wanted me to represent him. I went sound asleep during the meeting and I don't doubt that Evelegh knew why, but some kind fellow apparently said that I had been working all hours lately and Evelegh was generous enough to ask no further questions.

By Saturday we had assembled sufficient vehicles and equipment to be ready to move. At 11 am Rau told me that the General, with a small tactical HQ, including himself, was going to fly to Bone, on the coast not far short of the border with Tunisia, that afternoon. I was to take all available signal resources by road with the aim of establishing communications from Bone eastwards to HQ 36 Brigade as early as possible. I had 4 LCVs and 2 other 3-ton lorries carrying food, petrol, water and a mass of other stores, and about 5 or 6 men in each of these 6 vehicles. There were also 10 DRs (despatch riders) on motorcycles. No one could tell us what the road was like or what the local French attitude to us would be. It was 375 miles.

8

TO TUNISIA: 1942

We had been told to take the inland road via Constantine, leaving at 1500. I have since learned that the reason for this route was that 36 Brigade was moving east from Bougie on the coast road, whilst 11 Brigade, starting from Blida, west of Algiers, would not want the inland road until later in the day. My little convoy, with its grossly overloaded 3-ton lorries and the new LCVs, could travel up to 30 mph with reasonable safety on the flat but much less when climbing through the coastal range of the Atlas mountains.

Our first long halt was in the mountains in the middle of the night, when I allowed 2 hours' sleep. There was no possibility of driving straight through because we only had 2 or 3 spare drivers or motorcycle riders. Taking turns as best we could, we continued until we reached Constantine in the early afternoon of Sunday. I was then a bit concerned about water as we had had to limit the amount we brought because of the excess weight.

As we entered the town there was an air-raid warning. I stopped at a largish house and asked Madame to be allowed to fill our jerricans from her tap. She objected because she was convinced that it was the arrival of my large army which was going to result in the whole town being destroyed by German bombers. I tried in vain to persuade her that it was unlikely to be a genuine alarm (in which I was subsequently proved right); that in any case our arrival was purely coincidental; and that the sooner we got water the sooner we would be gone. Eventually I had to insist, fingering my revolver as an added inducement. I'm afraid this did little for Anglo-French relations, as I have no doubt she told her neighbours that she had had to give way being in imminent peril of her life! We helped ourselves to water and went on our way as quickly as we could.

Winding through the mountains north-east of Constantine one of the despatch riders got a puncture. He had the necessary equipment to mend it himself and was told to do so and catch up the convoy in due course. As it was so slow moving, there should have been no difficulty but, as we learnt sadly the following day, he must have driven too fast round one of the multitude of S-bends: he had gone over the side and been killed.

We arrived in Bone at 2300 on Sunday night, 15 November, and tried at once to open a radio link forward to HQ 36 Brigade, which was then at Tabarka, about 70 miles east, just inside Tunisia, with its forward battalions in contact with German forces in the Djebel Abiod area. Our nucleus divisional HQ had set itself up in a cork factory. It seemed that the situation was none too healthy because, whilst we had fighter planes available, the tanker with their fuel had been sunk. Although initially we had nothing but Bren light machine-guns to defend ourselves with, we brought one German plane down in the sea.

By midday on Monday we had still been unable to get through by radio to 36 Brigade and so that afternoon I set off on a motorcycle, with one despatch rider as escort, to go to their HQ to try to solve the problem. As we left, German aircraft came over and LMGs opened up on them from both sides of a long straight stretch of road, their tracer making a sort of ceremonial arch for us to drive through. Approaching Tabarka, a section of the road was pitted with small bomb craters. My escort came off his machine in one of them and, being a small chap, was quite unable to right his bike unaided. It happened that most of our despatch rider section were rather small and had recently been equipped with what were then regarded as large and heavy motorcycles. So this was a problem which would occur again but it was counterbalanced by the excellent sergeant in command of the section, who had the figure of an international rugby forward.

So I entered Tunisia and reached HQ 36 Brigade in Tabarka. I cannot remember what the reason for lack of communication was: probably the not unusual attitude that rear links to higher HQs are commonly given a lower priority than those forward. Anyway, my arrival seemed to coincide with establishing this link.

On return to Bone next day, I found that the HQ had moved into the local yacht club. Whilst 36 Brigade were trying to battle their way through the hills and cork forests on the way to Bizerta, 11 Brigade had moved east from Blida aerodrome, to the south-west of Algiers, along the same inland road as I had travelled as far as Constantine, and had then gone on eastwards into Tunisia, aiming for Medjez-el-Bab. Divisional HQ had to follow one of the brigades eastwards, accepting that its communications with the other would be tenuous because the only lateral road between the 2 was the long and twisty road between Beja and Djebel Abiod. Radio communication, with the sets available then, was uncertain over such a distance, particularly at certain times of day. More vehicles having arrived to augment Divisional HQ, we moved via Souk Ahras on to the 11 Brigade axis, setting up HQ at Souk el Arba.

During the first of these moves we learnt to our cost that our normal practice of moving our convoys at a density of 30 vehicles to the mile (vtm) did not pay when the enemy dominated the sky. This was quickly changed to 6 vtm but this had the snag that the HQ was spread over perhaps 4 or 5 miles and so the wireless sets designed for intercommunication between vehicles on the move, having a range of only a mile or 2, were useless. To try to ensure that some sort of links were kept going, I developed a system of riding on the pillion of a motorcycle, driven by my batman, Whiteside, and climbing from it on to the ladder which was attached to the left rear of each LCV. As these vehicles were normally lumbering along at a steady pace, this was not as difficult as it sounds.

After moving in this rather unsatisfactory way to Beja and then forward to Oued Zarga, it was decided that in future we would send half the HQ to the new position to open for business there before closing with the other half in the old position. This proved to be a much more efficient system, particularly in view of the difficulty of maintaining radio communication over these great distances: usually only Morse was possible anyway and so there was no question of commanders or staffs talking to one another even when stationary, let alone on the move.

This does not purport to be an account of the war in Tunisia. (The best that I have found is that by Gregory Blaxland, *The Plain Cook and the Great Showman*, published by William Kimber and Co Ltd in 1977. It is no longer in print but is at present obtainable through public libraries.) I shall merely continue to record the principal incidents which affected me, together with such background as seems necessary.

The first such incident was a few weeks later when the Allied drive to break through to Tunis had been defeated by the combined obstacles of German resistance and mud. At this time of year, in this part of northern Tunisia, it seemed to rain torrentially for 2 or 3 days, followed by a rather longer interval of delightful sunshine. During the rain, and for a day or 2 afterwards, only tarmacked roads were negotiable by wheeled vehicles and they were dangerous because the wet mud turned them into patchy skating rinks. They were so bad that the rider of a motorcycle often had to travel with his feet sliding on the road on either side in order to remain upright. If, on arrival at his destination, he did not immediately clean the mud from the wheels, it would set hard and then the only answer was to take the wheels off. Mud favoured the side which remained stationary and any major movement had to take place during the unpredictable days of fine weather. In early January we withdrew some miles, to areas which could be more easily defended, until we should be able to build up our strength for a further offensive.

None of the vehicles available in First Army until then had been 4-wheel drive and the arrival of 6 jeeps in these conditions was naturally greeted with enthusiasm. I was lucky enough to be allotted one of them. During the withdrawal our divisional headquarters went back to Beja and I spent more than 24 hours travelling around the divisional area supervising the necessary rearrangements of our telephone lines. I sent my driver back to HQ on some chore in another vehicle, keeping my jeep to finish off the job in the forward area and then to return to HQ, driving myself.

At 10 o'clock on a lovely sunny morning I was nearly back, when I noticed the not uncommon noise of aircraft overhead. One could at that time safely assume that all aircraft were enemy: we seemed to have none in direct support. So, when there was a loud crash and my vehicle came to an abrupt halt with my head going through the windscreen, my reaction on recovering from being somewhat dazed was to look for a bomb crater. There was none. I had gone to sleep driving and had run into the back of a stationary French lorry. This had happened immediately outside an advanced dressing station and so I was taken in there and given the inevitable cup of hot, sweet tea. I soon realized that, if I didn't make a quick move, I should be detained. So I walked out and hitched a lift for the last mile or so to HQ. The jeep was a write-off and I was naturally rather unpopular!

My father, Hugh Hancock

My mother, Cicely Hancock

The family in Switzerland, 1921

Claude and Henrietta Hancock

Francis and Lucy Child

Francis and Kathleen Eliot

Olive Cairns

Aunts and Uncles at Lunt wedding, 1912. L to R standing: Cicely Sherbrooke, Cuthbert Sherbrooke, Cicely Hancock, Hugh Sherbrooke, Maimie Sherbrooke, Hugh Hancock, Penn Sherbrooke, Sybil and Dick Francklin. Adults sitting: Dorothy Sherbrooke, Marjorie and Geoffrey Lunt, Evie Duncan

9

MEDJEZ-EL-BAB: 1943

For the first month or so, the First Army in Tunisia consisted of 2 infantry brigades and 1 armoured regimental group, plus some parachute troops and 2 commandos, all under command of HQ 78th Division, which came under command of HQ 5 Corps, which was under HQ First Army, which was under Allied Force HQ in Algiers, some 400 miles to the west. It was truly said that 'Never have so few been commanded by so many from so far'!

By January, in spite of the arrival of 46th Division to the north and 6th Armoured Division to the south, 78th Division still had a very wide front with inevitable gaps between battalions and virtually no reserve. Divisional HQ was then in Testour. There had been little movement for a week or 2 and I noticed that there came, through the signal office, frequent reports to the effect that patrols had covered such and such an area and there was nothing to report. I realized that I was ignorant of the detail of the workings of an infantry battalion and had no idea of what sort of patrols were going out and what they did. As it happened that at this time a major of the Royal Canadian Corps of Signals, Orvile Gamble, had been attached to my company to gain experience, I managed to persuade my commanding officer, John Rau, that I should attach myself to one of these patrols, handing over my company to Gamble.

I went to see the commanding officer, Roddie Hill, of the 2nd Coldstream Guards, whom I knew when I was signal officer of 1st Guards Brigade Group in Scotland.

His battalion were holding Medjez-el-Bab and patrolling over a wide area to the east and to the north towards the foot of Longstop Hill. Patrols were then normally of 2 types: either reconnaissance patrols of 2 or 3 men whose object was to find something out without getting involved, or fighting patrols, perhaps 30 strong, who could fight for information, perhaps take a prisoner, and generally try to dominate no man's land, which was often 3 or 4 miles wide. He agreed to me attaching myself to one of the latter on the basis that I was under command of the subaltern concerned.

I had dinner at battalion HQ in Medjez railway station and then prepared myself for this patrol as instructed, the prime requirements being to blacken one's face and hands, to ensure that one had no equipment likely to rattle or make any noise and had no document in a pocket which, if captured or killed, could give information. Between Medjez and Longstop the land was entirely flat except for an occasional wadi and a very few scattered farms. During the next few hours the platoon which I accompanied covered, moving in a rough circle, a large part of this area, moving quietly and stopping to lie down at intervals to scan the land ahead. If an enemy patrol is doing the same thing, whichever is lying down when they meet is obviously at an advantage.

There was a tree-lined track, showing up white in the moonlight, leading north from Medjez. It reached a small farm after about a mile, and then, after another mile or so, a much larger farm, Chassart Teffaha. We did not know whether the latter was occupied by the enemy but it seemed unlikely as, within half a mile or so of it, we crossed this track without being spotted. I did, however, notice that there was a telephone cable of high quality with plastic insulation, which appeared much stronger than the rubber and fibre which we used, running between these 2 farms. In due course we got back to our own lines and I had learned something of what 'Nothing to report' meant.

When I told Rau about this cable, which seemed to be

there for the taking, we were short of much of the signal equipment we needed and particularly of telephone cable. Rau was a real squirrel with signal equipment and so I had little difficulty in persuading him that I should take a few men with me another night with a drum-barrow on which to wind this cable in. Hill of the Coldstream agreed and a night or 2 later I took 5 volunteers and, accompanied by the Coldstream signal officer and one of his men, we set forth to get this cable. Meanwhile a larger patrol had been sent further to the north with the probability that, if there were contact with the enemy, they would make it rather than our weak and untrained group.

When we were nearing the first farm, I left the battalion signal officer with his man and 4 of mine and the drum-barrow ready to wind in the cable, starting at that end. Meanwhile one of my men and I made our way, moving parallel with the track, as near to Chassart Teffaha as I thought prudent. I told the soldier to cut the wire there and, as he did so, we heard, from the direction of the small farm behind us, words of command in German followed by several bursts of light machine-gun fire and then further words of command.

My next job was obviously to find out what had happened to the party I had left near the small farm. With the lack of continued firing, my immediate reaction was that they must have been killed or captured: an appalling loss for such a relatively unimportant objective. I led my one soldier (I will call him Jones as I now forget his real name) south-westwards for perhaps half-a-mile and then turned south-east so as to approach the farm with the moon, which would shortly rise, behind it. I had noticed from my previous patrol that it is much easier on a flat plain to see an object silhouetted against the brightness of the area of moonrise than with the moon behind one. Soon after we had turned south-east, Jones and I lay down for a few minutes in the prescribed fashion.

It was lucky we did so at that moment because, almost at once, we saw a German patrol of 20 or more men lie down 50 or 60 yards away and facing us. The German-shaped helmet was unmistakable with the moon rising behind. My first reaction was that, even if they had not yet seen us, they could not fail to do so if we moved. Not having seriously planned for such an encounter, I had only a Sten gun and Jones, a despatch rider by trade, a revolver, which was the standard equipment for him. I saw nothing for it but to fire directly they got to their feet and hope in the subsequent confusion to be able to make off to our right, the south-west, which seemed to be near the end of the German line. With this aim I took out of my pockets my 4 reserve magazines and laid them ready for use in front of me.

Then I began to realize that they might well not be able to see us even if we got on our feet, provided that we remained doubled as low as possible. I whispered instructions to Jones to make off south-west as quickly as possible, whilst I remained ready to distract attention if necessary. If nothing happened after he had had a reasonable start, I would rejoin him a few hundred yards on. I saw no purpose in provoking an unnecessary fight against such odds but I have realized since that I had the considerable advantages of knowing where they were and of presenting a much smaller target: 1 or 2 persons against 20 or more. I found that I wasn't that brave (or foolhardy?). In due course I followed Jones and caught him up without being spotted.

The next question was what had happened to the other 6 chaps. It was hardly likely that all had been killed and yet this patrol had obviously not got prisoners with them. It might be that prisoners were being taken directly north by another escort. I had no reasonable way of approaching the farm and decided that I should get back to our own lines as quickly as possible to see whether they could throw any light on it.

It was about 0300 when I reached RHQ and saw the adjutant, who was of course aware of the firing, but he knew no more as the other 6 had not returned. I decided that I must at least find out what had happened and told him that I would go directly to the small farm and learn what I could. I left Jones behind because there was no way he could help. When I got to the farm there was no trace of anybody, not even of my drum-barrow or the cable. Finally I gave it up and walked back despondently to our lines as it got light.

Never in my life have I been more thankful than when I was greeted by Colonel Roddie Hill with the news that all 6 had returned safely half an hour after I had set out the second time. They had been lying down within a hundred yards of the farm, when a German patrol of about platoon strength put in a drill-book attack on the farm in case it had been occupied by us. Our 6 got a grandstand view of covering fire being given by the wing sections whilst the centre section entered the farm. The Germans then found the drumbarrow in the road and appropriated it, winding up their cable. Our 6 wisely returned to our lines by a roundabout route to the south-east.

I accompanied one more patrol some days later, also from Medjez but from a line battalion which had taken over from the Coldstream Guards and which shall be nameless. A subaltern was in command of an augmented platoon about 40 strong. When we were not too far from the foot of Longstop Hill, men were chattering as they walked along. At one stop it was discovered that about 12 men were missing; perhaps they had failed to get up after our last halt. A bit later the subaltern confessed to me that he was lost. It was a dark night with no moon and I then learnt that neither he nor anyone else had a compass with them: a mad omission on a flat plain of which they had no previous experience. I knew the area a bit by now and I had a compass: so I was able to lead them home and was very relieved to get there without being heard or spotted. The missing 12 men had been home a long time!

10

TESTOUR TO ALGIERS: 1943

In late February our Divisional HQ was still in Testour and our battalions were spread over a wide front, the reserves which we should have had having gone south to help the Americans hold the Kasserine area. Our own Royal Signals manpower was stretched to the extent that all duties were on a 2-man basis to cover the 24 hours, a tolerable arrangement for a limited period but progressively more tiring as the weeks went by. My No. 1 Company provided the communications at Divisional HQ and those off duty lived in an olive grove up a hill about a mile to the east of the HQ.

No. 6 Commando was 5 or 6 miles further to the east when the Germans put in a serious attack on this thinly help position. When finally the Commando was being overrun, their Royal Signals rear link wireless station was given a message to get through to Divisional HQ at the highest priority to warn them of the position. The corporal in charge, Corporal Lord, was told to get the message through and then abandon his truck, which had broken down, and get back on foot as quickly as possible. He sent his assistant operator on first, got the message through and was killed as he set light to his truck.

When the message reached Divisional HQ, I was told to organize the best possible defensive position on my side of HQ and, if attacked, hold it at all costs until I was relieved. I was to use all men who were not on essential duty at HQ, that is to say, men who should have been sleeping and eating during their off-duty shifts.

There was one road from the east along which enemy

wheeled vehicles would have to come. Even tracked vehicles would be very likely to get bogged down if they left the road. So I organized a defensive position astride of and covering the road and set all available men to digging and, as far as possible, concealing what they had dug. We had 1 or 2 anti-tank rifles but these were known to be remarkably ineffective, apart from a lucky hit on a weak point. Of more use, we had a supply of anti-tank grenades, which, whilst not strong enough to destroy a tank, could bring it to a halt by breaking a track. There was not time initially to dig these into the road and conceal them; so I arranged a few hidden piles of grenades on one side of the road strung together so that, if pulled by a string from the other side of the road just before the tank reached that point, there would be a good chance of disabling the tank and thus blocking the road for further vehicles. A small trench was dug for the puller of the string and covering fire would be available from either side. I gave this unenviable task to Second-Lieutenant Derek Emley, who gave me a somewhat sideways look and got on with the job: Colonel Derek Emley reminded me of this incident when we met a few years ago.

I chose my company HQ where I had a good view of the whole position and told my Sergeant-Major to arrange the digging so that we could all 5 (he, the clerk, the driver, the batman and myself) stand in the trench and just see out. This presented a difficulty as our heights were spread fairly evenly from the clerk at about 5 feet 3 inches to myself at 6 feet 6 inches. Each person's section of trench was dug according to his height.

Around 10 pm I took out a patrol of about 30 men, who came primarily from our QM and MT repair sections, with the aims of discovering if an attack threatened and of preventing the enemy finding out the weakness of our position. These men had, of course, no experience of such things but most were above averagely intelligent and they listened carefully to their instructions. I had confidence that they would, if required, give a good account of themselves. We met no one.

The company HQ trench seemed splendid until it rained in the middle of an exceptionally cold night and all the water drained down into my section! I arranged for a rum ration to be issued about 0500 and was glad of an excuse to take it round the whole position myself. Fortunately the rain that night was heavy enough for the German vehicles to get stuck in the mud and they did not come near us. A day or 2 later we were relieved.

I have read that, in the campaigns to clear Tunisia, of Eighth Army from the east after El Alamein and First Army from the west, First Army suffered much higher casualties in proportion to strength. Certain of 78th Division's battalions had high casualties, notable 2nd Hampshire's at Tebourba, where Le Patourel got his VC, and 3rd Grenadier Guards at Longstop Hill. 78th Divisional Signals lost all 3 brigade signal officers: first, Bretherton in 11th Brigade, who was sent on a dangerous liaison job because there was no liaison officer to send; then Paul Strange, who had taken over 1st Guards Brigade Signals from me; and later Geoffrey Hagger in 36th Brigade. Their company commander, Bertie Ashe, with whom I shared a vehicle and messing in the early days in Tunisia, was killed later in Italy.

In mid-March I was told that I had been selected to attend a staff course at Camberley starting in late May and lasting 4 months. I thought that this would mean staying with 78th Division until at least the end of April and thus having a reasonable chance of seeing the Tunisian campaign through to the end. Unfortunately Kenneth Thursby-Pelham, now the Brigadier Chief Signal Officer of First Army, thought otherwise. He insisted that I hand over at the end of March in order to have 3 or 4 weeks to set up the Signals Wing of a new First Army School, just over the border into Algeria, not far from Souk Ahras.

Peter Blake, who had been my Company Commander when I joined 1st Divisional Signals in 1939, took over my job in 78th Division and I started on my new task. There were to be several wings of this school for different arms, the first being mine for signals trade training and another for machine-gun training. Most of the signals work had to be done indoors and huts had already been erected for us: it was unlucky that the huts had been sited in a valley across which, a little higher up, was the only convenient machine-gun range. The noise was not conducive to good classroom instruction.

The administration of this school was in the hands of a tubby and pompous major of the Parachute Regiment who liked to maintain the fiction that he was the commandant rather than merely the camp commandant. I had been charged with the task of providing telephone communication between the School and First Army HQ, about 10 miles, and a 'quad' cable, a single rubber-covered cable with 4 wires, was laid. This would normally provide 2 circuits, with a pair of wires each, and I intended to connect these to our camp exchange. However, Parachute Pete, as he was known, insisted that he must have his own private line. There were inevitably differences of view between him on the one hand and the wings on the other and these sometimes had to be resolved at First Army HQ: if he had his own private line to 'higher authority' and the rest of us had to take our chance on one busy public line, I foresaw that we might have trouble. So I arranged to get hold of a pair of superposing units, a useful device which I suppose is now found only in a museum. They enabled a third conversation to be conducted on the quad cable without interfering with the other two; moreover, because it used 2 wires, instead of 1, in each direction, the 'phantom' circuit had half the resistance of the physical circuits. I never disclosed to Pete the existence of this high-quality circuit and kept its telephone discreetly hidden in my office, allowing only those running other wings to use it.

I managed to make one visit to 78th Division in mid-April and found that the general advance towards Tunis had really started; I was sad no longer to be a part of it. I finally left Souk Ahras by train for Algiers, a journey scheduled to take 24 hours, but the railway service was quite inadequate for the load that had been put on it and no one expected schedules to be kept. There was a standing order for military personnel travelling by train that they must take 7 days' rations with them. My journey took 2 days instead of 1, because of a minor landslide, and my civilian travelling companions were glad of the help I was able to give them from my store of rations.

In Algiers I happened to discover that an old friend, Dick Wheeler, in the Royal Navy, was at Allied Force HQ. Our parents had been friends during the First World War and we had met in our prams, though our first real meeting was at Marlborough. Dick's eyesight was not good enough to go through Dartmouth and so he had come to Marlborough in order to enter the navy later as a pusser. When we went our several ways from school, we agreed a bet of sixpence on which of us would reach the rank of rear-admiral/major-general first. In due course Dick sent me a well-polished old sixpence, although this was hardly fair as he had been invalided out of the navy in 1946 with TB. He went to work for the Duchy of Lancaster, ending with a KCVO.

At the time of my visit to Force HQ he had distinguished himself in another way. The night before I arrived, there had been a rowdy and alcoholic party, which adjourned to the naval operations room, where there was a large chart of the Mediterranean covering the whole of one wall, with ship positions marked with flags on pins. I believe that Dick took the lead in crying, 'Let's sweep the Mediterranean.' This they did with a large broom, starting at Gibraltar. Not until they got to Malta did someone intervene!

I learnt that there was a section in Allied Force HQ which dealt with airborne forces, and that it was headed by Major-General Browning. So I asked to see him and told him that I had some gliding and a little power-flying experience: please could I join airborne forces when I had done my staff course? As I would have 2 or 3 weeks at home before going to Camberley, it was arranged that I should be attached for a few days to 6th Airborne Divisional Signals on Salisbury Plain. This bore fruit in the end but not as soon as I hoped.

I sailed home in a troopship which was considered fast enough to travel unescorted. One evening many of us were in the dining saloon on a deck below sea level watching the film, then fairly newly released, *The Foreman Goes to France*. It ends with a battle scene, with guns firing and numerous explosions. We found it rather too realistic when the whole ship shuddered. In fact a bomb dropped from a high-flying aircraft had hit the sea close to our ship but had fortunately done no damage.

The commanding officer of 5th Corps Signals, when I was with 78th Division, had been Robin Yolland, an old friend who had taught me on my Q Course. Halfway between our 2 units was a White Friars monastery where they made tolerable wines. So I arrived home with a carboy (about the equivalent of 24 bottles) of white wine; and again we reached Liverpool on a Sunday with no Customs open.

11

CAMBERLEY, WENTWORTH, HAMMERSMITH, CAMBERLEY: 1943–44

While I had been in North Africa, Gerry had been living with her parents at Mytchett and working in the Canadian troops' canteen. She was also taking her turn on the local fire-watching roster, for which duty she was required to wear a tin hat which was most becoming! As the Ovens' house, Mytchett Heath, was only about 4 miles from the Staff College, they were kind enough to allow us to stay with them for this 4-month course. In the 2 or 3 weeks before the course started we had a brief holiday staying at the Spread Eagle Hotel in Midhurst and then I spent a few days with 6th Airborne Divisional Signals near Tidworth. There was a charming and obviously highly competent commanding officer, Paddy Smallman-Tew; sadly he was killed in the early days of the Normandy landings.

The wartime staff course was limited to teaching the essentials of staff work at divisional and brigade levels with only brief references to the workings of higher-level headquarters. Having, in a signals capacity, worked at a variety of levels, I found I had some advantage over the majority of students who had spent their time wholly in their own regiments. I had the further advantage that I was the only student who had taken part in the Tunisian campaign, which had come to a successful conclusion whilst I was on the way home.

Nevertheless it was a fairly hard-worked course and I learnt much: most importantly, how little I knew of the jobs of the divisional and brigade staffs. Had I attended such a course before going to North Africa, I am sure that I could have done my job there more competently. This was when I concluded that the senior signal officer at any formation headquarters can do his job better if he is fully qualified to do the job of the senior staff officer at that headquarters: a dictum which I stated publicly on more than one occasion later in my service. It was one which was sometimes not too well received either by staff officers of other arms, who felt that signal officers would be encroaching on their preserves, or by signal officers who, perhaps highly qualified technically, felt that this was an unnecessary hurdle.

An odd feature of this course was that, out of 180 students, I was the only Royal Signals officer, whereas Royal Signals then formed about 7 per cent of the army. It can be argued that Royal Signals had had to expand due to the war at about twice the rate of other arms and were therefore desperately short-handed: winning the war came first. I am, however, convinced that sending only one officer on this course was a gross error. To have sent, say, 6, half the proper proportion, would not only have paid dividends in the long run but would have ensured that there was a small field of officers available from whom to choose Royal Signals officers for the directing staff.

For one of the indoor exercises, I was one of a group of students required to set up and operate a mock divisional HQ in the Staff College library. To this end I was helping to move a heavy filing cabinet, when it fell on the end of my finger, slicing off a small piece. I was taken to the Cambridge Hospital in Aldershot, where, under a general anaesthetic, they took a piece out of my forearm and sewed it on the end of my finger. I was back at work next day, with my one war wound incurred in an indoor battle at the Staff College!

In the army, as opposed to the other two services, one is (or was in my time) required to see one's annual confidential report, and to initial it to show that one has seen it, not to indicate agreement with it. The Staff College report, however, has always been an exception: it is not seen. I got the impression that I had done quite well on the course, an impression that, a few years later when I happened to get a job which included custody of all past Staff College reports, I discovered was wholly justified. I was therefore very disappointed when, at the end of the course, I did not get a general staff job at a division or brigade HQ, the jobs for which the course was specifically designed. I was posted to be GSO 2 Signals at 21st Army Group Headquarters, that is on the staff of the Signal Officer-in-Chief (SO-in-C), Major-General Leslie Phillips.

I duly reported to the HQ, which was then in the club-house of the Wentworth Golf Club. On arrival, when summoned for interview by Phillips, almost his first question was, 'What do you think of being given this job?' When I replied that I had just worked hard for 4 months being trained for a non-Signals job at division or brigade level and was therefore feeling frustrated by getting a Signals job 3 or 4 levels higher, he said, 'Don't you realise that you've been given the best major's job in the corps? After all, if you reach my level, what job would you like to have?' I replied without hesitation that I would like to command a division. His answer was, 'There are more than 20 divisional commanders in 21 Army Group but there is only one SO-in-C.'

I found that I was taking over from Finlay Austin, who was going on promotion to a highly secret job, which I later learnt was to command a regiment whose task was to reproduce the training radio signals of a whole army in East Anglia, thereby, in conjunction with dummy tanks and other visual indicators, leading the Germans to believe that, after our assault in Normandy, the Allies had even larger forces ready to strike in the Calais area. This succeeded to the extent that, long after D-Day, large German forces were kept ready around Calais instead of being sent to Normandy to repel our invasion in the first and most vulnerable weeks. One would not think that command of such a regiment was a dangerous job but, only 2 or 3 months later, Austin was killed by a bomb on his flat in Pall Mall.

The most interesting job that I was given, just after my arrival, was to write an appreciation on the problem of how to ensure that the training wireless communications of the Allied armies in the United Kingdom did not give away the date, location and strength of the invasion force. Assuming that most of these signals were being intercepted, they inevitably gave an indication of the organization and thus the strength of the forces available, but it was hoped that the dummy army in East Anglia would confuse that issue. When the time came, 3 or 4 weeks before D-Day, to move forces down to the embarkation areas, radios would gradually be closed down as equipment was packed up and, if nothing were done to prevent it, the enemy would have a good idea of the locations of the ports of embarkation and thus of the probable destination in France. Moreover, the gradual shutting down of radios would indicate the date of the attack. The best scheme that I could think of was to impose complete wireless silence throughout all ground forces in the United Kingdom for irregular periods from a couple of days up to 10 or 15 days, completely haphazardly. This would be most unsatisfactory from the point of view of training but, in due course, General Eisenhower decided to accept that disadvantage and it was put into effect.

About October 1943, HQ 21 Army Group moved from Wentworth to St Paul's School Hammersmith, where GHQ Home Forces had been when I was adjutant of 1 HQ Signals in 1940. Soon after the move, Phillips moved to the War Office to be SO-in-C for the whole army, handing over his job as SO-in-C 21 Army Group to RTO Carey, a much more approachable chap.

In the middle of December I developed a grumbling appendix and it was obviously sensible to have it removed soon, so that I would be fit again well before the invasion. Carey asked me whether I would like him to hold open my job for me while I had the operation. It seemed to me that, by being available for posting again in January or February, I would have a second chance of getting a decent job at a lower level in an active formation, and Carey accepted this view. How wrong I was! Because there was such a shortage of staff-trained officers in Royal Signals, I was sent back to Camberley as the one signaller on the Directing Staff.

Gerry and I needed to find some accommodation a bit nearer to the Staff College than the four-and-a-half miles from her parents' house at Mytchett if we could. I knew that I would be working to all hours and, as no petrol was to be had and I would have to use a bicycle, I wanted to live as close as possible. Moreover my in-laws were aiming to go over to their house in Donegal and proposed to let Mytchett Heath. No army quarter would be available and so a search was necessary in an area of serious shortage. I go on my bicycle and rode in ever widening circles around the Staff College, ready to ask anybody who might help. When talking to the village blacksmith in Sandhurst, he mentioned that his wife did some work for a Miss John who was thinking of leaving her house. It turned out that there were 3 Miss Johns living in a very small detached house with about a half an acre of garden, only one-and-a-half miles from the Staff College. They wanted to sell but had a horror of agents. We did not want to buy but it happened that 18 months earlier, when I was 25, I had got control of the small amount of capital left to me by my parents, about £2,000 I think. We agreed to buy the Miss Johns' house for £1,120.

It had no electricity and in wartime it was difficult to get a permit for a new installation. However, by going to see the appropriate authority in London and persuading him that I could not be expected to do the amount of homework I would have by oil lamps, we got our permit. There were 2 small bedrooms and a bathroom upstairs, with a sitting room, dining room and kitchen downstairs. We were allowed 1 ceiling light and 1 socket in each room. The installation, including burying cable for about 20 feet from the road, cost £32.

The most part of the Directing Staff (DS) were GSO2s, ie majors, but they were given the local, unpaid, rank of lieutenant-colonel to distinguish them from the students, who were about half majors and half captains. Each GSO2 was responsible for a syndicate of 10 students of all arms, with the result that in any one syndicate there was usually available at least one student who knew more about the particular subject under discussion than the DS. Most of the students were of course in the army for the war only and came from a great variety of backgrounds.

In one syndicate I had 2 prospective MPs, 1 Liberal and 1 Labour, who reckoned as politicians do, that they knew the answers to most problems. One day we were discussing minor tank tactics and, after somewhat heated discussion by these 2, I asked a Royal Tank Regiment student, whose practical experience had been confirmed by the loss of an arm, to go to the blackboard and give us the answer. He was quite unable to make himself heard until he took hold of his false hand and rotated it on its noisy ratchet through 360 degrees!

Each such DS had a full-time job running syndicate discussions, correcting written work, and mugging up the next subject for discussion. Some of the longer and more complex papers and exercises were written by the 3 or 4 spare DS excused syndicate work, but a good deal had to be done by syndicate DS in their 'spare' time. My particular extra task was to write the papers dealing with units of Royal Signals and to arrange some wireless voice procedure exercises.

I also had to examine in draft and correct all other papers for their signals element. It had been normal practice to issue with the paper on any major unit its own wireless diagram, including its rear link. I soon found that rear links seldom tied up with the paper on the next level above. So I got it agreed that I would produce, on one sheet of paper, all the wireless nets for an infantry division and on another sheet the corresponding ones for an armoured division. This meant very large diagrams, about 1,300 wireless sets each, but I was able to get them photographically reduced to manageable size.

I used to bicycle into the Staff College to arrive a little before 9 am, returning normally about 5 pm, unless there was an evening outside lecture by a visiting senior officer or politician. Then at home I would be able to start the day's paperwork, getting to bed around midnight. I usually managed to take at least half of Sunday off.

Having worked at HQ 21 Army Group until Christmas, I was of course aware of the main elements of the plans for invasion of France due, as far as I knew, to be implemented in early May. One other DS was in the same position. We were concerned to find that the biggest paper exercise of the course was called the Battle of St Lo and that it bore a very strong resemblance to the actual plans for invasion. We debated together whether we ought to draw attention to such an apparently glaring breach of security and concluded that, if we did so and any action were taken, the cat would be even further out of the bag. If we did nothing and if the substance of the Staff College exercise should, by some remote chance, reach some German authorities, it seemed unlikely that they would believe that the British could have been so careless as to use the real plan as a basis for an exercise. We were rather worried when early May went by and nothing happened but were relieved by the news on 6 June: D-Day.

In order to prepare a TEWT (Tactical Exercise Without Troops), the DS responsible normally wrote the gist of the battle and drafted a series of questions which, in due course, the students would have to answer after making a reconnaissance on the ground. Then the whole of the DS would go out on the ground and make their proposals for the 'pink', that is the pink paper issued to DS as guidance towards a correct solution. It was always emphasised that there was no one correct solution, though some were better than others. In one case, during the DS reconnaissance, I came up with a solution that was markedly different from anyone else's: I reckoned that it would surprise the enemy just as it surprised the DS. However, the assistant commandant, Brigadier Julian Gascoigne, and most of the other DS, considered that my ideas were tactically unsound. The day was saved for me when the commandant, Major-General Douglas Wimberley, lately commanding 51st Highland Division in Eighth Army, intervened on my side.

I was, one day, conducting a syndicate discussion about a large-scale movement exercise, involving the production by students of a complicated graph 7 feet long. It was a situation that would be most unlikely to confront them at divisional level or below but, if they understood this, they would find their own movement problems relatively simple and the principles were the same. Douglas Wimberley walked into the room and listened to the discussion for a short time and then intervened, 'This is no doubt good academic training but I hope you realize that, in the field, it doesn't happen this way. You just say "Get in your vehicles and go!"' No doubt true in the desert.

Wimberley's PA went into his office one summer's morning to see him having apparently gone berserk, running round the room, stripped to waist, and shouting, 'Get out, GET OUT!' She fled. Apologising later, he explained that he had had a wasp inside his shirt.

One of the most important things for the senior signal officer at a headquarters is to discover as far in advance as possible what plans the commander and staff are contemplating, so that he can deploy his inevitably limited resources as effectively as possible. The chief gunner and engineer officers are in the same position. I noticed that when members of the DS were demonstrating the issue of oral orders at divisional HQ, they always remembered to call the CRA and CRE, or their representatives, to the order group, but usually forgot to call the signaller. It seemed to me that this was, in part at least, due to his long-winded title: OC Divisional Signals. So I arranged to see General Phillips, SO-in-C, and bicycled over to his home in Yately one Sunday morning. I suggested the title CR Signals and this was soon accepted. I think it has helped.

It was normal for the GSO2s DS in wartime to stay for 2 courses, ie about 10 months, although a proportion were required to stay for 3. Towards the end of my second course I decided that I would pull any string I could to get an active job outside Signals. One of the outside lectures in early November 1944 was given by Lieutenant-General 'Boy' Browning (husband of Daphne du Maurier, the author), who was then commanding First Allied Airborne Army. After his lecture he came, as was normal, to a small drinks party attended by the DS. Having met him briefly in Algiers, I asked him whether he would consider me for a job in one of the airborne divisions. As 6th Airborne Division had taken part in the D-Day landings and 1st Airborne Division had been to Arnhem in September, it seemed obvious that both would be used again fairly soon. So I was delighted when, a week or so later, I received a posting order to be GSO2 1st Airborne Division.

12

FULBECK, OSLO, WENTWORTH, GWALIOR: 1944–45

The headquarters of 1st Airborne Division was in the small village of Fulbeck in Lincolnshire, a mile from Leadenham, where my father had been the rector up to 1923. More significant, the officers' mess was in Fulbeck Manor, owned by my sister Joyce and her husband Francis Fane. Francis was away delivering newly constructed ships to their users and Joyce and their 4 children were living in a cottage at the bottom of the garden. The headquarters itself was in Fulbeck Hall, owned by Francis' brother Harry, whom I had last met in Tunisia and who was then, I think, in Italy.

A number of the staff were, like myself, replacing Arnhem casualties. I was lucky to have good officers to work with, particularly the GSO3, Philip Somerville. The GSO1 was pleasant but idle, which meant that he was quite happy for me to deal directly with the GOC, Major-General Roy Urquhart of Arnhem fame. This speeded up routine business a lot and was quite logical in that, in operations, it was planned that Urquhart and I would travel by glider whilst the GSO1 and GSO3 would parachute. There would thus be a reasonable chance that one pair or the other would arrive.

It was obviously wrong that, as GSO2, I should not have qualified in parachuting. Until about 1944 I had not been eligible because, before that, one used to drop out of a hole in the bottom of the aeroplane and, if tall, was liable to hit one's head on the way out. Then 6 feet 3 inches had been the limit, and I was 6 feet six-and-a-half. When the Dakota was introduced one jumped out of a door in the side and height was no longer a problem. So I did a parachute course at Ringway near Manchester in February. The last of the 8 jumps one had to do to qualify was at night. I had developed a sharp attack of 'flu and had a temperature of 102 degrees but I was determined not to have to waste another fortnight doing the course again. Fortunately the only damage from my jump in the dark was to a knee, which recovered in the next 2 or 3 weeks.

A rule had been introduced to stop husbands in operational units from living out with their wives. If, however, my sister, in her cottage in the mess grounds, invited my wife to stay, I did not feel it necessary to intervene. Moreover, I felt it would be unreasonable for me not to visit my sister, and if I happened to stay the night...! No one asked tactless questions.

Roy Urquhart kept the division busy with exercises that winter and I learnt a lot about the practicalities of setting and running divisional exercises after absorbing 3 courses' worth of theory at the Staff College. For 2 of the nights we were out on one exercise, there was a record low temperature for Lincolnshire, -9 degrees F or 41 degrees F of frost.

Meanwhile 1st Airborne Corps Headquarters (GOC Lieutenant-General Gale, BGS Brigadier Geoff Bourne) was busy planning about 15 different operations for our division with 21 Army Group, the last of which was to seize the Kiel Canal in early May. None of these plans materialized. Finally, in late April we moved to airfields in Suffolk and Essex for a major exercise, during which Urquhart and the GSO1 were called to Corps Headquarters. An hour or so later I got a message to summon the divisional O (Order) Group within 30 minutes and to be prepared, after the GOC had given his orders, to give out a movement order for all units to move at once from their exercise positions to certain airfields. It was unlucky that most of the units in the southern part of the exercise area had to go to the more northern airfields and vice versa.

The war in Europe was nearly over and surrender was anticipated in the next few days. The division's task was to occupy Norway, a vast area for a mere 12,000 men. We could do no more than move to 4 main centres: Oslo, Stavanger, Bergen and Tromsö. We were told that 'heralds', presumably a few specially briefed representatives of the Foreign Office, would be flown in to Oslo on, if I remember rightly, 8 May; that a small advance party of Divisional Headquarters, accompanied by about 120 men of the Independent Parachute Company, would follow the next day; and that main bodies would fly to the 4 main centres over the next 2 or 3 days.

I was very privileged to be detailed to take the advance party into Oslo. Together with the Parachute Company we travelled in about half a dozen Lancaster bombers, bringing 1 jeep with us. As we approached Gardemöen airport, some 25 miles outside Oslo, we were somewhat concerned to see that all the anti-aircraft defences were fully manned. However, the German troops behaved entirely correctly. I sent for the senior German officer and told him that the company would be remaining on the airfield, whilst I would take my divisional HQ party into Oslo to make administrative arrangements for the main body arriving in the next few days. In addition to my jeep I required 2 more cars to convey my party to Oslo and back. The German officer made heavy weather over providing them until I pointed to the car he had driven up and said I would have that for one. I was at the time unfamiliar with German badges of rank and thought that, as the officer in question was wearing 2 silver bars, this would be the equivalent of 2 'pips' for us, ie a lieutenant. Had I known that I was talking to a lieutenant-colonel, I might have had less self-confidence, which would have been a mistake.

By the time we reached our rendezvous in Oslo, the sight of one jeep arriving with a small Union flag on the bonnet had drawn an enormous crowd. There was no sign of a German uniform and it was later that we learnt that the German forces had already handed over to the Norwegian

Underground, who were in complete control of the situation.

Next day there was a tragedy. The first part of the main body was due to arrive at Gardemöen airport. Our planes had enough fuel for such a journey but not sufficient to divert elsewhere if they could not land. This was a risk that was thought necessary in the interests of taking control of Norway quickly, before any of then very large German forces there had second thoughts. After a number of aircraft had landed successfully the weather closed in and cloud obscured the hills surrounding the airfield. The only available aid to landing was a talk-down radio manned on the airfield by an RAF warrant officer, who had an impossible task. Four Dakotas crashed in the vicinity and about 100 men were killed: the day after the war had ended.

One of the arrivals that day was the DAAG (Deputy Assistant Adjutant General ie the major on the staff responsible for personnel), Major Henry Wigram. For the next few days he and I had the task of arranging the transport of the arriving troops from Gardemöen to Oslo by train. They were taken from the airfield to the nearby station by rather decrepit German Army lorries. On a hot day I noticed that half the loading area of a lorry was being wasted by transporting large sackfuls of something and, through an interpreter, I told the driver to off-load the sacks. This he did; and then told me, through the interpreter, that the lorry would now be no use because it ran on the fuel contained in the sacks. By the time he had loaded the sacks again, he must have been hot and tired!

One evening, when we had finished our job on the airfield, Henry and I went into Oslo and had a brief stroll through the streets. A young Norwegian couple, who had obviously been celebrating, were approaching us when the girl thrust her escort on one side and strode up to Henry, who apparently had something I hadn't, and said, 'You, you are English. For you I am free!' Her escort had different views and somewhat apologetically led her away.

Norway's National Day is 17 May and this was less than

10 days after VE Day. Nevertheless the authorities managed to stage a great celebration to welcome back Prince Olaf, arriving to represent his father, King Haakon. One of the principal events was a march past by all the many thousand schoolchildren of Oslo, each one of whom had been equipped with a small Norwegian flag: a very moving sight.

At this time there were in Norway no less than 400,000 German soldiers, left perhaps because there might have been an Allied invasion there, but more probably because Hitler had decreed no withdrawal. Just outside Oslo there was an armoured division, fully equipped, which had never fired a shot in anger. If this occupation force had been transferred to Germany a few months earlier, the war would no doubt have gone on a good deal longer. A small but welcome by-product was that a supply of wine had been imported for the use of these 400,000, including one-and-a-half million bottles of the best French champagne. As we had taken over Norway with only 12,000, there was an adequate supply.

We learnt something of the remarkable achievements of the Norwegian Underground. For example, they had established a small factory for making sub-machine guns in an Oslo cellar. The German authorities decided one day to requisition the building above, although they had no knowledge of what went on below. Only 24 hours' notice was given to evacuate the building. During that time the Norwegians managed to reduce all the machinery, materials etc. to loads small enough to be carried on bicycles unobtrusively and to re-establish the factory elsewhere.

One morning Roy Urquhart decided that the GSO1 must be replaced and required him to leave Norway that day. This left me acting as GSO1 for about a week, until a replacement arrived. It happened that Urquhart had already planned to make a 4-day trip to visit our troops throughout Norway, starting next day. He decided to go ahead with this, thus leaving me apparently in operational command of Norway! There was, however, a higher headquarters, on a different floor in the same building, headed by a general whose name now escapes me: let us say General X. He had overall responsibility for Norway but only dealt with the major political issues. General X was a charming ex-Guardsman who, having delegated operational responsibility to GOC 1st Airborne Division, was extremely correct in respecting that position, even when a 27-year-old major had been left in charge. One day he wanted to make some minor operational move. Not only did he ask my permission but even walked down to my office to make his request.

The new GSO1 was Tom Pearson, a very welcome change, competent, firm and a delight to work for. Nevertheless, time was going by and I had still taken no part in active operations other than 6 months in Tunisia. So I asked to be posted to a unit in active operations against the Japanese. I was appointed to be 2IC of 1st Airborne Corps Signals, then in England but due to go to the Far East shortly.

There were in Norway at the end of the war no less than 200,000 Russian prisoners living in very poor conditions and on a near starvation diet. Obviously we did everything we could to get food to them as quickly as possible but even by the middle of June the situation was very far from satisfactory. We had had to require the German prison guards to continue to keep control because, if Russian prisoners were let loose, we felt that the Norwegian population would suffer.

The evening before I left, a telephone call came through from the Brigade Commander in Tromsö to say that a Russian general had just landed at the local airfield and would be with him in about 15 minutes. He would obviously want to see the local Russian POW camp. What was the policy? The answer was 'Be as helpful and polite as possible but on no account is he to see the POW camp, even if it means escorting him back to his aircraft!' I never heard what happened.

I returned to England and, with 10 days' leave, Gerry

and I flew to Belfast and thus on to Donegal to stay with her parents at Aughnagaddy House near Ramelton. It was our first experience of civil airline flying: we each had to be weighed and then to be allotted a seat appropriately. We could not have been made more welcome, not only by Gerry's parents and sisters but by their many friends. No one was in a hurry and one had to relax: a real holiday. I then joined my new unit at Sunningdale and Gerry went back to stay in London with an aunt, Connie Prideaux, her mother's elder sister, a widow.

A nucleus of HQ 1st Airborne Corps, including about 50 men of the Corps Signals, had already left for Gwalior in India, a state about 130 miles south of Agra. In the third week of July I flew with a subaltern and another 20 or 30 men to join them. Air trooping was not then the relatively comfortable way of travelling that it later became. We went by Dakota, sitting on canvas seats facing sideways, having to refuel at Nice, Malta, El Adem and Lydda. This took us 24 hours and we were then given a 3-day break before tackling the second half of the journey.

I spent one day seeing the sights in Jerusalem and the next swimming. It was, of course, very hot and, knowing that I was susceptible to sunburn, I was careful to sit in the shade when not in the water. The shade in question was a form of straw matting on poles and I assumed that the amount of sun coming through would be innocuous. I was very wrong: that night, knowing that I was somewhat burned, I rubbed myself with oil, which relieved the irritation but resulted in my getting hotter and hotter until, in the small hours, I felt rather ill. So I had a cold shower to wash all the oil off, which reduced my temperature to normal proportions. By the time I saw a doctor I had 2 enormous blisters covering the whole of my shoulders. He treated them and bandaged me with layers of cotton wool. When we took off in the middle of that morning, I was feeling utterly miserable and hardly noticed that the next hop, to Habbaniya in Iraq, was extremely rough. It was so bad that the subaltern with me was violently sick all the way, so much so that the doctor there insisted that he was unfit to continue.

As we left the plane for refuelling, on this hot July afternoon, we noticed a considerable detachment of airmen marching into camp from the desert. We were told that they had been to bury a man who had died from the heat that morning. Feeling hot in the night, he had stood under a cold shower for several hours and, when he came out, the normal mechanism of the body for putting up with the heat no longer worked.

Having refuelled again at Dhahran in the Persian Gulf, we flew on to Karachi, but that was apparently as far as our Dakota was prepared to take us and we were put into a transit camp there for a week. Another Dakota then took us on to Bombay, where we went into another transit camp at Kalyan. There we were told that we would have to make the last leg of our journey to Gwalior by train and that, on average, we could expect to wait a month before a train would be available. I insisted that there were operational reasons, though I did not know what they were, why we must get there more quickly. I asked to ring up the Corps HQ in Gwalior but was told that long distance calls like that did not work in India. I did succeed in getting through but the voice at the other end was too faint to be comprehensible. I assured the camp authorities that I had been told that it was essential that my detachment got to Gwalior urgently. After much argument we went on in 2 weeks.

The day before we left, we heard the news of the first atom bomb. By the time we got to Gwalior, nearly 2 days later, it was clear that the war with Japan was over. I then learnt that 1st Airborne Corps had been going to undertake, no doubt with other forces, the recovery of South Malaya and Singapore. Although Fourteenth Army was by now doing well in Burma, there is no doubt that the Japanese could, and would, have continued to fight for many months, perhaps a year or more, had it not been for those 2 bombs. The casualties which would have resulted for both sides would probably have been far greater than those resulting from the bombs. I may be biased by being one of those who might well have been one of those casualties, but I am quite certain that the decision to drop those bombs was right. They saved a great many Allied lives and there was probably a net saving of Japanese lives too.

HQ 1st Airborne Corps and the 70 men of its Corps Signals settled down to a month or so of inactivity, while we waited for a decision on our future. With nothing much to do I quickly found that far too many men were reporting sick with minor complaints. I started an early morning physical training parade and also arranged with the Chief Signal Officer, Brigadier Richard Moberly, for him to require me to establish enough local line communications to keep everyone reasonably busy. Health returned to normal.

In due course it was decided that all ranks of the HQ and Signals would be posted individually to fill gaps elsewhere. I received a posting order to go to the Indian Signal School at Mhow as an instructor. This was not at all what I wanted and I asked Richard Moberly for help. He spoke to the BGS, Brigadier Geoffrey Bourne, who arranged for me to go to Delhi to see the DMO (Director of Military Operations) at GHQ, Brigadier Roddy McLeod, with a view to becoming one of his GSO1s. Apparently I passed muster because a few days after my return to Gwalior, in early October, I received a posting order from the Military Secretary's branch to be GSO1 of MO2 and 3, dealing with internal security and future plans respectively.

However, by the same post came a posting order to be 2IC of the 2nd Battalion, the Wiltshire Regiment, then stationed on the Frontier, that is, in the tribal area near Afghanistan. It was explained that GHQ India had decided that, now that the war was over, it was a good moment to broaden the experience of officers at about 2IC level by exchange postings: gunner, sapper and signal officers on the one hand, swapping with infantry officers on the other. Evidently the Adjutant-General's branch who dealt with such regimental postings had not been in touch with the Military Secretary's branch who arranged staff postings. It seemed that I might have a choice.

A job on the Frontier in an infantry battalion seemed a chance not to be missed but I decided that I should first consult Richard Moberly, who, through Geoff Bourne, had been kind enough to get me the chance of the MO job. He took me to see Geoff Bourne, who considered that I would be very foolish to give up the chance of a job in MO from the point of view of my future career. While we were talking, General Gale, the Corps Commander, happened to walk in and wanted to know what we were talking about. He immediately took the other point of view, saying that I should on no account miss the most unusual opportunity, for an officer of Royal Signals, of service in an infantry battalion, particularly in a fairly active area. Gale and Bourne argued about it heatedly and I then withdrew to think it over. I rang the Adjutant-General's office to say that I was delighted with the posting to the Wiltshire Regiment and would they please get the MO job cancelled, only to be told that the double posting had just come to light and it had been decided that I was to go to MO in Delhi. At least it had the temporary advantage of promotion to lieutenant-colonel.

13

DELHI: 1945–46

The Director of Military Operations (DMO) India was Brigadier Roddy McLeod, late Royal Artillery. He had a reputation for being fierce with all and sundry but this was only true when he was dealing with those whom he found out being incompetent. He was at this time a widower with a teenage daughter at school in England but, when in the spring of 1946 he became engaged to a widow, Molly Thomas, in the WAC(I) – Women's Army Corps (India) – he was generally thought to have mellowed.

He had 2 GSO1s working for him: Lieutenant-Colonel Jack Masters (later John Masters, the well-known author), whose branch, MO1, was responsible for the North-West Frontier, and myself, looking after MO2, Internal Security, and MO3, Future Plans. I took over from a man who before the war had worked in newspapers and, no doubt as result, was impervious to noise where he worked. His office, shared with 3 more junior staff officers, was on the corner of 2 corridors and got its ventilation through the doorways opening on to those corridors. The hubbub was, to my way of thinking, such as to make concentrated work impossible. I quickly managed to acquire a more peaceful office with a window on to the outside world and a door which could be kept shut.

I shared this room with the GSO2, Howard Rowse, and GSO3 of MO2, Wilshaw, and with the GSO2 of MO3. Rowse had been in charge of sales of Austin motor cars in Ceylon before the war; he had become invaluable in his present appointment, having a phenomenal memory for past internal security operations and their legal implications. He also had a caustic wit. On one occasion a rather plain member of the WAC(I) came into our room and, looking round said, 'Internal Security?' Rowse immediately answered, 'Yes, do you want some?' The poor girl fled.

Wilshaw was primarily responsible for keeping up-to-date a large wall map of India with the location of every major unit and the minor units when detached. I soon found that, whilst he was a useful officer in other ways, he had no head for detail and his map was invariably wrong. He was a likeable chap but I had no choice but to get him moved elsewhere. He was an Anglo-Indian and so stayed on in the Indian Army after partition. It was amusing to meet him again in 1961 when, as a colonel from MO2 in the War Office, I had occasion to visit the Indian Defence College, the equivalent of what was then called the Imperial Defence College. Wilshaw was a brigadier ex-CRA (Commander Royal Artillery) and I was delighted to find that he harboured no grudge at all. As a brigadier he had probably had a staff who looked after the detail for him.

There had not been much work for MO3, Future Plans, during 1945 and one GSO2 had coped with it but, by November, there was a need to look forward as far as possible. More significant, the internal situation was deteriorating due to the many agitators. Marches to demonstrate against British rule occurred in some of the bigger cities. It was reported that in Bombay there had been a large crowd with banners such as 'Go home, Tommy', whilst their band played 'Will ye no' come back again'!

The situation was aggravated by unrest in the 3 services. Their British elements included too many men whose only interest was to return to Britain and be demobilised. Some of the Indian units were thought to be somewhat unreliable because of the political agitation. There were some 50 to 60 battalions scattered round India, which, of course then meant the whole sub-continent, what is today India, Pakistan and Bangladesh. As far as possible, wherever there

Harry Tabor May Tabor

Gerry and me: engaged

Gerry's parents, Robert and Beatrice Ovens, with David Gribbin (best man)

Rachel Hancock and Honor Ovens (bridesmaids)

Arrival in Oslo, 9 May 1945

Roddy Mcleod

L5 - Sentinel

Taj Mahal taken from the Sentinel

were two Indian battalions together, we tried to station also a Gurkha or a British battalion as well.

Making plans for appropriate action in the event of a worsening situation as well as dealing with a multitude of day-to-day problems was a big job for MO2 and so the DMO obtained a further GSO1 to run MO3 as a separate section, whilst giving me 3 more GSO2s and one GSO3 to run an operations room on a 24-hour basis.

Meanwhile it had become necessary to produce a lengthy plan for action by all 3 services in the event of a really widespread insurrection. The army was far larger than the navy or air force and the heads of these 2 services were subordinate to the army Commander-in-Chief, General Auckinleck. It followed that it was the army's job to co-ordinate plans. So, within 2 or 3 weeks of arrival, I found myself chairing a committee of about 25 grade one officers of all 3 services, meeting 3 times a week, when I was probably the youngest person there and the one with least knowledge of India.

After the first meeting McLeod called me in to find out what decisions had been taken. I had got the wrong answer on pretty well every item. Having explained to me the error of my ways and made clear that it was the chairman's job to decide beforehand what, in his opinion, was the right decision in each case and only to vary from that view with very good cause, he said, 'Well, you haven't been here long and so I suppose I had better run this meeting myself'. This needled me, as it was probably intended to, and I asked to be allowed to sort out what had gone wrong and run the next meeting. I took McLeod's advice and did my homework very fully before the next meeting, including thinking out in advance who in this committee was going to support the MO view on each item. It worked and from then on I had the confidence that McLeod trusted me and would back me, a happy relationship for which I was profoundly grateful over the years to come.

The document that we produced included draft contributions from each element of all 3 services and was inevitably lengthy. One such draft came to me from the Army Signals Directorate and was signed by the SO1, Pat Mansergh, a chap I knew well as we were exact contemporaries and so had been on the same 'Q' Course at Catterick. As with most such contributions, I had to make minor changes to it in order to fit it into the plan as a whole. So I rang up Pat and gave him the gist of my proposed changes, inviting him to come and check them. He said there was no need as I knew the signals implications as well as he did. When the plan was finally issued, McLeod received a virulent minute from the SO-in-C India, Major-General Vulliamy, to the effect that he did not like his personal drafts being cut about by the DMO's junior officers. McLeod asked me to prepare a suitable reply. I did, he signed it and no more was heard. In my experience it is rare for an officer of high rank to be so petty-minded.

Although this plan was voluminous and had to be distributed widely, it was necessarily graded 'TOP SECRET'. With the problems of security in the 3 services in India, particularly at this time on a matter of internal security, it was recognized that it would inevitably leak. The plan therefore deliberately glossed over the action that would be taken if matters got really serious, eg a repeat of the mutiny of 1856. A plan for this was also made and this was restricted to a very few officers at GHQ and to Army Commanders personally and to Heads of the other 2 Services. I was sent to visit Army Commanders to discuss this plan and I took the opportunity whilst travelling to visit some of the commanders at the next level down. Whilst it was helpful to me to see some of the problems at the lower levels, it presented difficulties when talking to the more astute of those who had seen the main plan but not the extra secret plan within it.

A short document had to be produced for sending to London as the joint civil and military view on some matter of internal security. Drafts had been passed to and fro without agreement until one morning I cleared our latest version with Roddy McLeod and he said that it was time to get it decided. I was to take this version to his opposite number on the civil side, Philip Mason, and see whether he would agree it. Mason read it carefully and said, 'I don't think that this is quite right'. Pressing a bell for his secretary, he added, 'Please sit down and listen and see whether you can accept this'. He then dictated a new version with no hesitation. It was clear, concise and expressed perfectly what we had all been reaching for. I had no hesitation in accepting it. This charming and clear-thinking man greatly impressed me. It has not surprised me to find, since the war, that amongst other activities he has become an author of stature, *The Men Who Ruled India* being perhaps his most important work.

Auchinleck had very clear views on how troops should be used in aid of the civil power. It was the duty of the police to maintain public order and only when they were obviously unable to contain a situation should military help be provided. When the army was called in, it would be prepared to shoot if this was the only way to retrieve the position but if they did shoot they would shoot to kill. As long as crowds knew that this would happen if soldiers appeared, they would have a healthy respect for the army and would be more likely to disperse at the mere sight of them. The civil authorities in general and the police in particular liked to be able to call in the army more often, expecting them merely to reinforce the police.

In order to get the C-in-C's views over to the police, it was decided that, before issuing any directive on the subject, there would be a meeting in Delhi of the chief constables of all provinces, to be chaired by the Chief of Staff, Lieutenant-General Sir Arthur Smith, assisted by the senior civil servant in GHQ (the Permanent Secretary? I forget his title) to try to deal with their arguments in advance. When the day came General Smith and the DCGS, a major-general, were both away or sick. Roddy McLeod was away visiting the North-West Frontier. So it fell to me to chair this meeting of very senior police officers who had spent their whole careers dealing with internal security problems. I was 28 and had been in India less than 6 months. However, the Permanent Secretary was extremely helpful and gave me all possible support. At least the policemen went away quite clear that there was no point in arguing further.

In February 1946 the internal situation worsened markedly. The impatience of British troops to return home and be released from the army was balanced by their clear task in aid of the civil power; but it was worse for the RAF, whose role was less obvious, and there were cases of men refusing their duty. The RAF referred to these incidents as strikes until General Auchinleck insisted that they must be denounced as mutiny.

The most serious of such actions originated in the RIN, the Royal Indian Navy. The officer strength of the RIN had been built up at the beginning of the war by requiring every merchant vessel based at an Indian port to transfer one officer to the RIN. Naturally merchant skippers did not willingly part with their best officers and, even by the end of the war, the RIN was in general poorly officered. Moreover, it had been widely penetrated by political elements demanding immediate independence.

Ships in Karachi and in Bombay were taken over by their crews, the officers being locked up on board. In Karachi very direct and immediate action was taken: a frigate which was tied up alongside was summoned to surrender by a company of the Parachute Regiment. They refused and one mortar bomb was dropped on board with no apparent result. In fact a man was on his way to hoist a white flag when he was directly hit by this bomb. This episode was repeated and in the end 5 men were killed before surrender was achieved. This was a sharp lesson, news of which spread rapidly, and there was no more trouble in Karachi either with the RIN or the civil population.

In Bombay it was a different story. Mutinous ships were afloat in Bombay harbour and direct action was more difficult. The RAF were at standby to bomb them but the commanders concerned were naturally reluctant to order such action, which would inevitably have resulted in large casualties and much damage. The civil population, no doubt encouraged by the RIN having apparently got away with it, started to riot and troops had to be deployed on a wide scale. It took several days to restore order and more than 400 people were killed.

Quite frequently at this time I found it necessary to return to the office after dinner and one evening I came in at about 10 pm with the intention of 2 or 3 hours' work. My first call when coming in was always to the operations room and there I found a captain on duty who had only recently arrived from England. He had been told to be at Auchinleck's house at 10.30 pm to brief the C-in-C on the current situation and was understandably nervous. I told him that on this occasion I would go instead. Having said my piece and answered questions, Auchinleck said, 'Well, let's relax and have a whisky and soda'. Stupidly, without thinking, I said, 'If you don't need me any more, sir, I am afraid that I ought to get back to my office for an hour or 2'. Stupid for 2 reasons: first, I missed the chance of what would have been a fascinating half-hour with one of the foremost commanders of World War Two; and second, it resulted in an inquiry through the Chief of Staff next day as why staff officers were being required to work excessive hours. I'm afraid that Roddy McLeod had unnecessary trouble sorting this out.

Whilst all this was going on I was living in a large single officers' mess, waiting impatiently for Gerry to join me. The war was over but personal long-distance travel was not yet available on demand. Gerry, meanwhile, was staying with her parents in Donegal and with the vagaries of the Irish posts her application to go to India was dealt with less than expeditiously. She arrived in Bombay towards the end of March 1946, having travelled in very crowded conditions in a troopship, sharing a state room for one with 8 others. We stayed one night in the Taj Mahal Hotel in Bombay and then set out on the 24-hour train journey to Delhi.

14

INTERLUDE IN THE AIR: 1946

During my efforts to co-ordinate the production of the internal security plans, I got to know the SASO (Senior Air Staff Officer), Air-Commodore Wheeler and, through him, his brother, a colonel. One evening they asked me and 4 or 5 others to a small private dinner party. The main course was officially goose and it tasted very good. Later the truth was whispered. The 2 brothers had spent part of a Sunday morning on the Viceroy's estate and, with a .22 pistol, had shot a peacock. Not only had they been poaching one of the Viceroy's birds but, for Hindus, peacocks are, I learnt, holy.

In the middle of December Wheeler, the RAF one, told me that he had heard that the Americans, who were busy withdrawing their air forces from eastern India and Burma, had decided to sell their light planes at very modest prices. No American was allowed to buy one, to prevent any accusation of fiddling. He, Wheeler, was getting one and, having learned of my interest in flying, advised me to do the same. I contracted to buy a Sentinel as it was known to British forces in Burma, or, to give it its American name, an L5. My one had done only 40 hours' flying and would cost the equivalent of £400.

An RAF friend and I went by train to Calcutta and thence on to an American air station. The paperwork completed, we stayed there overnight and early next morning started to fly the 700 miles back to Delhi. We refuelled twice and I learnt as much as I could. We diverted slightly from the direct route as I wanted to see the Taj Mahal near Agra from the air and to take some photographs. It was some time later that I found out that this was breaking a strict rule: very reasonably, it was laid down that no aircraft was allowed to fly within several miles for fear that an accident would damage this priceless building. Sadly my photographs were very poor due to a fault with the camera.

My pilot was going to give me further instruction in the next few weeks but, unfortunately, he was posted elsewhere. I had also to pass a medical examination and was apprehensive that I would have difficulty with colours. Fortunately the Indian doctor tested me with coloured wools instead of the more sophisticated system, designed by a Japanese, with pages of coloured dots where a number is picked out in carefully selected shades so that it is visible only to someone with normal colour sight: other pages present a number which can be seen only by someone with a particular colour abnormality. With the coloured wools I was able to persuade the doctor that any error I made was due to his limited English rather than my colour sight.

I was required to take a basic flying test before being allowed to take a passenger or to leave my parent airfield. One requirement was to shut off the engine at 2,000 feet and glide in to land. I was practising this one hot Sunday afternoon and circled the airfield, waiting for a green light to give me clearance to land. Willingdon aerodrome had very little traffic and, after a long wait, I reckoned that either the control tower had gone to sleep or that they had given me a green which due to the bright sun I had not seen. So I shut off my engine and began to make a fairly steep descent. Then I saw a red Very light and turned away sharply, getting my engine going again. I had been coming in straight on top of a Dakota. When I finally landed I went to the control tower, where they insisted that they had given me a red light. They did not pursue the incident, which may have been due to kind-heartedness, to idleness, or to being unsure that they had given me a red.

I talked to Roddy McLeod about this aeroplane and he bought one too. Whilst he was still inexperienced with it and before he had passed the necessary test, he flew off one day to Agra, 130 miles away, taking a passenger. On arrival at this unfamiliar airfield he misjudged his landing and damaged his machine but, fortunately, neither he nor his passenger was seriously hurt.

One Sunday morning I decided to make a long flight into the foothills of the Himalayas to the north-east, approaching an area which was marked intriguingly on the map as 'unexplored territory'. The machine cruised at 105 knots and carried about 30 gallons of fuel, which was enough for 4 hours. As I planned to be away for 4 or 5 hours, I would have to refuel and so I put about 8 2-gallon cans of petrol in the back. Just before I left the plains I searched for a deserted flat area where I could land to refuel: not too difficult as I only needed about 200 yards. Full again, I had a most enjoyable flight at around 6,000 to 8,000 feet in the valleys between hills of 10,000 feet or more. On one occasion I found myself level with, and quite close to, a farmer working on one of his terraces and we exchanged cheerful waves.

I used the machine on duty once. Another officer from GHQ and I had to go to Cawnpore to meet the Army Commander of Central Command, General Scoones, to discuss internal security problems there. Scoones had had to travel all night from Agra in a none too comfortable train and seemed a little upset that his juniors had arrived fresh after a pleasant 1-hour flight.

When the Airborne Corps HQ and its Signals had been broken up in Gwalior, all ranks had been posted to jobs all over the Far East. One of the staff officers, Bob Chaundler, had come to GHQ with me and became GSO1 SD (Staff Duties, ie responsible for the organization, provision and movement of troops). When in Gwalior we had met Dick Duyf, a Dutch sugar farmer, who had invited us to come and stay if opportunity offered. With an aeroplane available, we decided that we could manage this between lunch on a Saturday and Sunday evening. We exchanged telegrams about the length of landing strip required and off we went.

I had said that I could manage with 200 yards, preferring 250. Dick had replied that he had marked out 400 yards. On arrival I thought from the air that the strip looked much less than 400 and was careful to touch down at the very beginning: just as well as it turned out to be a bare 200. Although from the air the strip appeared to be in a large area of uninhabited scrub, before I had even switched off the engine, numerous locals were swarming round to examine this strange mechanical bird. However, Dick soon appeared and arranged for the protection of the plane from the curiosity of all.

We had a pleasant evening with the Duyfs and next morning were taken over the farm and factory. It was a satisfactorily self-contained process. The sugar-cane grew to perhaps 7 or 8 feet tall and was not unlike bamboo to look at. It was cut by hand and loads were brought in to the factory on ox-wagons. Machinery squeezed the juice out and the remaining woody part became the fuel to drive the machinery. The juice was then either dried to become brown sugar or separated from molasses, leaving white sugar. The molasses were used to make rum and treacle.

After lunch I took Dick up to see his estate from the air and he then asked me to take up his Indian foreman. I had to make sure that his flowing robes did not get tangled with the controls. I learnt from Dick afterwards that his foreman would do well out of this since, having been nearer to heaven than others, his garments were worth selling at so much per square inch. Bob and I then flew back to Delhi without incident.

All this flying was great fun and a marvellous antidote to the stresses of my job. I had written about it to Gerry in Donegal, which I am afraid added to her frustration in having still not got a passage promised. No petrol being available, she had no form of transport other than a pony and trap.

Bob Chaundler and I had been considering where to arrange for accommodation, for our wives in the hot weather, it being normal for families to go to hill stations for most of May to August, husbands joining them for whatever leave was possible. We agreed that Nainital would, from what we had heard, be likely to suit us. The normal journey to Nainital consisted of an all-night train journey east to Bareilly, a few more hours in another train north to Kathgodam, and then an hour's taxi ride from the plain at less than 1,000 feet to Nainital at 6,000. If we were going to see the place and choose suitable accommodation it would mean at least 36 hours' wearisome travelling unless we could go by air. As I had already discovered that it was easy to find an adequate strip on which to land almost anywhere on these northern plains, we planned to fly to near Kathgodam and take a taxi from there up the hill. On this basis we could make the return journey from Delhi in one day easily and we selected a Sunday a couple of weeks after his family had arrived.

On the Saturday evening Bob rang me up to say that he had had a rush of work and would have to spend Sunday in the office: would I take his wife instead? So early next morning we foregathered on Willingdon airfield and I was introduced to Irene Chaundler. I don't think either of them mentioned then that Irene had not flown before. We had a pleasant and uneventful flight as far as Kathgodam in, I think, about 90 minutes. Flying over this small town and railhead, I realized that, whilst it was pleasantly cool sitting quietly 1,000 feet in the air, it would be hot on the ground and a 2 or 3 mile walk into the town was not an attractive prospect. So I studied the possibilities of landing really close to the town itself and realized that the river bed, dry in March, included some apparently dead-level stretches. I flew over one such line at about 50 feet and reckoned that it was straight for more than 200 yards with no obstacles. So round again and down we went. All was well until, just before coming to rest, the right front tyre hit a sharp stone and burst. The wheel dug into the ground and the plane turned sharply through 180 degrees and stopped. I turned round to Irene, expecting to find her nearly hysterical. But I did not then know her: she was blessedly calm and, having not flown before, had not realized that this was not the normal method of landing.

We were quite unhurt and the plane appeared to be intact except for the burst tyre. The local police soon arrived and they agreed to put a guard on the plane for the next few days for a modest payment. Arrangements were also made for a telegram to be sent to Bob in Delhi to tell him of this contretemps and that we would come back on the night train. We collected a taxi and had a much more frightening journey, climbing up the twisty, mountain road to Nainital. There we made our arrangements, had a meal and returned to Kathgodam, where we were lucky to get a lift in a military lorry to Bareilly and then caught the night train back to Delhi.

Bob, meanwhile, had not received our telegram and by late afternoon was understandably anxious. Enquiries, via the inadequate telephone service of those days, finally yielded the tentative information that a light aeroplane had crashed in the vicinity of Kathgodam. It wasn't until next morning, when we returned, that he learnt that we were alright.

It happened that the following Thursday was a public holiday to celebrate the end of the war against Japan. Mountbatten, the Commander-in-Chief in the Far East, was coming from his HQ in Ceylon and he and Auchinleck were to take the salute jointly at a victory parade. As far as I was concerned it meant a very convenient day's holiday. Roddy McLeod very kindly offered to lend me one of the wheels off his damaged plane in Agra and I arranged for it to be sent to Delhi. An RAF corporal, who used to do the minimal maintenance on my machine in his spare time, agreed to come with me by train on the Wednesday night to Kathgodam in order to fit the wheel and fly back with me to Delhi. This we did but not without incident.

I found that there was a smooth bullock cart track

across this river bed about 200 yards long, sufficient to take off in still air. So I collected about a dozen children and gave them half a bar of chocolate each to clear loose stones from this track. The wheel was fitted but it was not practicable to connect the brakes; I would therefore have to land at Delhi with enough runway for the plane to come to rest unchecked by brakes.

One of the routine actions before take-off in this plane was to put the flaps half down, which enabled it to become airborne at a slower speed. With no excuse, I forgot. I had to concentrate on keeping the plane very straight during the take-off run because my track was little wider than the spacing of my wheels. When I reached the end of the 200 yards and we were doing about 60 knots, I found to my alarm that we were not airborne. The track then dipped and rose again 50 yards further on. I pulled the stick back hard and the plane stayed in the air but about dead level so that we hit the far rise and then, mercifully, rose into the air and stayed there. I looked over the side and saw that one of the wheels had a chip out of it and, assuming that that tyre had burst, I made note to be prepared to land as far as possible on the other wheel.

The next problem was that the elevator control was rather stiff and the manual control, which one should have been able to set so that the plane would naturally fly level, was not working. We got back to Delhi with no further trouble and I flew over, but not too close to, the parade which was then marching up between the 2 large government buildings, North Block and South Block. I turned off to Willingdon airfield and approached as I had planned, so as to land at the very beginning of the tarmac and with the weight on the sound wheel. To my great surprise the plane landed evenly and came to a complete halt within 10 or 15 yards.

It turned out that, although there was a chip out of one wheel, the tyre was intact. When I had hit the far side of the dip on take-off, the tail wheel must have hit something: it had turned through 90 degrees and, on landing, the axle had dug into the tarmac, making an effective drag anchor. Further investigation showed that the cable controlling the elevator, a 7-strand steel wire, had only 2 strands left at a point where it went over a pulley: hence the stiffness of the control. We were very lucky to get back unhurt but I'm afraid that my helpful corporal must have been reluctant to fly with the Army again.

15

DELHI, PUTNEY, MYTCHETT: 1946–48

Reasonable accommodation was not easy to come by in New Delhi, due, no doubt, largely to the enormous size of GHQ: more than 2,000 officers, headed by 57 major-generals and above. When Gerry came, all that I had been able to find was one room in a boarding house. We continued at first to use the young Mohammedan bearer who had served me adequately when living as a grass widower in a large mess. But the new regime did not suit him and he no longer suited us; so he was soon replaced by an older Hindu, Lal Chand, who was used to dealing with wives as well as husbands.

I used to go to the office, a mile or 2, on an autocycle, a bicycle with a motor attached. This was a satisfactory and cool way of travelling, except that this machine kept developing punctures until we discovered that the bearer, the young one, liked taking it to be repaired so that he could ride it and no doubt make a small profit. We also had a 1937 Chevrolet which I had acquired at a modest price during the winter. When I went first to take delivery of it, I noticed that it was firing on only 5 of its 6 cylinders. The salesman asked why that worried me as many cars managed perfectly well on 4.

During April Roddy McLeod and Molly Thomas were married. On the night before the wedding one of the other GSO1s arranged a stag party for Roddy, whilst Gerry had a party for Molly and the wives.

About the end of April it was time for Gerry to go to the hills and I took her up to Nainital one weekend, planning to join her for a month's leave at the beginning of June. There were 3 classes for which tickets were issued on Indian railways: first was reasonably comfortable and was mainly occupied by the British; second had basic upholstery and was appropriate for servants; third had hard wooden seats; and those who had no tickets (I presume) travelled on the roof. Our bearer brought his family and they got into a second-class compartment, which had a seat on one side only and thus could reasonably accommodate 5 or 6 persons; he was pleased to find that, when we started, there were only 21 in it.

The main-line train took us during the night to Bareilly and there we changed to the Oudh and Tirhout branch line, otherwise known as the Old and Tired. Timekeeping was rather casual and, if late, the usual excuse, which we learnt was often genuine, was trouble with a tiger on the line. So we came to Kathgodam and made the hair-raising journey up the hill in a taxi.

We had given up our room in the boarding house with no regrets and I shared a bungalow occupied by Jack Masters, my fellow GSO1, whose wife had also gone to the hills. May was very unpleasantly hot, just before the monsoon broke, and I usually slept on a camp bed in the garden.

I joined Gerry as planned and found that she was very bored. Regardless of the heat, she wanted to come back to Delhi with me at the end of my leave. I soon saw her point. Life was comfortable enough but soon became monotonous. One could play tennis, walk and sail in dinghies on the Nainital Lake. There was a thriving club with weekly dances. Because of the mountains around, the wind on the lake was quite unpredictable and, as there were reeds near the banks, one was strictly instructed that, if one capsized, one must stay with the boat until rescued. We were told that the goddess of the lake required at least one body drowned each year and that, in default of an accidental death, it was the custom to throw an old woman in.

Our boarding house was up the hill above the lake and the club was at lake level. It was therefore usual, after the Saturday night dance, for ladies to travel home by *dandi*, a light canvas-sided chair carried on 2 poles by 2 men on the flat or 4 uphill. It was not considered de rigueur for men to travel that way and one was expected to walk alongside. I found that the carriers thought it fun to go a good deal faster than I could reasonably manage, having just come from the plain at about 700 feet to Nainital at 6,000.

We returned to Delhi about the end of June and moved into a pleasant, large bungalow with 2 grass widowers. Soon after I had got back to work I had my sixth or seventh go of 'Delhi belly'. On each occasion the doctor had given me a course of a sulphur drug, which had soon put me right on the first occasion but had had progressively less effect on each subsequent occasion. By this time I was feeling pretty run-down and told the doctor that I thought something more had to be done. My normal weight had been about twelve-and-a-half stone, none too much for my height of 6 feet six-and-a-half inches, and it was now down to under 10 stone. After exhaustive, and exhausting, tests it was decided that I had tuberculosis. It was considered that one of the causes was that, from November to February, I had had lessons in Urdu from 7 to 8 am every day and the munshi teaching me had coughed pretty regularly.

It appeared that there was a considerable incidence of this disease in the services soon after the war and the authorities had taken a very generous view of the situation by introducing a 'long term treatment scheme', which entitled each case to up to 18 months' treatment at government expense whilst remaining on full pay. In the military hospital, I was required to lie still and do nothing, until about the end of August, whilst arrangements were made for me to be shipped home. I was officially put into what was then called medical category E, defined as 'permanently unfit for any form of military service'.

Meanwhile Gerry had had to dispose of an autocycle

and an aeroplane: we had already got rid of the car. In answer to an advertisement, an Indian family came to inspect the autocycle, accompanied by someone who purported to know something about them. There was much talk which Gerry did not understand but she happened to catch the words *'tik hai'* from the 'expert', and so she knew that it had been pronounced in good order. She therefore declined to bargain, which was very disappointing for the buyer, and she got the asking price.

The aeroplane was sitting at Willingdon airfield, about 2 miles away, unable to move as the spare parts ordered had still not arrived. Gerry had to cycle there in the heat several times to interview the RAF corporal who was keeping an eye on it, causing lifted eyebrows as to whether he, rather than the plane, were really the object of her visits! We were lucky that, although Americans were not allowed to buy these planes direct from the US authorities, there was no objection to them buying indirectly. This, coupled with a bank strike, resulted in an American, who had cash that he could not put in the bank, paying the equivalent of £300 for it. I had had a lot of fun with it at a cost of only £100.

Soon after I went into hospital, Gerry was invited to stay with the Beresford-Peirses (Lieutenant-General Sir Noel B-P was in charge of welfare for all forces in India) until I should be shipped home. Meanwhile Roddy McLeod arranged with the Director of Movements for Gerry to travel in the same hospital ship as me, on the books as a VAD, which she had trained as early in the war. One way and another all these very busy people took a great deal of trouble to look after us both. The Director of Movements, whose name I forget, came to see me and greatly encouraged me by telling me that in 1924, having tuberculosis, the doctors had given him 6 months to live and here he was doing a busy job in 1946.

When I left Delhi I went by train – nominally on a stretcher, with 2 soldiers to look after me – to Poona, not too far from Bombay. At one station, towards evening, I asked the soldiers to go up the platform to discover if there was any arrangement for an evening meal. After they were gone the guard came to have a chat and, whilst we were talking, we noticed that the soldiers had walked back down the platform, inadvertently passing our carriage and on down to the end of the train. At that moment, with no warning and without any action by the guard, the train drew silently out of the station. The guard and I agreed that this was a moment to do what I have often wanted to do, to pull the communication cord. We did: the train came to a halt and, in due course, backed into the station to pick up my escort. After 3 or 4 days in Poona hospital, I was sent down to Bombay and into the hospital ship, with Gerry to look after me.

From Bombay the ship went to Kilindini, the port for Mombasa, in Kenya, to pick up Italian prisoners who were ill and to take them back to Italy. Gerry overheard a shouted conversation between ship and shore: 'How many beds have you available?' 'I don't know. How many patients have you to send?' 'I don't know.' It gave one little confidence in the efficiency of either party.

After filling up with fuel and water at Aden, the ship had to go up the Red Sea with a marked list to starboard, as they had filled the tanks on one side of the ship and not the other. In the considerable heat of the Red Sea, I was lucky to have a fan over my bed. I noticed one afternoon that smoke was coming out of it and, as there was no nurse or other attendant in the ward at the time, I reached up and unplugged it. I then rang my bell and, when in due course the sister came, I told her what had happened. She was horrified: I should have waited for her to get the electrician!

We disembarked the Italians at Naples and then had a marvellous view of Stromboli erupting at night.

Arriving at Southampton, all officer patients were put into a train but no one would tell us our destination: too secret, although the war had been over for more than a year. Gerry had to find her own way to London to stay with her aunt, Connie Prideaux. Meanwhile the trainload of officer patients ended up at ten o'clock at night in some remote place in North Wales and we were taken to a new hospital which was not yet open and was not equipped or staffed to receive us.

I was taken the next day to a military hospital in Chester. Whilst there I was visited by my cousin, Ronald Lunt, and his wife, Veslemøy. One Saturday, when in Norway, I had been invited to a Norwegian dinner party with dancing afterwards and asked to bring a friend. Ronald was then SCF, Senior Chaplain to the Forces, to 1st Airborne Division, and I asked him to come. He maintained at first that he could not because he had to prepare a sermon for next day but was eventually persuaded. On arrival we were greeted by our host and his very attractive great-niece. Ronald somehow appropriated Veslemøy for the whole evening, and they were married in Norway that summer. Ronald had now become headmaster of Liverpool College.

I was soon moved to a hospital which specialised in tuberculosis near Hindhead, Surrey, which was much more convenient for Gerry to come and see me. After 3 or 4 weeks there, it was decided that I would have to have an operation to cut out the affected part of the lung and that I needed a few months to build up strength before the operation. To this end I was sent to Scio House in Putney, a small nursing home for about 15 patients, originally established after the First World War as a home for incurables. It had an elderly and devoted staff, several of whom, including the matron, who, I suspect, was close on 80, would have retired years earlier if it had not been for the war. Fresh air and good food worked wonders and, before Christmas, the doctors decided that I did not need the operation: a long period of rest would put me right. The doctors in question, Dr Todd, assisted by Dr Teare, ran a large TB sanatorium at Midhurst and treated Scio House as a small outstation.

Gerry, meanwhile, had settled into a small flat in

London. For Christmas I was allowed to join her for a few days and even to go to a theatre, provided that we had a hire car each way and that I took no material exercise: a very sensible approach which certainly raised my morale a lot.

The first 3 months of 1947 were the period of the great freeze. Not only was it bitterly cold but there was a serious fuel shortage. Only medical establishments and the like could be kept properly warm: so I was in the right place. Putney was reasonably handy and Gerry trailed through the snow and ice to come and see me frequently. I had a number of other visitors too: busy people, including Roddy McLeod and my uncle Geoffrey, now the Bishop of Salisbury, were very generous with their time.

During this winter I occupied myself sorting out my own pay and allowances. A new army pay code had been introduced in 1946. One of the general principles was that no-one ought to get less under the new code than the old but there were certain rather complicated exceptions. 'Corps pay' had been an addition for those who had certain academic qualifications but was abolished under the new code. Those who had been drawing it were allowed to continue to do so as long as they continued in the same appointment or a 'similar' one. The Army Pay Office had interpreted the word 'similar' narrowly and I argued that they were wrong. Much correspondence ensued without success until eventually, losing patience, I asked for the matter to be referred to the Army Council. The pay authorities capitulated within a few days. As result I received an extra 5 shillings a day for several years.

The Pay Office in India had failed to register that I had left, with the result that for several months I was paid both in India and in England. I realized that this was happening and put the money on one side until the time came, about 5 months later, when I was asked to refund the overpayment, by which time I owed more the £500. I was told that initially this would be recovered from my pay at the rate of about £15 a month but would I please make arrangements to pay it back more quickly. I replied that, as I had been underpaid in 1941 (Chapter 6) and had had to pay interest on an overdraft, I considered it fair to continue to pay at £15 a month whilst obtaining interest on the rest. There was no reply for about a year. In March 1948 I received a rude letter to the effect that it was disgraceful that an officer should advance such an argument and would I please refund the balance of around £350 at once. I suspect that someone was in trouble with his accounts near the end of the financial year. I replied that I had 2 outstanding travel claims in India which had still not been paid, amounting to some £60. I was prepared to return the £350 less this £60. To my surprise they said 'Done' by return of post. These 2 cases taught me some lessons which were valuable in my next appointment.

In March and April I was allowed up for gradually increasing periods and then out for short walks. In May I left Scio House and we went to stay with my sister Rachel in Devon and then took care of their house and dog whilst they went away for a holiday. She had married John Sutton, in the RAF, in August 1941. John was a flying instructor at Cranwell when they married and not long afterwards had to bail out of his plane because it caught fire. This happened not far from where he and Rachel were living and Rachel was the first person on the spot. His hands were badly burned but recovered. Later he became a distinguished bomber pilot, ending the war as a Wing Commander, DSO, DFC and AFC. His father having died recently, he took over the family wine business in Exeter and a year later declined the belated offer of a regular commission in the RAF: he was too firmly committed.

In June we spent a month in Switzerland. Having always heard that that was the place to go to convalesce after TB, I asked Dr Todd whether he would recommend it. He said that there would be no harm in a month's holiday there but that it was essential to recover in the same climate as that in which one was going to live.

We went to Leysin, which in the past had been exclusively visited by TB cases but now welcomed ordinary tourists as well. Part-way through this pleasantly restful holiday, we got the awful news that my brother-in-law, Francis Fane, my sister Joyce's husband, whose business was taking newly built vessels from builders to new owners, had set out down the Clyde in a ship with a crew of about 10 and had, 2 years after the end of the war, hit a mine. It was later established that the ship had gone down with all hands. Joyce was left with the task of bringing up, on her own, 4 children then ranging in age from 14 to 8.

We spent August in Donegal with Gerry's family and then returned to England, where I had to have a check-up at Midhurst. It appeared that my condition had worsened and I was immediately readmitted to Scio House. In November I had improved again and I was allowed to join Gerry in a small flat at Mytchett provided that I remained almost entirely in bed for some time.

At the end of March (1948) I attended what was expected to be my final army medical board. I was now considered fit to take on a job if it were not too physically arduous. I asked whether, if all went as well as it could, there was any reason why in the course of time I would be unable to take on any army job. They said that there was not and thus they had, reluctantly, to agree that, if I were allowed to stay on in the army, I might in time reach the top medical category: but no TB case such as mine had until then been allowed stay on and it would be setting a precedent. Anyway, the outcome was that I stayed.

While all this was going on, much more important, Gerry was expecting our first infant, due in May.

16

CAMBERLEY: 1948–50

The posting authorities were trying to find a reasonably quiet job for me within working distance of my home at Mytchett. It was lucky for me that Roddy McLeod had recently been made Assistant Commandant at the Staff College at Camberley, only four-and-a-half miles from Mytchett. He got me over there to meet the Commandant, Major-General Dick Hull, who, it may be remembered, had commanded Blade Force, the spearhead of First Army in Tunisia. As result I was posted to be DAAG (Deputy Assistant Adjutant General) at the Staff College, starting in April (1948). This was really 3 separate jobs: personal staff officer to the Commandant, personnel matters for the staff and students, and supervision of the civilian staff. I had, of course, long since reverted from temporary lieutenant-colonel to my war-substantive rank of major and was fortunate to keep that rank as, on a peacetime basis, I was not due for promotion to major until August 1950.

This proved to be an ideal job because it was not too arduous and few things were so urgent as to require long hours without warning. Not only was it interesting in itself but, whenever I had the time and inclination, I could attend lectures and demonstrations arranged for the students.

The first significant event was the birth of our first infant, Margaret, about midday on 12 May. Poor Gerry had had much more than the usual prolonged problem of the arrival of a first infant because it was very large, over 10 pounds. However, she and Margaret prospered and we were lucky to be able to rely on Gerry's mother to keep the house running. Gerry's mother, known to everyone as Moppy, then aged 68, had run the house right through the war. I particularly appreciated having her and Gerry's father, then 80, having lost my own parents so young.

Of the 240 students and about 35 officers on the staff, a large proportion had recently returned from service abroad. Many, particularly those who had been in the chaos of Indian partition, had problems to do with their pay which it was my job to try to sort out. I had so many unresolved cases at one moment that I travelled to the Officers' Accounts Office in Manchester to try to deal with them on the spot. I found that not only did this speed decisions in some cases but improved relations with some of those in that office, smoothing the path of later cases.

Some of these problems resulted from regular overpayments over a period, often amounting to fairly large sums which the authorities were trying to recover. I went to discuss the policy for these cases with the appropriate branch of the AG's (Adjutant-General's) office in London. There I learnt a point of law which was valuable not only then but on several later occasions. If an overpayment was made, it followed from 'a mistake of fact' or 'a mistake of law'. If the mistake arose because the authority believed that the recipient was eg married not single, or at place A not place B, or made any other mistake as to the facts of the case, it was a 'mistake of fact' and the authority was entitled to reclaim such excess payments for a period of up to 12 months but no more. If, for example, the payments had been made monthly for, say, 2 years, only 12 months' worth could be reclaimed.

On the other hand, if the overpayments arose from a misinterpretation of the law by 'a person in authority', who might be a very junior staff officer or civil servant, it was a 'mistake of law' and no repayment at all had to be made. Although this was the legal position, it did not stop the pay authorities trying to recover money to which they were not so entitled. Moreover, I was asked to keep this knowledge of the law to myself, presumably to reduce the chances of someone retaining what he was legally entitled to, an attitude which I regarded as wholly reprehensible. I did all I could to prevent such unjustified recoveries, which otherwise often left the individual, who usually had not known that he was being overpaid, on very short pay for a long time.

The case which I had successfully argued whilst in the Putney nursing home, for the continuation of corps pay, made me popular with a number of officers who had had their pay increased by 5 shillings a day because 'the Hancock appeal' had been treated as a test case.

A feature of this job for which I was profoundly grateful was that I had a secretary, Miss Kinsman, who was a highly competent and most patient shorthand typist. With her help I learnt to dictate my letters and thus avoided much wearisome waste of time then and in many different jobs later on.

The 1946 pay code seemed to have hit certain ranks badly. The students at the Staff College then were about half majors and half captains and I found that some of the latter could easily be in serious financial difficulty. There were no married quarters to be had except for some of the Directing Staff and others had to find what they could. I went into the detail of a specimen case of a married captain with 2 children in which the essential outgoings, with no luxury of any sort, were £55 a month, whilst his net pay was £50. His father, an impecunious parson, had given him £25 but this was now exhausted. What was he to do? The Commandant, Dick Hull, took up the whole question of pay rates, using this case as a lever, and, before he handed over to his successor in the autumn of 1948, a promise of certain improvements was given.

Another aspect of my job was looking after the 150 or so civilian staff. This was something quite new to me and it took me some time to learn about their pay and conditions of service. For example we were instructed by the War Office that we were to reduce the amount that we spent on overtime payments. At first sight this did not seem too difficult: we could do certain cleaning and labouring jobs adequately without any serious lowering of standards. But when the proposals were announced there was grumbling from most of the men, who did not want to lose pay, and delight from a few who would have more time in which to do a second job. Only a small proportion of the men were then trade union members but their union leader spoke up loudly. My superior for this side of my job was Colonel Stuart Knox (as it happened, late Royal Signals) and he took on this problem, achieving a reasonably satisfactory compromise.

In August 1948, whilst the Staff College had a mid-course break, the buildings and permanent staff were used for a 5-day indoor exercise run by the CIGS, Montgomery, for all general officers. On the first day, a Monday, Monty made his opening address and, amongst other things, said, 'I want you to make full use of your time here. In addition to your work on the exercise itself, I want you to study and report on a number of subjects. For this purpose I have divided you into small groups and the senior officer of each group is to hand in his report to me on Friday before we disperse.' When details were disclosed, this was generally most unpopular, because most of those present had been looking forward to a relaxed week meeting old friends and because the subjects themselves were generally such as to need considerable research and study, for which they would have neither the time nor the resources.

One of the subjects was 'Planning the careers of officers and the career structure up to the rank of Brigadier'. General Sir Neil Ritchie, one-time commander of the Eighth Army, was in charge of this one, with a lieutenant-general whose name I forget and Major-General Dick Hull to help him. The 3 met on the Monday evening and agreed that, as Dick Hull had his Directing Staff on the spot, they should write the report and have it ready by Friday morning. I was sent for and told to find 3 or 4 of those who, although on leave, were actually still at home in

Camberley. When I started telephoning, there were, not unnaturally, loud complaints about interference with leave. The end result was that, with help from the Military Secretary's Department, who were keen to ensure that the report did not upset their plans, I wrote the report, 3 of the DS approved it and the 3 generals signed it.

On the Wednesday of this week, the Prime Minister, Clement Attlee, was to come to lunch and attend the afternoon session of the exercise. He was due to arrive at one o'clock and, in case he arrived early, I was standing by at the front door from about 10 minutes to one. A few minutes before one, Montgomery came to join me on the doorstep. At 3 minutes past he said, 'He's late, isn't he?' I replied, 'Yes, sir, about 3 minutes'. 'Well, I can't afford to wait. Tell him to come in to lunch when he does come'.

Attlee arrived about 10 past and I gave him Montgomery's apologies for not waiting, which I had not been instructed to do. I took him to wash and then in to lunch. It was Attlee who apologised to Monty rather than the reverse. I suspect that, if Churchill had still been Prime Minister, the story would have been different!

I had 2 other contacts of interest with trade unions. In one case it was a small union representing a variety of the more skilled trades. We employed at Camberley a highly qualified lithographer who was clearly being paid far less than he was worth. He told me that he could not get his union to help him because he was the only person with his particular skills for many miles around: they weren't interested. He was paying 5 or 6 shillings a week in union dues, a large sum in those days, and so I asked why he didn't resign from the union. The answer was because, if he left Camberley for any reason, he would be unable to get another job: the closed shop. I fought his case with the appropriate financial authority and eventually got him a reasonable increase.

The other case concerned one of the college porters, a man who had been employed there for about 24 years. He was incorrigibly lazy and frequently left his work for other porters to do. I had been told about him by my predecessor, who had warned him on more than one occasion and had left me notes of the circumstances. The second time that he failed to do his share of the work in my time I decided that it was unfair to the others, a most loyal and hard-working group, to keep him on any longer. At 10 one morning I sacked him and he told me to expect a lot of trouble from his union. At 2 the local union secretary came to see me and, when I had given him the whole story, unreservedly endorsed my decision.

In the autumn of 1948 Dick Hull went to be DSD (Director of Staff Duties), an innocuous-sounding title for what was then probably the most demanding major-general's job in the army: the deployment, in peace or for minor operations world-wide or for war, of all elements of the army. It involved the execution of the policies produced by the DMO (Director of Military Operations) and the coordination of all other branches to that end. I did not realize at that time what an excellent choice Hull must have been for that job; but later, when I served him again in a similarly demanding role, I really began to appreciate his remarkable talent for this type of work. As Commandant of the Staff College he was not particularly highly regarded because directing staff and students saw little of him except when he had to address them collectively and, at that time, public speaking was not his forte. He was not at all easy to get to know well. Working for him personally, I found him straightforward to do business with but not someone in whose company it was easy to relax.

He was replaced by Major-General A D Ward, Dudley Ward, who incidentally did not appreciate any suggestion that he was connected with Penelope Dudley-Ward, a well-known actress of that time. He and his wife, Beatrice, were a delightful couple. I found him equally easy to work for and much more human. Incidentally we soon discovered that his father-in-law had been curate to my Hancock grandfather at Knaresborough around 1900.

Hull had tried to run the Staff College as nearly as possible on university lines: uniform was only worn for exercises and other expeditions outside the grounds or for special occasions. Although there were facilities for various games and sports, they were not particularly encouraged: officers could do as they wished in their spare time. Ward took a directly opposite view. He required that uniform be worn for all normal duties; all officers were expected to take part in the games and sports available; and the establishment was run much more like a normal regiment, albeit one with a particular specialist function.

Brigadier Roddy McLeod, Assistant Commandant to them both in turn, was primarily responsible for the instruction itself and I did not see a great deal of him in my job except when it came to reports and postings at the end of each course. There were at this time 240 students per course, which lasted one year, from January to December. They were divided into 4 divisions of 60 each, 2 living at Camberley, one 2 or 3 miles away at Minley Manor, and one 4 miles away at Blenheim Barracks in Aldershot. A colonel (local unpaid) was in charge of each division and he had 6 local lieutenant-colonels (GSO2s) to run his 6 syndicates of 10. There were also a few extra directing staff attached to divisions to write the exercises and instructional papers. The instructional work was co-ordinated by a fifth Colonel, with one GSO2 to help him; this was Colonel Knox, mentioned before, who had the extra job of being responsible for the administration of the place, carried out by the DAQMG and myself.

Reports and postings I found to be one of the most interesting parts of the job. Each colonel of a division, after consultation with his GSO2s, wrote a report on each of his 60 students at the end of each of the first 5 of the 6 terms into which the year's work was divided. These reports were studied by the Assistant Commandant and Commandant and passed to me for safe keeping. After the first 5 terms, that is to say about mid-October, students were assessed by their divisional colonels and the gradings and other comments formed the basis of each student's next posting. The comments would indicate, first, whether the chap should go to regimental duty (RD) or staff – about 5 or 10 per cent normally went to RD, having already been away from soldiers for too long – and, second, the type of staff job for which he was best suited. For those going to staff jobs the crucial decision was whether it should be to a grade 2 or grade 3 job, ie as a major or as a captain. If the student was then a captain and going to a major's job, he was given acting (paid) rank. If the reverse, he was allowed to keep his major's rank if it was substantive but, unless he did very well, his future was probably limited.

Whilst this was going on, the Military Secretary's Department sorted out the staff jobs which they wanted filled from this year's output from the Staff College and sent us a list. It was then my job to match the 2 lists against one another: not to appoint student A to job No. 23, but to assess the degree of match which existed, having allowed not only for suitability but also for geographical location (eg a student who had recently been abroad for a long time should probably be given a home posting); for ensuring as far as possible that the 3 main staff branches, G, A and Q, each got their fair share of high and low grade staff officers; that there was similar fairness in allocation of quality to different theatres; and to consider a number of personal problems.

When I had done my homework, there was a meeting lasting 2 long days of the Commandant, Assistant Commandant and the Colonels. We went steadily through each of some 220 staff jobs, allocating individuals to each. I had to keep the score and warn the meeting when a tendency was developing towards, for example, as usually happened, putting too many of the high-grade officers into G appointments. After this I had to send the proposed postings to the Military Secretary's Department, where they were again studied in detail and there were always some points of disagreement. Moreover, each change inevitably had consequential changes. So there was then a further meeting at the Staff College but this time with the Deputy Military Secretary and one of his staff present.

Final decisions were then taken. As result, on a given day, I placed in each student's letter-rack a slip of paper telling him about his next job. This was done before lunch. One year, one of the divisional colonels, Willie Pike (late RA, not the Grenadier Guards Willie Pike referred to in an earlier chapter who was GSO2 at the Staff College at the same time. Due to physical size, the latter was known as 'Big Willie' and the colonel as 'Little Willie') told me that evening that 2 students' wives had rung him up to say that their husbands had been posted to grade 3 jobs and surely there was some mistake! He added that this remarkable action by the wives confirmed to him the correctness of these lowly postings.

In the break between courses in January 1949 we left Margaret, aged 8 months, with a kind neighbour and went for our first continental holiday since the war, taking Moppy (Gerry's mother) and my sister Bridget with us. It needed careful planning because the exchange regulations stopped one taking more than £50 abroad for a holiday. Our car was a 1937 Rover which had a grid at the back for strapping on the larger items of luggage. The rest had to go inside with us and there was little space to spare. We set off for the French Riviera, having booked into a small hotel in Villefranche. It happened that for the first 2 days Bridget sat in the back and then exchanged with Gerry. Gerry immediately complained of the discomfort of this back seat and we soon found that I had stowed chains, in case of snow, under that seat and the springs were too weak to protect the passenger. Poor Bridget had assumed that the car was made that way and had not liked to complain. We took about 3 days travelling each way and had a pleasant week in the Riviera sunshine.

I had regular medical checks and, towards the end of 1949, the most recent board had upgraded me to the extent that I could do any job in a temperate climate. I was long overdue for regimental duty but was still too junior to hope for anything above the rank of major. At that time the Parachute Regiment recruited its officers from volunteers from all arms. John Mogg, a GSO2 on the Directing Staff, was leaving at this time to take command of one of their battalions. He asked me to come as his second-in-command. I much wanted to accept, not only because he was the sort of chap for whom I would have been delighted to work but also because it would have given me a practical insight into the functioning of infantry. Unfortunately the battalion had to be available to go anywhere at short notice and my medical category would have prevented me going too. So, very sadly, I had to refuse.

Roddy McLeod was going to be CRA (Commander Royal Artillery) of 7th Armoured Division in Germany and asked me to go as his signal officer. Unfortunately, a few days earlier, Dudley Ward, the Commandant, in an address to the students at which I had happened to be present, had said that he considered it wrong for a senior officer to have a group of more junior officers who tended to follow him around. Perhaps this was a dig at Monty and others who adopted this policy. I accepted his view and, as I had already worked twice for Roddy McLeod, thought that I ought not to do so again at once. I put this to Roddy, who I suspect did not agree with Dudley Ward but was too loyal to say so, and so this was pursued no further. I was posted to 2nd Infantry Divisional Signals in Germany as that CRA's signal officer.

Signa, our converted lifeboat

Jack Profumo on Gan, 1961

De Cumont, Iceland (De C in Mac)

Nigel Henderson, Iceland (H without hat)

Military Committee's last meeting in the Pentagon

Briefing at SEATO

River travel in Brunei: John Simpson, CO Royal Brunei Malay Regt, Dick Worsley, BES, and me

John Simpson, Headman and me

17

HILDEN: 1950–52

We drove with the usual overloaded car from Mytchett to Harwich. On top of the luggage in the back seat were Margaret in a carrycot with our bulldog alongside her. Each night there were a troopship and a civilian ship crossing to The Hook. We had to go in the troopship but, as the troopship would not take dogs, we had planned to send ours by the civilian ship. I went to ask for a dog ticket but I found that this could not be issued unless I could produce an export licence for the dog! Because exchange controls were strict, the authorities had to make sure that we did not sell our dog abroad and so gain a little foreign currency to which we were not entitled. Fortunately the person concerned had a little common sense and said that, whilst the dog could not be taken officially, if we liked to hand her over to the chief cook she would arrive in Holland overfed and free: she did.

No reasonable quarter was immediately available in or near Hilden, where the Divisional Headquarters and Divisional Signals lived, and so we were given a tiny flat belonging to Divisional Headquarters as a temporary measure. A childless couple had the ground floor and we had the first floor of a very small house. We were also required to take over the attics and therefore to sign for their contents. These included a pile of a dozen mattresses. When we moved out a month later, the Quartermaster counted these mattresses and flipped the corner of the pile; a cloud of moths flew out, as he had obviously expected. He said that we should have to pay for these mattresses.

We learned later that the QMs of Divisional Headquarters and of Signals were at daggers drawn and this was a way of scoring points. It was, however, unsuccessful because we got our Medical Officer along and he certified that the moths were more than a month old.

After a time we were told that, as no nearer quarter was available, we could go and look at a rather large house at Heiligenhaus, about 15 miles to the north. It was certainly much too large but we were desperate to get out of our claustrophobic flat. It had 9 bedrooms, 5 bath and shower rooms and its own swimming pool. However, because of the size, we were entitled to 2 German maids, and, like any other quarter, to a third share of a boilerman. As there were no other quarters near enough, we were given a boilerman of our own. The central heating and hot water for this house used up to one-and-a-half tons of coke a week in the winter, stoked by our staff and provided for us free.

The owner of the house was living in a corrugated iron bungalow at the bottom of the garden. We never met him but we were shown an album of photographs of the main rooms in this house as it was when the army took it over. It had certainly been luxuriously furnished. In due course we learnt the history. It had been an officers' mess for a GCLO (German Civil Labour Organisation) unit. There had been 3 officers living in this mess. One Saturday night only 2 of the officers were in and they said that they drank rather a lot and went to bed, taking their dogs upstairs with them. They slept solidly and when they came down on Sunday morning they found that all the more valuable items of furniture had been stolen. There was reason to suspect that the owner and the senior officer, a major, were in cahoots but this could not be proved.

It was alleged that this major was involved in a number of financial rackets that could not be proved against him: eg demanding and obtaining antifreeze for the 100 vehicles in his unit and selling this very profitably to German civilians, since his vehicles were all air-cooled Volkswagens;

and running a public dance, using his official labour force for the purpose, whilst he pocketed the proceeds. He was finally caught out and sacked for 'Conduct unbecoming...' in that he had a naked lady in the officers' mess, the evidence for which was a photograph circulated widely to try to obtain an identification!

It came to my notice that a certain regiment was selling on the black market around 100 bottles of gin a month for the benefit of mess funds. I reported this to the brigadier concerned but I believe little or nothing was done about it. I do not suppose that the scale of such activities was such as to have any material economic effect but, in my view much more serious, many soldiers, both officers and other ranks, were beginning to believe that this was acceptable behaviour. The high pre-war standards of integrity seemed to have disappeared.

In due course I had to go back to England to attend a medical board and I had lunch with General Dudley Ward at the Staff College. Knowing him to be an officer of the very highest integrity, I told him all about this and found that he was as horrified as I expected. When I heard only a few weeks later that he was to take command of the new 1st British Corps which was being formed, I was delighted, feeling that the problem was in safe hands. It was. I do not know how he achieved it but when I was posted back to Germany in 1963, standards were what they should be. Shortly after my arrival then, I was required to be president of a court martial to try an officer for falsifying travel claims. The sums involved were trivial but this could not be tolerated and he was dismissed the service; he was lucky not to be cashiered, when his pension too would have been forfeited.

I was delighted to have the opportunity to take up sailing again, encouraged and helped by my CO, Geoffrey Bell. It was a thriving sport amongst the British forces in Germany, very few units being out of reach of a suitable lake. Baldeneysee, a long narrow lake which is really no more than a widening of the river Ruhr, was not far from our house in Heiligenhaus and Gerry and I went there most weekends. She was very long-suffering because we sailed mainly in small dinghies which required only one person unless there was a strong wind: so she was not often invited to crew unless it was rough. However, she won the ladies' race in slightly larger 2-person dinghies.

The boats were maintained by a highly efficient German staff and fully rigged ready for racing. There were regular races on Saturday and Sunday afternoons and one only had to ring up to book a boat to find it all ready to cast off for the first race. After a time we found that some of the newcomers to the sport had become proficient racing helmsmen without knowing how to rig a boat!

September was normally the month for the annual major manoeuvres and so it was, we found, convenient to take our main leave of the year in October. Brigadier Dick Jelf was CRA and I his signal officer. The Jelfs lived in a large country house some miles to the north of us and they were kind enough in our first year there, 1950, to have Margaret, aged 2, to stay whilst we were on leave. She developed chickenpox the day after we took her there but they were not concerned as they thought that their small twins might as well get it over, which they did.

We drove south into Austria, spending our first night there in a very old inn. The rooms on each floor were built round a square well and on the top floor there was a pulley system for bringing the luggage up: most efficient. When we wanted a bath, wood was brought up and laid in a small stove which was built under a water cylinder at the end of the bath. It produced very satisfactory hot water.

From Austria we went into Italy, mostly sleeping in the car, whose front seats folded back for the purpose. We had a Primus stove on which to prepare our breakfast but we mainly went to restaurants or had sandwiches for other meals. In Venice we had to leave the car in the main car park and use water transport. Having thus far been economical with our accommodation, we stayed for 2 nights at the Danieli, which was delightful and at that time not so astronomically expensive.

We went on down to Florence and Pisa and then slowly back to Germany by a more westward route. One night, in northern Italy, I asked a farmer for permission to camp in his vineyard. He willingly allowed this with a spate of Italian which meant nothing to me. The following morning, when we went to thank him, it appeared that we had caused some offence by not taking up an invitation to drinks the previous night. We were of course profusely apologetic and I think he realised that it was merely that we had not understood him. It was a pity that we missed the drink session, which would probably have been interesting in spite of the language problem.

Shortly before Christmas we got the sad news that Gerry's father had died in Donegal. He was 82.

We wanted to ski that winter but Gerry had another infant on the way. She nobly said that she would be quite happy sitting in the sunshine, keeping an eye on Margaret aged two-and-a-half. So we went to Ehrwald, which, together with Lermoos about a mile away, had been taken over as an army leave centre. This meant an all-night train journey and the trains ran only every 5 days in each direction. I had arranged for 15 days' leave but I got the impression, probably wrongly, that my newly arrived Commanding Officer, Bill Blaker, took the view that the purpose of leave was to charge one's batteries for further work rather than to be enjoyed. We therefore had a problem when, a day or 2 before we were due to start back from Ehrwald, Margaret got measles. We reckoned that I must return as planned and that Gerry would have to follow 5 days later when Margaret was expected to be fit to travel.

However, for my last day's skiing, I went over to Lermoos and, while having lunch there, happened to meet our divisional commander, Major-General Colin Callander. I knew him better than the average major would expect to do because his house was some distance out from Divisional HQ in the same direction as ours and we had dined in each other's houses. He asked after Gerry, and I told him our sad story. He at once said, 'This is nonsense. You must ring up Bill Blaker and tell him that I have said that your leave is to be extended until Margaret is fit.' So, not unwillingly, I obeyed orders. The sad part was that, throughout, the weather was bitterly cold and the sun hardly shone at all: so Gerry had a rotten holiday.

Gerry's mother, Moppy to all, came to stay with us in time for the arrival of our next infant, in June 1951. It had apparently become evident that Gerry was going to have another over-large baby but the doctor seemed unwilling to hasten it at all. Eventually Gerry went into the military hospital on Friday, 8 June, the doctor saying that this was just a precautionary measure and not to expect any news for a few days. So on Saturday afternoon I went to sail as usual. I came in from the first race to be called to the telephone and told that we had a son and that Gerry was alright. A little later I happened to look at the results of the first race and found that I had been marked down as retired. I queried this with the score-keeper, who said that he had understood that I had hit a buoy: I assured him that I had not, I had had a boy.

Hospitals then were much less welcoming to visitors than nowadays. Even so the BMH Wuppertal carried this to extremes when they would not allow Gerry's mother to visit her at all. Husbands were the only visitors permitted. If this was because of possible extra infection, it was somewhat illogical to have the window cleaner in the room!

Early in 1951 I was moved from 2 Squadron of the Divisional Signals to 3 Squadron. This meant that I was no longer concerned with gunner signals but with the 3 signal troops with the infantry brigades and the small troop attached to the sappers. I found this a less satisfactory job because I had no soldiers directly under my command. Whilst it gave me direct access to the brigade commanders, if there was any general policy question to be settled, I had to go to my own commanding officer, who in his turn would have to discuss it with the divisional commander. I thought that my position was largely unnecessary and that my CO, the CR Signals, should have dealt direct with the brigade commanders. This was one of the reasons that 12 years later I was glad to support the introduction of integration of brigade HQs with their brigade signals. I will go into this much argued re-organisation in due course.

In October, when Hugh was 4 months old, we wanted to do a similar trip to the previous year. Gerry was still feeding him and so he came too. Margaret was invited to stay by a kind family in the unit. We were using 'Paddipads', the earliest paper nappies, for Hugh and therefore had in the back of the car 2 very large cardboard boxes of spares. When light snow was falling at the Italian customs post on the Brenner Pass, we had to change Hugh's nappy to demonstrate to the customs officials that we really weren't smuggling.

It was about this time that we were persuaded to move house into one of a group of new quarters which had been built in Hilden. As we were due to leave in February, after 2 years in the job, it meant that we should no longer have the 15-mile drive, in winter snow, which was often tiresome.

I was told that I was going to be posted to the School of Signals at Catterick, a proposal which did not at all accord with my ideas. I had avoided the degree course at Cambridge, offered to me again in 1946, particularly in order to serve in the army more widely and not only in Signals. I pleaded, through the usual channels, that I had already spent a disproportionate amount of my service at teaching establishments. At the same time I wrote to Roddy McLeod, who had recently been promoted to major-general and appointed Director of Military Operations in the War Office. The result was that I was appointed to be GSO2 in MO4, which was exactly what I wanted.

18

WAR OFFICE MO4: 1952–54

We went back to live at Mytchett Heath and Gerry's mother came to spend each winter with us, going to Aughnagaddy to her other 2 daughters for the summer. It was a straightforward commuting journey for me to the War Office each day, Ash Vale station being far enough out of London to be reasonably sure of a seat on the train.

The Military Operations directorate was then divided into 5 sections, MO1 co-ordinating, MO2, 3 and 4 dealing with different parts of the world and MO5 handling home defence and anti-aircraft matters. MO4, headed by Lieutenant-Colonel Abdy Collins, a sapper, covered the Middle East, which for this purpose meant Libya, Egypt, Sudan and all the East African colonies, Southern Rhodesia (now Zimbabwe), and the High Commission Territories in South Africa; and the countries east of the Red Sea as far as Persia (now Iran). MO4a, my section, was concerned with the African countries and MO4b, headed by Tony King-Harman, had the Asian part. I had 2 GSO3s and he had one. One of my GSO3s handled Libya, Egypt and the Sudan and the other the rest, although there was, of course, a good deal of give and take. The 5 of us shared an office, whilst Abdy Collins had his own room next door.

It was each person's job to keep up-to-date with all significant events in his territories. The most important regular task was to prepare briefs for Chiefs of Staff meetings. The Chiefs of Staff met every Tuesday and the Vice Chiefs every Thursday. Directly the agenda for a meeting was received the officer concerned with each item had to start assembling the relevant material, some of which he would have readily available and some of which would have to come from other War Office branches. The subject matter might be operational but commonly dealt with the whole gamut of military subjects and it was the MO officer's job to consult every single branch which could conceivably have an interest and make sure that their views were adequately represented. Thus one might be dealing on the same day with the building of married quarters for troops in the Canal Zone of Egypt (we had 2 divisions there then), rumours of an insurrection in Uganda, and the future ruling of Libya if the elderly King Idris's wife should prove not to be pregnant after all. It was a fascinating job.

The DMO, Roddy McLeod, used to hold a meeting of his 2 deputies, the Director of Plans, and his 5 GSO1s every morning at 9.30. Each colonel was expected to be up to date on every subject concerning his area. This meant for most of them getting into the War Office before 9 am, a very early hour by the Whitehall standards of those days. However this was not convenient for whatever train it was that Abdy Collins took. He normally arrived at the door of the War Office between 9.20 and 9.25, having read *The Times* (essential reading) on the way, and was met there by our chief clerk who would have ready all the relevant telegrams which had arrived overnight. Sometimes one of the GSO2s was there too, ready to walk up the 2 floors with him and brief him on the way. He was very quick-witted and I don't suppose that he was ever caught out. Certainly one could not risk guessing or pretending to know: Roddy dealt very firmly with one GSO1 who tried that.

The Director of Plans was Brigadier Dick Craddock, a delightful chap with a very ready wit. If 'Morning Prayers', as they were commonly called, got too serious he could be relied on to lighten the meeting without offence to anyone. Roddy knew his worth and tolerated an interjection from him in a way that he would not have from most others.

The DMO was allotted a fairly generous travel budget, which enabled his staff down to GSO2 level to travel to the relevant theatres at least once a year. I am sure this was a sensible provision as it meant that briefs were prepared with real first-hand knowledge. It gave the army an advantage over the other 2 services, which organized their equivalents of MO on a functional basis and so often had no one available with real local knowledge.

My first such trip was to the Canal Zone and to Libya. In Tripoli I was invited to a diplomatic/military cocktail party, where I happened to discover that the dental wing of the local British Military Hospital had just refused to make false teeth for the Libyan Prime Minister. No doubt this was correct by the rules but was, in my view, an obviously silly decision. I reversed it on the spot and assured the local military authorities that I would take full responsibility in the War Office: I knew that I could count on Roddy's backing if it should be required.

In the autumn of 1952, Abdy Collins, my boss, became ill and for a few months was in and out of hospital. I had to act for him in his absence, which I found difficult because not only did I have to co-ordinate the whole of MO4, as well as doing my own job, but had to spend a lot of time briefing him whenever he returned to duty. I was probably not as considerate of his health as I ought to have been but I had no idea that he was seriously ill until quite suddenly he died of cancer.

It took 3 or 4 months for a successor to come and during this time I enjoyed running the section myself. Roddy was kind enough to certify that I was doing the job satisfactorily and so I was paid appropriately! I remember only one tiresomeness: it concerned 13 briefs on Friday the 13th (of February). The problem arose because the CIGS, General Sir John Harding, liked to be given short briefs with the minimum of accompanying documents, whereas the VCIGS, Lieutenant-General Stratton, liked very full briefs with ample supporting documents. All in MO were aware of this, not least of course the DMO himself; when the DMO was standing in for the VCIGS he seemed to prefer the longer briefs. So we all had to draft accordingly. On this occasion the CIGS was going on a trip around the Middle East starting on Saturday the 14th and required briefs on 13 different subjects. All 5 officers in MO4 worked hard on Thursday the 12th and I went home pleased that we had served up 13 good clear short briefs.

Roddy had evidently read them very early next morning and sent for me to tell me that they were no good because, regardless of the CIGS's taste for short briefs, these were not nearly full enough. So we all toiled hard on Friday the 13th and by about 5 pm handed in 13 very full briefs, which Roddy approved and gave to the CIGS. I was told later on by the MA to the CIGS, very confidentially, that the CIGS had complained forcibly to Roddy that the briefs were too long! We never heard a word about them officially.

A new GSO1 was appointed about April, Tommy Bulkeley of the Scots Guards, a delightful chap whom I had known at the Staff College in 1948-49 when he was a GSO2 and I was DAAG.

1953 was coronation year and, working in the War Office, I was entitled to enter the ballot for window seats. I drew 2 ground-floor window seats facing Northumberland Avenue, along which the procession would pass going to the Abbey. Gerry and her mother and I came by a very early train and they sat in the window whilst I stood on the pavement just outside and we all got an excellent view. The star attraction was the Queen of Tonga, a very large lady; and squeezed into the carriage alongside her was a very small man. Some wag pointed out that she had brought her lunch.

For my efforts in standing in as GSO1 for some months, Roddy McLeod had recommended me for the MBE and this was duly presented by the Queen. The investiture started at 11 am and I was one of the last, after 1 pm. Nevertheless the Queen greeted me as though I were the one person she wanted to talk to: most impressive. And next day I read in the paper that she had come down on the night train from Scotland: what energy.

My father-in-law had left Aughnagaddy equally to his 3 daughters. Gerry and I knew that we would never want to live there and equally her sisters had little interest in Mytchett Heath, which was owned by Moppy, their mother. Mytchett, however, needed money spending on it, money which Moppy could not afford; moreover, there were 2 small flats in it which were let and provided Moppy with a small income extra to her then very inadequate army widow's pension. After some family discussion we all agreed that the sensible and fair answer was for Gerry to surrender her share of Aughnagaddy to her sisters and for Moppy to leave such capital as she had to those sisters. Meanwhile she would make over Mytchett to Gerry and we would pay her regularly a sum of money equal to the profit on the flats. Thus Gerry's sisters would have half of Aughnagaddy each with the prospect of a little capital in due course, whilst we would have Mytchett Heath less payment of a small regular sum to Moppy. Moppy would no longer have the problems of running Mytchett Heath and could make her home in either house.

Whitehall was officially open for business in those days on Saturday mornings, although it was generally accepted that, if there were no special emergency, offices would be manned at about one-third strength. One Saturday morning I was rung up by the Chiefs of Staff Secretariat, who said that the Minister of Defence, Field Marshal Lord Alexander, needed to be briefed urgently for a Cabinet meeting later that morning on matters to do with the Middle East. He wanted the CIGS, who could not be located, and failing him, the most senior relevant officer available. If none more senior could be found would I please cross Whitehall to his office at once. It was interesting for me to meet this great man, whom I had once set eyes on as my divisional commander in 1939 (as described in Chapter 3). Having answered his questions, I left the room to be greeted in the corridor by one of the secretaries saying that they had now located the CIGS and he was waiting on the end of a telephone: did the Minister wish to see him? I went back in to ask Alexander, who said, 'No thank you. Tell him that you have told me all I needed.' I hope that when talking to Harding I put it a bit more tactfully.

In the autumn of 1953 there were 2 major and continuing problems confronting my part of MO4. First, it had been decided that Britain must cease to occupy the Canal Zone of Egypt, where we had 2 divisions and a base large enough to support that force and considerable reinforcements if they should be required. After much debate it was decided that a large part of this force would move to Cyprus, and barrack building started there. But the cost of moving the base with several hundred million pounds' worth of stores would be prohibitive. Under financial pressure, the Chiefs of Staff proposed to leave the base and all its stores where they were, under the care of Egyptian contractors who would be required to maintain the equipment in a state of readiness for any British force to pick them up on the way to an emergency in any of our colonies. A signal to this effect was sent to the BDCC (ME), the British Defence Co-ordinating Committee (Middle East), which consisted of the 3 Commanders-in-Chief and their Political Advisor. General Sir Brian Robertson (son of the Field Marshal who was CIGS in the 1914 War) was at that time the Chairman and it was not difficult to detect his skilled hand in the drafting of the reply which concluded 'It must be remembered that, compared with the Egyptian, the vulture is a bungling amateur'.

Relations with Egypt at this time were not good and it was a distinct possibility that either the Egyptian regular forces, or irregulars unofficially sponsored by their government, would attempt by force to throw us out or to make life so uncomfortable as to accelerate the departure that we already contemplated. Plans to secure our position if there should be some flare-up were reviewed and, just before Christmas, the Prime Minister, Churchill, required the

CIGS, Harding, to brief him on the action we would take in such an event. Churchill demanded much more detail than was held in Whitehall and would not listen to the argument that it was not Whitehall's job to know which company would assault which house in Ismalya. The result was that on Christmas Eve I was told to go to the Canal Zone on Boxing Day and bring back all the details of plans down to the lowest level.

When I returned a few days later I got the impression that there was no longer any serious prime ministerial interest in the subject. I suspect that it was Churchill's usual ploy to keep, as he thought, commanders at all levels on their toes.

The second of MO4's problems starting that autumn of 1953 was the Mau Mau rebellion in Kenya. For a number of years there had been intelligence reports that Kenyatta and others were putting in the spadework to foment trouble, with a view to ejecting the British and taking over the country for the Kikuyu as opposed to any other tribes. To this end secret oath-taking had been organised in schools, with oaths graduated in horribleness. Murders, primarily of white settlers in the more remote areas, became widespread. To control this sizeable country the only support available beyond the police were one British infantry battalion and, I think, 2 KAR (King's African Rifles) battalions. There was also a battalion of the Kenya Regiment, a white territorial force which was embodied for the duration of the emergency. Quite soon it became obvious that reinforcements from outside were required. Over the next year or so 2 more British battalions were added, making one British brigade; then a second brigade was sent; and finally a third one. With hindsight, I suspect that, if these reinforcements had all been sent in the first 2 or 3 months, the emergency would have been brought to an end sooner and with less loss of life.

19

MAU MAU: 1954

In March 1954, about 6 months after the start of the operations against the Mau Mau in Kenya, the Colonial Secretary, Oliver Lyttelton, decided to go to Nairobi for talks on the future constitution. Sir John Harding, the CIGS, now a Field Marshal, was to accompany him. It would have been normal on such a visit for the latter to take with him the GSO1 of the MO Directorate responsible for that part of the world. On this occasion, however, Tommy Bulkeley, the GSO1, had a horse running at Sandown and did not want to go. I expect he gave some other reason. Anyway, I was lucky enough, as the GSO2 concerned, to take his place.

I had only once before this set eyes on Harding; he was walking towards me along a War Office corridor with his MA, Charles Harington, who was nearly my height, whilst Harding must have been nearly a foot shorter. As I approached, Charles gave me a large wink over his head and I had great difficulty keeping a straight face. So I realized that on this trip, when there would be press photographers about, I would have to keep my distance.

Harding, his ADC and I travelled by BOAC via Cairo. Due to some fault in the aircraft we were delayed in Cairo for 24 hours and so, unexpectedly, we had to go through Egyptian customs. I was carrying 2 black Whitehall despatch boxes. As one of them contained details of the British plans for action in the Canal Zone if the Egyptians became tiresome, this could have been embarrassing. However, they were not tactless enough to ask to see inside!

During our enforced wait in Cairo BOAC arranged for those passengers who wished to do so to go to see the pyramids and the Sphinx. I had not realized before that the pyramids were made of large, perhaps 6 foot, stone cubes.

When we set off again we joined the passengers on the next day's BOAC flight and amongst them there happened to be the Governor of Uganda, who was returning to Kampala, our next stop. A guard of honour by the local KAR (King's African Rifles) battalion had been arranged there to greet the CIGS. This presented a problem of protocol because a Governor is supreme in his own colony and therefore he ought to inspect the guard; on the other hand, the guard had been specifically assembled for the CIGS, whereas the Governor was not expecting it and was somewhat casually dressed. Signals flew back and forth to Kampala, and for all I know to Whitehall too, and in due course a masterly compromise was reached: they were to inspect the guard jointly.

We arrived in Government House, Nairobi, in time for lunch and went off to the local GHQ directly afterwards to be brought up to date on the current Mau Mau situation. It was a very hot afternoon and we were all shut in a small hall with shutters on all windows for security reasons and I found it desperately hard to keep awake. Harding seemed to radiate his usual energy. He gave me the impression of having a mainspring which was kept fully wound at all times.

The chief subject of the briefing was to tell us about an operation planned to take place in Nairobi in the near future. All members of the Kikuyu tribe, from which Mau Mau had sprung, who worked or lived in Nairobi were to be arrested. Doubts were expressed about the practicability of this since almost all businesses, hotels, etc. depended on their labour. A day or 2 later I reported to Harding that I had learned that the Deputy Commander had held a 'confidential' meeting of the heads of all the principal businesses to warn them of this impending round-up and so all security must surely have been lost. Harding was obviously furious, not so much, I suspect, with the inevitable cancellation of an operation of doubtful merit, as with the incompetence it indicated. All he actually said in my hearing was, 'I thought that I had got a reliable commander here.'

On arrival in Nairobi, prior to Lyttelton's arrival, the CIGS spent a few days visiting some of the troops deployed against the Mau Mau. This was a time when the press at home had been accusing the army in Kenya of needless killing: a headline had appeared 'BOB A KNOB.' The CIGS was anxious to counter this and was naturally concerned when a company commander of the Kenya Regiment said that the army should have, in the Kikuyu Reserve Areas where about one-and-a-half million people lived, the same powers as in the Forest Areas, where they could shoot on sight. Harding turned to the brigadier and said loudly, 'If those are really this officer's views, the sooner he resigns his commission the better.' When we got into the car and left, the ADC said 'Did you know, sir, that when you were talking to that officer the press were listening?' 'Yes, that's why I spoke so loud!'

The Governor, Sir Evelyn Baring, and Lady Baring were charming hosts and made us all very welcome although it must have been a tiresome invasion. Not having stayed in a Government House before, I had not appreciated that it was customary to maintain formalities comparable with a royal residence: eg everybody, ladies included, stand up when the Governor comes into a room and acknowledge him with a slight bow; and the Governor is served at the table with his food first. After a few days, when I had realized what a delightful and approachable man Baring was, I asked him whether he did not find such customs irksome. He said that he had found it much worse in Rhodesia, where, when he arrived, he had never managed to get his hand on a doorknob: it was always opened before he could get to it.

A year or so before, when white settlers thought that the Governor was transferring power too rapidly and too fully to the black population, there had been a march by white

C.I.G.S. TOURS MAU MAU TERRORIST AREAS IN KENYA

C.I.G.S. IN KENYA. Field-Marshal Sir John Harding, Chief of the Imperial General Staff, followed by Gen. Sir George Erskine, C.-in-C. East Africa, walking through the undergrowth during his recent visit to Kenya. BELOW: The Field-Marshal (second from left) watching a member of the Kikuyu Home Guard demonstrate his skill with bow and arrow.

settlers on Government House to demonstrate their views. The result was that at this time the guard on Government House was provided by a company of a British battalion instead of the usual KAR guard. One evening, after a long day of travelling over rough and dusty roads to visit widespread detachments, we returned to the comfort of Government House. I was enjoying a leisurely bath before dressing for dinner when I heard a yell from Harding, who had a room adjoining mine. Feeling sure that the Mau Mau must have got in, I put a towel round my waist and rushed in next door. The CIGS was already in his dinner jacket and had wandered out on to his balcony. Looking down, he had seen a National Service sentry who had parked his rifle against the wall and was enjoying a cigarette. Harding told me to deal with the matter. I returned to my room and telephoned to the Company Commander concerned and told him what had happened. Going down to dinner a little later, Harding asked me what action I had taken. I told him that I had left the Company Commander to take the necessary disciplinary action. He said, 'That's not good enough. I want the Commanding Officer here in my room at 9 o'clock tomorrow morning.' He was! I was not present. It must be unique for a soldier on guard duty outside the local equivalent of Buckingham Palace to be caught without his rifle and smoking by a CIGS in person.

After a few days of visiting units on their various operational duties, we heard, on a Friday evening, on the BBC news, that there had been riots in Khartoum and that the corporal on guard duty outside Government House had shot some of them. Harding decided to go to see for himself. On Saturday evening we took off in an RAF aircraft for Khartoum and arrived in time for breakfast with the Governor-General. Afterwards Harding had an hour alone with him and then we left for the Canal Zone to meet the BDCC(ME) – British Defence Co-ordinating Committee (Middle East), consisting of the 3 Commanders-in-Chief and their Political Advisor – who were militarily responsible for the Sudan.

After take-off I was busy dealing with papers resulting from our stay in Kenya and noticed that Harding across the gangway was also writing. In due course he handed me 5 sheets, which were a brilliantly clear appreciation of the Sudanese problems, concluding with recommendations of which the most urgent one was that a squadron of Hastings transport aircraft should be moved from the United Kingdom to the Canal Zone at once. The signal was to be sent to the VCIGS for consideration by the Cabinet Defence Committee. I checked later and found that the signal reached the VCIGS about 1 am on Monday morning and the Defence Committee met at 11 am under Churchill, who was then Prime Minister. When we left the Canal Zone to return to Nairobi about 5 pm on Tuesday, the Hastings were flying in: a pretty rapid reaction in peacetime for the usually ponderous Whitehall machine.

On the Monday morning there was a meeting of the BDCC to consider the Sudanese situation, attended by Harding with myself in the background. Eventually, without prompting from Harding, they decided that they must have more transport aircraft in case they needed to reinforce the Sudan. With a nice smile, Harding said that he had already made this request!

On return to Nairobi it appeared that Harding would be spending the next 2 or 3 days attending meetings with Oliver Lyttelton and that he would not want me. So I arranged to attach myself to a KAR battalion for 24 hours to try to learn a little of the practical results of our paperwork in Whitehall. Arriving one afternoon, I accompanied a patrol that night whose task was to lay an ambush covering a path in the Forest Area, where no one was allowed to be. It was therefore legitimate to shoot on sight. As apparently happened more often than not, we had an undisturbed vigil.

Next morning the whole battalion formed up in a single line with about 5 yards between each man and the next. We then had to advance in line through a mixture of forest and banana trees. It was not at all easy to keep station because more often than not one could not see one's neighbour and the sun was directly overhead. A Mau Mau who chose to try to conceal himself whilst the soldiers swept past seemed to have a reasonable chance of getting away with it. The total results that morning, after 3 or 4 hours, were one Mau Mau killed by my platoon (his only crime was to be carrying a supply of torch batteries) and one soldier slashed by a panga in the next-door platoon.

I returned to Nairobi that afternoon to find that Harding and his ADC had already left for England. I followed by the next available aeroplane.

20

LATIMER: 1954

After returning from Kenya I had only a further 6 weeks or so in MO4 before I was due to join a course at the JSSC (Joint Services Staff College) at Latimer in Buckinghamshire. This establishment had been set up soon after the war to try to remedy the ignorance of officers of one service about the other 2. During the war there had been a number of joint HQs which would have run more smoothly if the staff officers serving them had had at least some knowledge of all 3 services.

It was about one-and-a-half hours' drive from Mytchett to Latimer, rather much to do by the day, and it was not worth uprooting the family for only 6 months. So I decided to live in at Latimer from Monday to Friday, which enhanced the value of the course as I got to know my contemporaries in the other services better. The course was run on similar lines to that at Camberley in that we discussed problems in syndicates and there were a number of central lectures. We did paper exercises in which each student normally took the part of someone in another service.

We also did brief attachments to establishments of the other services. I remember being slung across from one warship to another on a breeches-buoy and being put in the tail of an RAF Coastal Command Shackleton off the coast of Cornwall and invited to try to hit markers representing submarines with a machine-gun. The fumes from the machine-gun came back into my compartment and as soon as I had nothing further to do I became unpleasantly airsick. Like seasickness, it seems to be an ailment that has little effect if one is fully occupied. In this case I persuaded the pilot to let me drive back to RAF Farnborough, under his supervision, and I had no further trouble.

Towards the end of the course an evening was devoted to a series of playlets put on by the students to poke fun at the staff. I am no actor and I took part only on the understanding that I had no word to speak. One of the senior directing staff, a Captain RN, when sitting in on syndicate discussions was wont to go to sleep, or at least to appear to do so. I borrowed a naval captain's jacket, walked on to a staged syndicate discussion, settled down in a chair at the back and gently dozed. It caused prolonged mirth. Late that evening, after a fairly alcoholic end-of-course party, the Commandant, Rear-Admiral K Edden, congratulated me on my performance and told me that what he had particularly enjoyed was that the Captain I had impersonated had asked him what I had been supposed to be doing!

I was by this time a fairly senior major but I was still in a low medical category. If I could not persuade the doctors to upgrade me fairly soon, I would be likely to remain a major indefinitely. At a medical board that autumn I pointed out to the board that they had said, 6 years earlier, that, if all went well, I could hope to be upgraded in time and that all had apparently gone well. They said they were not prepared to upgrade me until I had done a tour of duty in a bad climate. So I rang up the Royal Signals posting branch and said, 'Please post me to a bad climate!' They complied and I was sent to Singapore.

21

SINGAPORE: 1955–56

Very early on a bitter cold morning at the end of December 1954, Gerry and I and our 2 children, Margaret, 6, and Hugh, 3, arrived at Blackbush airport, not far from Camberley, to travel by air trooping to Singapore. There were a number of other service families and 30 or 40 unaccompanied soldiers there for the same flight. Since we had to land in countries in which British uniforms would not be accepted, the soldiers had all been issued with civilian clothes: identical suits. We sat at Blackbush for the whole day, delayed by fog, ice or snow, and finally set off early the following morning.

After 1 or 2 refuelling stops, we arrived at Karachi in the afternoon of New Year's Eve and were required to stay in the plane when the air hostess announced that we had to wait for the 'doctor'. A very scruffy individual appeared with a spray-gun, which he squirted all round, and we were then considered safe to land. In buses we went from the airport out into the desert and in due course saw that we were approaching what appeared to be a desert fort, square with very high battlemented walls looking like the stage set for a Foreign Legion film. We went in through a large gateway (no drawbridge) labelled Mrs Minnewallah's Grand Hotel. Inside was a courtyard with 2 floors of bedrooms built on the inside of the walls on 3 sides. On the fourth side were the main rooms with, sitting at the entrance, Mrs Minnewallah herself, a massive lady on a small stool.

As we were due to leave again in the middle of the night,

the families, including us, were primarily concerned to get something to eat and then go to bed. Most of the soldiers had other ideas: some managed to fix a game of football with the locals and one, who wanted to get into Karachi and had no local currency, was given his fare by a generous beggar!

We took to the air again in the small hours and were given orange juice all round in which to toast the New Year. This niggardly treatment was compounded by seeing the air hostess helping herself to the medicinal brandy. We approached Delhi as it was getting light and I noticed that the inboard port engine, and it alone, was emitting a lot of sparks. At Delhi we were given a very poor breakfast in the airport restaurant, which had not been cleaned after a New Year's Eve party.

When we arrived in Calcutta in the afternoon, we were told that one of the engines was out of order and that we would have to stay the night. I asked the pilot which engine it was: answer, the inboard port! He evidently preferred to breakdown in Calcutta rather than Delhi.

We were all put up comfortably in the Great Eastern Hotel but the delays had consequential problems which, as OC Troops on the plane, I had to ensure were solved. The air hostesses were most helpful with the urgent one, the supply of 'Paddipads' for babies. This system, relatively new in England, had not reached India but somehow supplies of some substitute were provided. The next problem was finding some harmless occupation for all the single soldiers, as well as a small quantity of local currency for all. The Calcutta Club was kind enough to make its swimming pool available and I persuaded the Gurkha Lines of Communication paymaster to come into Calcutta and give a small advance of pay to all who wanted it. The advance had to be repeated because we were stuck in Calcutta for 4 nights, whilst signals went back and forth between Calcutta, Singapore and London to determine which end could provide a spare engine. When we finally left Calcutta I was suffering from a severe tummy upset and, on arrival in Singapore, went straight to bed.

One of the families on board consisted of a corporal's wife and 7 children. When greeted by her husband, he was heard to say, 'I didn't know you were bringing Heather.'

There was no military accommodation for us and so initially a friend, David Gribbin, my best man, had booked us into a boarding house; minimum accommodation and not much privacy. However, we soon found a better one where we had our own tiny bungalow in the garden and meals were brought to us. We were lucky to stay there only a further 6 months until we were allotted a married quarter. Families often waited a year or 2, depending on a points scheme, but we scored well because we had not had a quarter since leaving Germany nearly 3 years earlier.

My job in Singapore was to run what was then called the Signal Training Squadron Far East. Its job was to provide trade training, both basic (Class 3) and upgrading (to Classes 2 and 1) for Locally Enlisted Personnel (LEP); that is to say for Malays, Indians and Chinese enlisted in British Army units in Singapore and Malaya as well as a small number of Chinese from Hong Kong. I had a mixture of British and local NCOs as instructors. For administrative purposes I came under command of the Commanding Officer, Lieutenant-Colonel Gerard Mellor, of Singapore District Signal Regiment, which was in a barracks next door to my hutted camp, and through him to GOC Singapore District, whilst for my operational function I was directly responsible to Brigadier Derek Good, Chief Signal Officer Far East.

Before leaving England I had exchanged letters with my predecessor, Bob Blackman, and had got him to arrange for me to attend a 3-week intensive language course in Malay immediately on arrival. As I arrived 5 days late and was incapacitated with my tummy bug for a further couple of days, I had to scratch from that course. I fixed to go on another course a few months later after a new, and excellent, British squadron sergeant-major had arrived. Sadly this invaluable man died suddenly of a heart attack at the end of the first week of my course and I had to withdraw again. I have no natural facility for languages and in Malay I was always too limited to be really effective.

When arranging my trade courses and attendance at them, I dealt directly with each of the signal units throughout the theatre. Sometimes units were difficult about booking vacancies and not taking them up, which meant a waste of the limited resources available and, on occasion, I had to get the CSO to lean on certain commanders. Some of the problems seemed to arise from the feeling of distant operational units (this was still in the time of the Malayan insurgency) that mine was only some small squadron whose arrangements did not really matter. So I got the authorities to change the title of the unit to Signal Training Centre Far East (STC). This made a material difference because distant units did not know how important or otherwise we were and they soon came to realize that I was strongly and directly supported by the CSO. The change of title had also one quite unforeseen result of considerable advantage to me personally, as I will relate in due time.

In about August or September we moved into a small quarter on Kent Ridge. This is a narrow ridge facing south-west and set back about a mile from the sea. In clear weather one could see to Sumatra 50 miles away, the direction from which considerable storms reached us: Sumatras. Being up on this ridge meant that we often got a breeze which others missed and we thought that this advantage outweighed the snag of having a smaller than average house.

On each of the major holy days of the Malays, the Indians, the Chinese and the British there was an appropriate celebratory meal in the barracks. All the chores on one of these days were allotted to soldiers of the other faiths. It was rather shaming that it was only at the British Christmas that soldiers were apt to get tiresomely drunk. On Christmas Day 1955, the Adjutant of Singapore District Signal Regiment appointed the most newly joined subaltern to be Orderly Officer: with hindsight a mistake. A Duty Field Officer of the week had also been nominated but, not unnaturally, this subaltern did not like to call on a major for help on Christmas Day if he could avoid doing so.

After the midday Christmas dinner for the British, which was held for the District Signal Regiment and the STC jointly in the Regiment's barracks, one soldier was left behind, drunk. One or 2 others were outside the dining hall and it is on their evidence that I rely. The Malay lance-corporal in charge of the clearing-up party went up to this soldier and told him that it was time he left. The British soldier lumbered to his feet and made as though to push the lance-corporal out of the way, calling him a black so-and-so. The lance-corporal, although a lightweight, was a member of the regimental boxing team and, thus provoked, punched him. The man fell, hitting his head on the concrete floor, and was permanently damaged.

Very varied versions of this incident circulated amongst both British soldiers and LEP that afternoon and in the evening tempers were running high. It was only then that the Orderly Officer saw fit to report to the Duty Field Officer that a nasty situation seemed to be building up. The latter went to investigate, driving down to the barracks in his private car. The focus of the trouble was the fence dividing the Regiment from the STC, with British rank and file on one side and LEP on the other. The latter were led by the small Indian element who were naturally far less peaceable than the Malays and Chinese. The Duty Field Officer foolishly tried to deal with the problem by driving into the middle of it in his car, which was promptly pelted with missiles; from which side I do not know, probably both! He reversed out of trouble with a damaged car and rang me up as he believed the STC to be the principal party responsible.

Gerry and I had had 2 subalterns to Christmas dinner and we had just finished our meal. I drove the mile to the barracks and left my car at the guardroom. I then walked quite slowly towards the rear of this shouting mob and spoke to the first soldier I came near, telling him to go back to his barrack room and stay there. I repeated this to the next and then to a few more until gradually I got to the front, when the more vociferous found that they had no one in support. So my STC soldiers dispersed peaceably. Those from the regiment then found that they had no one to fight or shout at and so they too faded away.

Next day, Boxing Day, Mellor agreed that there was no point in cancelling a family holiday we had planned to Hong Kong, leaving in a troopship that afternoon. We also agreed that the planned promotion of the Malay lance-corporal would have to be postponed. I spoke in the strongest terms to all my soldiers before I left, having learned my speech in Malay with the help of my Malay Sergeant-Major.

The ship was due to arrive in Hong Kong on New Year's Eve and we had planned a good New Year party with friends, the Mansfields. Ged, a Commander RN, had been on the same course with me at Latimer and had been posted to be Staff Officer Operations to the Flag Officer Second-in-Command of the Far East Fleet or, in naval shorthand, SOO to FO2IC, based in Hong Kong. Ged, having a seagoing appointment, was not entitled to have his family with him and, if they chose to come, got no allowances or help with accommodation. Joan and their 2 small girls had managed to get to the Far East free by travelling in an ammunition ship and had had a hideously uncomfortable voyage. When they got as far as Singapore the ship had business in the Naval Base for a few days and so they had been to stay with us. In Hong Kong, within the limited means available, they had found a rather pleasant small flat on the fourth floor of a block looking over part of the harbour; that is to say, it seemed pleasant until one realized that it was in the red light district.

It was foggy as our ship approached Hong Kong but this did not seem to the passengers an adequate reason for failing to dock until the following morning. The real reason was that the Captain wanted an excuse to keep his mainly Scottish crew away from the bright lights on New Year's Eve.

However, we settled ourselves comfortably into the Repulse Bay Hotel in what used to be a quiet seaside area on the south side of the island. Its charges were modest. Hong Kong was then about the cheapest place in the Far East for all sorts of goods. Although Singapore was not expensive, prices in Hong Kong were often about half.

The Mansfields had a small car and insisted on us borrowing it so that we could see something of the colony, both the island and the New Territories on the mainland. Not having foreseen such a generous offer, we had not brought driving licences but Ged got over this problem by pulling the necessary strings to get me an immediate driving test.

Altogether we had a delightful break and returned refreshed to the steamy heat of Singapore. Another break that we had was to drive *en famille* to the various stations in Malaya where there were signal regiments or independent squadrons which were in the habit of sending pupils to the STC. Combining business and pleasure in this way worked out well.

Gurkha Signals had their own arrangements for trade training, in Gurkhali, except for the most skilled trades, such as radio technician. The STC taught such trades in English, if only because there were not enough Malay or Gurkhali words available, and so we also took a few of the brightest Gurkha Signals soldiers on these 6-month courses. Towards the end of one such course one of the best of these men went down with tuberculosis just before his final written exam. He had passed the practical test with flying colours. I went round to see him in the military hospital, where I found him flat on his back with a large notice saying 'STRICT BED', which I knew from my own experience meant that one was not supposed to move unnecessarily in any way. He looked at me as I came in at the door and, as I was in plain clothes, took a second or 2 to recognize me. He then leapt to his feet and stood smartly to attention.

After I had got him back into bed and talked to him a bit, it was clear that his one worry was that he would be sent back to Nepal having failed a course, which would be a long-lasting disgrace to his family. I went off and consulted his doctor who agreed that, as he would be likely to pass his exam, it would be worthwhile allowing him to make the effort to take it in bed. I returned and told him that we could arrange this if he liked. His reply was, 'Last night I not sleep well at all. Tonight I sleep very well.' He passed.

Having been in Singapore for more than a year, I thought that it was time that I had a medical board in the hope that they would recognize that I had survived in 'a bad climate' and would upgrade my medical category. The first reaction was that, as I had previously been graded by a War Office board, no lower-grade board was entitled to consider my case. I pressed the matter, pointing out that I needed a fairly urgent decision if my career was not to be circumscribed for medical reasons. So the medical authorities at GHQ were persuaded to seek guidance from London.

When the reply came, a copy was sent to Commandant Signal Training Centre Far East, the doctors evidently not realizing that this was me. It said that GHQ Far East should convene a medical board but that the Director of Medicine 'remained of the opinion that this officer should not be upgraded above LE', the category in which I already was. When I saw this, I remembered that, by great good luck, Colin Callander, the divisional commander who had been so helpful when I was skiing in Ehrwald, was now Military Secretary and thus responsible for officers' careers and postings. I sent him the letter I had had, pointing out that this was the equivalent of saying, 'Yes, you may hold a court martial on this officer as long as you find him guilty.'

Within a week I was ordered to fly to England for a medical board. The members asked me little except about the recent riots in Singapore and, being obviously still unwilling to take the responsibility for upgrading me, referred me to Dr Geoffrey Todd, the civilian head of the TB hospital at Midhurst, who also had responsibility for Scio House, where I had been. Having studied my history, Todd asked what I would have to do beyond what I was already doing if I were upgraded. My answer was rather less, since I would no longer feel the need to prove that I was fit: I mentioned, for example, skiing, chasing Mau Mau and, in Singapore, doing the annual physical efficiency tests prescribed for those under 35, whilst I was 38. Not being a chap who shirked responsibility, he recommended that I be upgraded.

The need for me to insist on getting a decision on my medical category was demonstrated more quickly than I expected when, not long after this, I found my name on the annual list for promotion to brevet-lieutenant-colonel, a rank which I explained in an earlier chapter. Only a very few years later this odd system was abolished.

Yet another bit of luck came my way. I was posted in December 1956 to be GSO1 DCIGS Co-ordination in the War Office. I say luck because it so happened that at this moment Dudley Ward was handing over as DCIGS to Dick Hull, each of whom I had served when he was Commandant of the Staff College, and I am sure that they must both have had a hand in my selection.

Betty de la Mare
(wife of high
commissioner
to Singapore)

Bishop of
Singapore with
Jeff Jeffcoat
and John Barrie

Ken Kendra
with Gerry and me

Mike Carver's departure
L to R: Carver (C-inC), Naval Commander, Air Commander, Self representing Army Commander and Duncan Watson (Political Adviser)

Landing on RE road

C-in-C Nepal, Peter Hunt and me

Peter Hill-Norton and
HRH the Duchess of Kent

Cheese trees, Angkor

My father with me in sailor suit! 1921

Self with 5lb trout, 1970

22

WAR OFFICE DCIGS COORD: 1956–58

Our return to Britain in November/December 1956 coincided with the Suez crisis and there were no trooping aircraft or troopships available for such routine movements. So we had to come back first class in the *Chusan*, a large liner with a majority of cruising passengers. It happened that my sister Joyce's daughter Susan and her husband, John Dymoke in the Lincolns, with their one-year-old son, Francis, were coming back in the same ship.

We called in at Penang and then Colombo. Remembering that Howard Rowse, who had worked for me in Delhi, had, before the war, run the sale of Austin cars in Ceylon, it seemed probable that he had returned there. I sent him a cable from the ship, to which he replied with an invitation to lunch. He was a confirmed bachelor and it had not occurred to him that since 1946 we might have had children; equally I had not thought to mention them. He had arranged lunch in an excellent club, one which unfortunately did not admit children. A hotel had to be substituted. After that we had a day in Cape Town and then one in the Canary Islands, arriving in England on a cold December day.

Like most officers, I had had to revert in rank after the war. When I mentioned to someone rather older that I was bored with having had to do major's jobs for more than 15 years, apart from my brief period in Delhi, he very rightly pointed out that I was lucky not to have spent even longer as a subaltern, as had been a common fate between the wars. I had in fact been in 15 different appointments as a major, which certainly gave me a breadth of experience at that level. Anyway, I now had a chance to take on something new.

Dick Hull, the DCIGS (Deputy Chief of the Imperial General Staff), a lieutenant-general, had a large number of directors mainly at major-general level. His policy directors were the DSD (Director of Staff Duties, dealing with the size, organization and deployment of the army), the DWD (Director of Weapon Development) and the DGMT (Director General of Military Training, a lieutenant-general, Jim Cassels, of whom more anon). The DCIGS was also responsible for the DTA&C (Territorial Army and Cadets) and for the Arms Directors, that is to say, the head of each arm: DRAC (armour), DRA (artillery), E-in-C (engineers), SO-in-C (signals) and D Inf (infantry). The Scientific Advisor to the Army Council also normally channelled his advice through the DCIGS. An important part of my work was to prepare briefs for the DCIGS for the various meetings he had to attend and to obtain and coordinate contributions to those briefs from all the relevant directors or their staffs.

To help with this I had 2 GSO2s. When a brief had been completed and the DCIGS had read it, he would sometimes hold a short briefing meeting to allow him to ask questions and so that directors could emphasise points which they regarded of particular importance. Dick Hull was incredibly quick at reading and absorbing paperwork and at mastering new material; moreover, he never seemed to forget points of any significance at all. I remember an occasion when he had to attend a Ministry of Defence meeting, with his colleagues of the other 2 services, in order to plan the allocation between the services of the available fissile material for nuclear weapons. Having read the brief, he summoned the Scientific Adviser, grilled him for half an hour, and decided with him the line he should take at the meeting. Then, as on most other such occasions, I knew that I hardly had to read the minutes of the meeting: the decisions would be what he wanted.

The only time when I attended one of these meetings, I was fascinated to see his methods. This was a meeting chaired by the Minister of Defence, Duncan Sandys, at the FVRDE (Fighting Vehicles Research and Development Establishment) near Chobham. The object was to determine the general design of the next generation of tanks and the meeting was attended by 20 or 30 of the country's leading experts in this field, military and civilian. They sat at a long table, rather wider in the middle than at the ends, so that everyone could see everyone else. The meeting opened at 1030 and with a break for lunch was intended to finish between 3 and 4. By 1240 various divergent views had been expressed, the main problem being as usual the balance between weight of armour, firepower and engine power. There were broadly 2 different combinations which were supported. Duncan Sandys then turned to Dick Hull, who was sitting near to the centre of the table, and said, 'We haven't heard from you yet, DCIGS.' Dick Hull then spoke clearly but quietly, so that those at the ends of the table had to concentrate to hear him, and for no more than 5 minutes. The logic of his masterly summing-up was such that without further dissent his conclusions were accepted and the afternoon session was cancelled.

One unusual element of this job was to be the army's representative in the Lords or the Commons when the army estimates were being debated. One sat behind the main rows of members, technically outside the chamber; it was referred to colloquially as being 'in the box'. One heard all that went on and, when it seemed appropriate, wrote a short note to the minister on the front bench to give him the answer to any point which he might not have expected, or to answer a note he might have sent back. Attendants, who were allowed into the chamber without formality, were always immediately available to convey these notes. In particular, towards the end of the debate, it was sometimes necessary to list a number of points for use in the closing speech. Although my normal job covered a wide field, obviously one person could not answer everything and so I was equipped with a list of telephone numbers of key members of other departments to ring up at home, where they had to remain on call until the debate closed, normally at 10 pm.

This was the period of the first big cuts in the services, coincident with the abolition of National Service. There were many amalgamations of regiments in the cavalry and the infantry and corresponding reductions in other arms. The territorial basis of infantry recruiting made such amalgamations of great local importance and, in particular, people wanted to know where the new infantry training depots were to be located; often there would be only one where there had been 3.

I was in the box one evening when a Welsh member of the opposition asked the Secretary of State to explain how it had come about that the Colonel of the Welsh Brigade had announced the location of their new depot before the House had been informed. What had actually happened was that the Adjutant General, who also happened to be Colonel of the Welsh Brigade, had disclosed the location at what he considered to be a confidential meeting of the commanding officers concerned, and these included Territorial Army officers who were interested in local politics. One could hardly expect them to keep an item of such local importance to themselves and the AG should have realized this. I dreamed up some story for the Secretary of State to tell the House why such premature disclosure was unavoidable in this case, and I was in the AG's office ready for his arrival in the morning to tell him what I had said so that he could stick to the same line with the press.

John Hare was Secretary of State for War and on one occasion he planned a tour of military establishments in the Middle and Far East. It would have been normal for him to take the colonel of the relevant MO branch with him but, for some reason which I forget, MO had not got any appropriate chap available. So Dick Hull offered to lend me. Some days before this projected trip, the Army

Estimates debate was due in the Commons. On such occasions it was normal for the Secretary of State to make the opening speech and for the under-secretary, in this case Julian Amery, to close the debate. The prime task in closing was to deal with the controversial points which had been raised but Julian Amery wanted to find some new and fairly innocuous announcement which he could make in closing. The evening before the debate he walked the few doors along the passage into Dick Hull's office and asked whether he had any suggestions.

It happened that at that time the DSD's staff were preparing a paper for consideration by the Army Council on the possible reorganisation of the divisions in 1st British Corps in Germany into a number of self-sufficient brigade groups commanded by only very light divisional HQs. A meeting of the Army Council that morning had finished their set business early and so the CIGS had asked Dick Hull how this paper was coming on: could he give them an outline of the proposal off the cuff? As usual Dick Hull was aware of most of the arguments before he had even seen the paper, and he explained and backed the plan. The meeting regarded the proposal as so clearly worthwhile that they approved it without waiting for the paper. As it had no obvious political implications, Dick Hull suggested to Julian Amery that he could announce this change in his concluding speech.

He rang for me and told me I had half an hour to write out for Julian Amery the salient points of the proposal and the reasons for it. The following evening it was duly announced. I suppose Julian Amery had told John Hare what he intended to say but I do not know.

I spent the whole of the next afternoon until about 6 pm in John Hare's office, whilst he was briefed by a series of officers from different branches on the problems he would encounter during his tour. I went home to pack to be ready to leave the following day but I happened to turn on the 10 pm news when it was announced that John Hare was moving from the War Office to the Ministry of Agriculture and Fisheries. When I went in to the Secretary of State's outer office in the morning, the seals of office were being got ready for him to take to the Palace. Trip cancelled.

I learned, only second-hand of course, that Duncan Sandys insisted on John Hare's immediate move because he should not have allowed the brigade group plan to be announced without consulting the Minister of Defence first.

Dick Hull left his appointment in about March 1958 to become Commander-in-Chief of FARELF (Far East Land Forces) and was succeeded by Pete Pyman, who had been Commander of 1st British Corps in Germany. This was a very interesting change for me. Dick Hull knew the job from A to Z and remembered everything he had read or been told. He explored every subject fully and was then decisive. Most of the work that passed between him and me did so with brief covering notes in manuscript and, on average, I probably spent less than half an hour in total in his room in any one day.

I found that it was difficult to get Pyman to read anything like the quantity that Hull had read. If I put too much paper in to him, he would send for me and get me to summarise it for him orally. As often as not he would then ask what decision I would recommend. I spent about half of every working day in his office. All this made for more work for me but it was much more interesting; indeed, I seemed, in his early days, to be doing much of his job for him, which, having learned so much from Dick Hull, I felt fairly competent to do.

I was now due to command a regiment, and the policy was that, when selected for command, this normally took priority even if it meant curtailing one's present appointment. Around the relevant date there were only 2 signal regiments becoming available. One was a very large training regiment at Catterick which taught all the more technical trades to other ranks: a similar task to my job in Singapore but on a very much larger scale. The other was a new divisional signal regiment, which I would have to build up from scratch, in Colchester. I was given the choice and after some discussion asked for the latter. So I left the War Office in August 1958 after only about 21 months in the job.

23

COLCHESTER: 1958–60

I had learned over the years what a material contribution tradition makes to morale: the tradition that a soldier would risk anything rather than let the side down is very strong in most regiments. In Tunisia the 3rd Battalion of the Grenadier Guards was required to hold Longstop Hill to the north of Medjez-el-Bab against massive and determined attacks. Their losses were appalling but they held on. Shortly after the action, I had occasion to visit the only company commander who had survived unwounded. He was in command of the remnants of the battalion and was still holding a small defensive position. There was little I could do to help, except listen to a chap whose real worry was what had he done wrong? His friends had been killed or wounded and, as he was physically untouched, in what way had he failed in his duty? The remarkable achievements of this battalion seemed to me to be a lesson on the merits of *esprit de corps*, based to a large extent on long and worthy tradition. I now tried, in a small way, to make my soldiers aware of our own relatively brief history, in the hope that, if the occasion arose, they too would maintain the standards of the past.

At this time 1st Divisional Signals was technically 'in suspended animation'; there was a nucleus of about a dozen men who were nominally on its strength to look after regimental property and actually attached to another unit in Bulford. My task was to build up a whole divisional signals, that is to say, the unit for the provision of communications from divisional HQ to brigades, and to be prepared to exercise technical control of the signal squadrons serving such brigades as might be put under command of our divisional HQ.

Whilst the initial administrative work of assembling men and equipment was going on, I decided to find out what I could about the history of 1st Divisional Signals (in which it may be remembered I served briefly in 1939). In the 1870s there was a signal troop of the Royal Engineers under command of Lieutenant Kitchener, later Lord Kitchener of Khartoum. This troop led, through various changes, to the formation in about 1907 of 1st and 2nd Divisional Signal Companies RE, serving their respective divisional HQs. Royal Signals was formed in 1920 from the Royal Engineers.

I sent a subaltern, Gordon Oehlers, to research the War Office library for a few days and as result he produced the basis of a useful short pamphlet tracing the history of 1st Divisional Signals.

I must explain here that, until about 1959, units of Royal Signals took their titles from the formation HQ which they served. Thus 1st Infantry Divisional Signals served HQ 1st Infantry Division and when that HQ changed its name to HQ 1st Division, its signal unit followed suit. But in 1959, as result primarily of the initiative of Brigadier Guy Tucker, who was Deputy SO-in-C, all units of Royal Signals were given numbers and called regiments. The same applied to independent squadrons. These numbers were to remain fixed whatever duties the regiment or squadron was subsequently called upon to perform. So we were renamed '1st Signal Regiment'.

At the same time the Signal Regiment which trained boy soldiers for Royal Signals, 6th Signal Regiment, decided to ally each of its troops to one of the divisional signal regiments and we were asked to suggest a suitable name for our troop. We proposed Anzio Troop because 1st Division made the assault landing at Anzio in Italy and the Division at the time was commanded by Major-General Ronnie

Penney, late Royal Signals (who was seriously wounded a few days later).

The Regiment began to assemble in Cherry Tree Camp on the south side of Colchester, already occupied by 30th Signal Regiment. We were the cuckoo in their nest. They moved out gradually, initially I think to Bulford, with a view to being located alongside the School of Signals, which was planned to move from Catterick to Blandford. Cherry Tree Camp was made up of huts in quite good condition and adequately supplied with baths, central heating, etc, but it was planned to demolish it because temporary buildings cost too much to maintain. We were therefore due to move in the spring of 1959 to Sobraon Barracks, which consisted of about 6 large blocks, built around 1900. Each block had 2 barrack rooms on each floor and each room held about 16 men. The 32 men on each floor had only 5 wash basins and 2 showers and there were no more than 2 or 3 baths in the whole barracks. Each barrack room was heated by an old solid-fuel stove so that those distant from the stove froze even when those nearest to it scorched. The move was by no means an improvement from the point of view of men's comfort.

It had, however, some advantages apart from economy of upkeep: good stores and a good parade ground and good officers' and sergeants' messes. It also had a good solid Victorian house as the commanding officer's quarter. All this building up and moving was a quartermaster's nightmare. No sooner had we taken over Cherry Tree than we had to start arranging to take over Sobraon, which, until then, had been occupied by 3rd Divisional Signals, who were going down to Salisbury Plain. However, I was lucky to have an excellent QM, who, by coincidence, was supported by a Regimental Quartermaster Sergeant who had been in my section in 1st Divisional Signals in 1939 and I had recommended him for his first promotion, to lance-corporal.

Another stroke of luck was that the Commanding Officer of 3rd Divisional Signals was David Price. Normally a new

CO takes over a going concern and can gradually make such changes as he sees fit, but I found that, starting from scratch, I was continually having to make small decisions on how we would do this or that. The advice I got from David Price was invaluable. Moreover, the operation of taking over his barracks could not have gone more smoothly.

During that first winter the Regiment grew in strength and received its weapons, vehicles and equipment. Our prime task was individual and troop training until, by the summer of 1959, we were fit to go on a regimental exercise and then to stage a joint exercise on Salisbury Plain with our Divisional Headquarters, which had also been building up from nothing.

Fairly early on we had had our first guest night in the officers' mess and invited as our chief guests the Mayor of Colchester, a lady, and her husband, known as the Mayor's Escort. Colchester Council at that time was normally about evenly divided between Conservative and Labour and a civilised arrangement had been made that the office of mayor would alternate between the 2 parties. This mayor was Labour. As she was female and as we still had relatively few officers, we decided to make this first occasion one for wives as well. Although Colchester had long been a garrison town (some say since Boadicea!), she seemed to know little about how the army was organized nowadays. She did not realize that there were civilized messes for the sergeants and for the corporals, or that the NAAFI provided good club facilities for the rest. It happened that that night our corporals' mess was also having a special party and so I sent word to them to ask if I might bring my guests to them for a brief visit. This was a great success and I think she learned a lot that evening.

We were the first regiment to be issued with the then new radio relay equipment, which enabled us to provide much more efficient and reliable communications than in the past, particularly for a formation which was expected to be mobile. Unfortunately, it was planned to mount the radio relay sets in 15-hundredweight trailers, which were unnecessarily big and heavy and would be most unlikely to be given space in aircraft if the divisional HQ and signals were airlifted to some trouble spot. So I gave my technicians the job of making suitable mountings to put the sets in the small trailers which were towed behind Land Rovers.

To make sure that nobody told me that I wasn't to do this, I arranged with the SO in C, Richard Moberly, and with my late boss, the DCIGS, Pete Pyman, for me to bring samples to the inner courtyard of the War Office for their approval and I managed to sell them the idea. Without such a scheme we could not have provided adequate communications on an exercise in Libya the following spring, nor for overseas operations had they occurred.

During the summer of 1959, we managed to get the Corps yacht, a 6-berth sloop, made available for the regiment for a month and we arranged three 10-day cruises, giving about a dozen newcomers an introduction to this sport. Also whilst in Colchester we had renewed acquaintance with Harry and Pat Clive. Harry and I had been at the same prep school but did not really get to know one another until 1939–40 at the Royal Signals OCTU. He had left the army fairly soon after the end of the war and was fruit farming in Suffolk, only about 25 miles from Colchester. He and Pat also enjoyed sailing and they had a 30-foot Hillyard. They very kindly lent it to us for 2 short cruises with our children. By 1960 Harry had hurt his back and they had to get rid of their boat. So, if we were to sail again, something had to be done: in the next chapter.

By the autumn of 1959 the regiment had trained for its role to a reasonable standard and 2 major exercises were planned. The first was to be in Northern Ireland, in November, with the Divisional HQ in the normal way. We were to take off from airfields on Salisbury Plain. The second was for the Divisional HQ to control an inter-brigade exercise by 3rd Division in Libya, with the Signal Regiment providing umpire communications for both sides.

A reconnaissance party was to go to Libya in November whilst the Northern Ireland exercise was staged.

Just before this busy November started, we were told that the army was to have another bout of economy: 1st Divisional HQ and 1st Signal Regiment were to be abolished with effect from April 1960; 5th Division in Germany was to be renamed 1st Division and 1st and 5th Signal Regiments were to amalgamate in Germany with the title of 1st Signal Regiment. So, in that November, my 2IC, Reggie Glanville commanded most of the Regiment on the Northern Ireland exercise; one Squadron Commander, David Sylvester-Bradley, commanded the Salisbury Plain element of this exercise; and the remaining major, John Cooper, went with the GOC and the recce party to Libya. Meanwhile, I went to Germany to plan this amalgamation. The adjutant was left to hold the fort in Colchester.

In January I was operated on in Colchester Military Hospital for varicose veins, timing it so that I would just be fit in time to go to Libya with the regiment in February. The exercise was not due to start until March but I insisted on the regiment going a month ahead in order to try out our new equipment in a very different terrain and, equally important, for us all to learn how to live and work in this hilly, rocky and near desert country.

There was to be a battle between 2 brigades. Umpires would be attached to each brigade HQ and to the HQ of each major unit within those brigades. The exercise director wished to be able to speak reliably to all those umpires directly from Control HQ and for all umpires on both sides to be able to talk to one another. In view of the likely distances, this was a considerable task with the equipment of those days.

I decided that the only possible way was to set up 2 communication centres, one in each brigade area, from which there would be an HF radio net to all the umpires with that brigade. Each communication centre would be linked to Control HQ by radio relay. The snag to such a system was that there was then no equipment designed to link HF radio to VHF radio relay so that people could talk freely from one to the other. We therefore had to train operators to listen to every conversation and to throw the necessary switches every time someone said 'Over'. Our month's start was very fully occupied with choosing the locations for the communication centres, laying all the necessary local cables and rehearsing the whole system.

It was essential to put the Control HQ radio relay and the communication centres on the highest ground available and, in at least one case, this meant the building of a rough access road for vehicles to get to the top of a hill. My linemen were equal to this. For my rehearsal I could not of course predict where all the operational units, with their umpires, would get to and so I chose what seemed likely to be the most difficult locations. One such was in a wholly unoccupied desert area and I sent a subaltern there with about 16 men for 10 days to live entirely on their own. He was a young man lacking in confidence and I believe this responsibility did him good.

Shortly after we had established ourselves in the vicinity of the intended Control HQ to the south of Derna, we were having an evening meal in the officers' mess tent when a soldier, not one of mine, staggered in covered in blood and managed to tell us that there had been a motor accident on the road a hundred yards away; his mate was lying there seriously hurt. Our MO gave such immediate help as was necessary to our visitor and then went to look at the casualty on the road. He gave immediate first aid and said that unless the man could be got to hospital within a few hours he had no hope of survival.

We had radio communication with El Adem RAF airfield about 150 miles to the east and they agreed to send a helicopter as quickly as possible to pick up the casualty. This was not easy at the time because our helicopters were not then equipped for night flying. We chose a suitable landing area and lit it with vehicle headlights. The man was picked up and taken to El Adem, where he was immediately transferred to an RAF plane to take him to Cyprus.

There he was in hospital on the operating table by about 3 am. No mean achievement; but sadly he died.

Having had our preliminary rehearsal, the exercise itself went very satisfactorily as far as control and umpire communications were concerned. The exercise director, Brigadier George Lea, had the use of a light aircraft with which to visit the widespread battle areas. He used to fly it himself. I could not resist drawing to his attention a scratch on the underside of one wing which had paint adhering to it matching exactly the paint of one of my radio aerials which had a bent top.

One irritating episode was that 2 of my soldiers decided to make off in a Land Rover, leaving indications that they were making for the Egyptian frontier. As relations with Egypt were at the time somewhat strained, it would have been particularly embarrassing had they gone there. Fortunately they were picked up by a British unit when going the opposite way, having run out of petrol halfway between Benghazi and Tripoli. The British Brigade Commander had them locked up in Benghazi and suggested that, as they were picked up in his area, he should convene a court martial if I would remand them. This, however, was not so simple. The brigade in Benghazi came under command of GOC Cyprus, whilst my regiment came under GOC 1st Division and through him under GOC-in-C Eastern Command in England. For this exercise, however, my regiment was serving the exercise director and through him GOC-in-C Southern Command, Lieutenant-General Sir Nigel Poett, who was the overall commander of the exercise. The lawyers would have had a field day if I had remanded these tiresome soldiers for the court martial that they plainly deserved. I discussed it with General Poett, who agreed that the crime did not deserve the enormous effort that, in this case, would be involved in a court martial. I should go to Benghazi and, if the miscreants could be persuaded to accept my award (they had to be given the option), I should give them 28 days' detention, the maximum within my powers.

I telephoned from our camp near Derna to Benghazi and, the Brigadier not being available, I told his Brigade Major what I proposed to do and that I would let him know how soon I could get to Benghazi. I was playing bridge that evening with the General, the AOC-in-C and one other when I was called to the telephone to speak to the Brigade Commander, who objected strongly to letting these 2 off so lightly and said that, as they were in his custody, he would not allow it. So I asked him to hold on whilst I got General Poett to the phone.

This settled it and General Poett arranged to borrow the AOC-in-C's personal aircraft next day as he wanted to go to Benghazi for other reasons and could then take me with him. We resumed our bridge until there was another interruption: a message for the AOC-in-C that one of his staff had backed a truck into the AOC-in-C's aircraft and it was unserviceable: a trifle tactless! A less comfortable plane was found and the trip to Benghazi went as planned. The 2 soldiers realized that they were very lucky to be dealt with so quickly and so lightly.

Back in England there was the sad task of winding up the regiment just when it had reached a high standard of efficiency and when all ranks knew that they had just completed a first-class job. About 100 men, headed by David Sylvester-Bradley, went to join 5th Signal Regiment, which was then renamed 1st Signal Regiment. This was, I think, the first time there had been an amalgamation within Royal Signals. Whilst at first sight it seemed preferable to disbandment with the whole regiment dispersing throughout the Corps, I soon realized that it was a mistake. It not only destroyed the present 1st Signal Regiment, as was inevitable, but also disorganized the new 1st Signal Regiment, who had to disperse 100 men and accept 100 new men. I recommended most strongly to the SO-in-C that it should never be repeated. Amalgamations make sense within the Cavalry or Infantry but not in a Corps such as ours where men are used to being posted around within it.

When there were left in Colchester only about 5 to 10 all ranks, headed by the QM and Chief Clerk, I paid a last visit to sign a few documents. The day before, a signalman, who had been absent without leave for 2 months, had turned up. I asked him where he had been.

Signalman: In London, sir.
Me: What have you been doing?
Signalman: Working, sir.
Me: What at?
Signalman: As a messenger, sir.
Me: Where?
Signalman (reluctantly): At the War Office!
Me: Why did you decide to give yourself up?
Signalman My girl wouldn't marry me until I had.
Me: Sensible girl. You have admitted being absent without leave. Will you take my award?
Signalman: Yes, sir.
Me: 28 days' detention.

He could have insisted on a court martial but would almost certainly have got more than this. It would have been very tiresome to have to go through that procedure since I had no adjutant and hardly any clerical staff.

Thus ended my short tenure in command and I was posted to the War Office to be Colonel of MO2. We moved back to Mytchett.

24

WAR OFFICE MO2: 1960–63

We left Colchester in April 1960 but I was not due to report to my next job until August. Welcoming this break, I bought an old 22-foot lifeboat of Norwegian origin and had it moved to the back garden at Mytchett with the aim of converting it, in the next few months, into a cruising yacht. It cost £40.

However, the new Signal Officer-in-Chief, Mickey Whistler, had other ideas. He wanted a study made of the recruiting, training and careers of officers of Royal Signals and appointed Colonel Jerry McGill to do the job, with me to help him. McGill was then working in SHAPE (Supreme HQ Allied Powers Europe, then in Versailles) and I suppose it was assumed that he would have time to spare. He hadn't. Moreover, out of England he did not have easy access to the sources of information which would be necessary. The result was that I did the work.

I had to forget about my boat and to spend 2 or 3 months writing to all sorts of people, both inside Royal Signals and outside, and travelling around to discuss our problems with many of them. I ended producing a voluminous document with 60 recommendations. Gerry and I then went to stay with the McGills for a weekend in the middle of July and the report was duly signed by us both. Over the next year or so nearly all the recommendations were implemented, to the considerable benefit of the Corps in my opinion!

I still managed a month or so's work on the boat. It was probably a good thing that I had been delayed because, over the next year or more, I was able to put in a lot of time in the train to and from London learning the elements of yacht design and making the necessary calculations: and doing it before being committed to building rather than afterwards.

Half of my job was very much the same as I had been doing in MO4, except that MO2 was concerned with the Far East, roughly everywhere from Pakistan eastwards. The other half was to look after our military advisers in Commonwealth countries and to liaise with the military advisers of Commonwealth countries in their High Commissions in London. The Director of Military Operations was now Dick Craddock, who had been Director of Plans when I was in MO4. I was very lucky to have a third thoroughly interesting and worthwhile job in the War Office. MO2 involved much enjoyable travelling for me but Gerry found that I was always away when it was cold in England and the solid-fuel boiler needed stoking.

I made one long trip, in October and November 1960, to get to know some of my area and the principal persons concerned, particularly our military advisers. I went first to Singapore to meet those concerned at HQ FARELF (Far East Land Forces) and then to Kuala Lumpur, Canberra, Wellington, Delhi and Rawalpindi to meet our MAs (military advisers). Each MA was responsible primarily to his High Commissioner and only secondarily to the War Office, but my job was not only to be the channel for military information about the country concerned but also to deal with the personal problems of the MA and such few staff as he might have.

I took advantage of being in that part of the world to see something of each of the countries concerned. Having already been in Singapore for 2 years and having travelled in Malaya, I did not spend long there, but in Australia I travelled extensively. First I went to Canberra to meet the British Defence Adviser, Major-General 'Joe' Kendrew, and his staff. I had known Kendrew earlier when he was Director of Infantry and thus one of the directors I had

had to co-ordinate on behalf of the DCIGS. I am sure that he was a most appropriate British representative in Australia: not only had he got 4 DSOs but he had captained the England Rugby team in 1935.

His staff had arranged a most comprehensive tour for me, making the most of the time available. It included a visit to the Australian Staff College at Queenscliff near Melbourne; then via Adelaide to Woomera, the base of the 2,000-mile range used by the British for testing rockets. I remember asking the Range Commander how he managed to warn the inhabitants of such a vast area when the range was to be used. 'No problem. There are only 12 farms and we have radio to them.' The majority of the range staff used to live in Adelaide and commute the 300 miles to Woomera daily, by air, having breakfast on the way there and high tea on the way back.

My next stop was at Maralinga, about 700 miles out into the desert north-west of Adelaide and about 20 miles north of the trans-continental railway. This was the base for testing atomic weapons. Brackish water could be obtained there from wells but it had to be distilled before use. They therefore had a distillation plant of sufficient capacity to provide water for the maximum number of persons present at one time. At times therefore there was water to spare and this was sprinkled on the desert to provide a fine cricket field, known locally as the Oval.

The afternoon temperature when I arrived was 111 degrees, cooling by night to 55, a change that felt bitterly cold. I was well looked after by a civilian batman and so, after breakfast, I took my host on one side and asked his advice on the tip I should give. 'Nothing: he's paid more than you are!' I suppose because he had to be persuaded to work in such an isolated spot.

I also went to Brisbane in order to visit the Jungle Training Centre not far from there. It had larger and more vicious mosquitoes than are found in most places but fortunately they are not malarial. I was interested to find that, due to an Australian act of parliament, any officer recommended for regimental command was required to pass a severe practical examination, conducted over several days, at this centre. An exam for promotion to Major or for entry to the Staff College is, or was then, the last such hurdle in the British Army's promotion stakes. Due to the war I had been lucky to avoid having to take any such exam.

I had a more relaxed week after this in Wellington, New Zealand. My host this time also was a high-grade rugby player and used much of his spare time coaching local school teams. In talks with the New Zealand Army staff, I learnt that they were most dissatisfied with the American tanks which they had bought for their one armoured squadron and which were breaking down far too frequently; moreover, the supply of spares was inadequate and much too slow. They would have very much liked to get rid of them and to buy British Centurions but, having spent their money one way, could not afford the cost of re-equipping. I knew that we, in Britain, would have been much happier if they had had Centurions to match our own armour and that of the Australians. If the 3 countries were called upon, by the ANZAM Pact or otherwise, to act together, uniformity of major items of equipment would be a great advantage.

I happened to know that we had in stock in Hong Kong a squadron's worth of old Centurions for which we had no use. They were not worth the cost of bringing them back to Europe and we did not know what to do with them. They were, however, in need of major reconditioning and could not be passed on to New Zealand in their present state, cheap as they would be. Hong Kong REME workshops were capable of putting them into first-class order but then their book value would double or more and it was no good asking our Treasury to agree to sell them for less than their book value.

It was clearly in the interests of all concerned to put these tanks in order and re-equip the New Zealand squadron with them. With the undercover co-operation of

Hong Kong, the tanks were brought up to a proper standard without this appearing on the books and New Zealand agreed to buy what were on paper worn-out tanks for a low price, knowing that they were in fact in very sound condition. As result, New Zealand got good tanks at a price she could afford; Britain, at the cost of workshop repairs, got rid of tanks which were merely an embarrassment and received reasonable payment for them; and our potential Commonwealth alliance was much more fit for war. It if achieved nothing else, I believe that this arrangement made my visit worthwhile.

In Delhi I was welcomed by Tommy Newton-Dunn, our Defence Adviser, and his wife, who put me up in air-conditioned comfort. One evening Tommy took me out to shoot duck whilst standing thigh-deep in a small lake. I had not realized how insecure I was: my first shot killed a duck but the recoil knocked me backwards and the dead duck and I were both completely submerged.

Before leaving London I had been asked which Indian Army units I would like to visit. I had chosen the Indian Parachute Brigade, stationed in Agra, only about 130 miles south of Delhi, because I had served briefly in airborne forces. However, Tommy told me on arrival that the Indian authorities, to be more precise the Indian DMI (Director of Military Intelligence), were being obstructive and he could not make out why. I pointed out that in England I was in a position to limit what the Indian Military Adviser and his visitors saw and that I would be quite prepared to be similarly awkward if necessary. Tommy agreed and advised that I should dig my toes in. As result, he and I were allowed to go to Agra, the detailed programme being left to our hosts.

On arrival at 11 am we had a rather prolonged chat over coffee with the Brigade Commander and then a visit to the parachute packing station. Lunch had been arranged with the 1st Parachute Battalion and they had clearly been told to 'push the boat out'. We had pre-lunch drinks until nearly 3 pm, with 2 bands playing in turns, then an excellent lunch, with all the best regimental silver on display, and of course more wine. Making the excuse that I had parachuted in the British Army, the Brigadier then formally presented me with a set of Indian Army parachute wings, requiring that I toast the occasion with a very large glass of port, which was followed by another 'one for the road'. We left about 4.30 pm with our sober driver. I insisted that he took us to see the Taj Mahal before returning to Delhi and I have photographs to prove the steadiness of my hand.

Clearly there was something going on in the Parachute Brigade which they did not wish us to see. On another evening the DMI and his wife insisted on giving Tommy and his wife and me dinner in a restaurant and then, as I left Delhi airport to get into a plane to fly to Pakistan, on a Saturday afternoon, one of the DMI's staff officers thrust into my hand a parcel which he said was a present from the DMI's wife. I could hardly decline it and was just more puzzled when, in the plane, I opened the parcel to find the most beautifully worked red silk stole, embroidered lavishly in gold: a most expensive present.

The new capital of Pakistan, Islamabad, was still under construction and I stayed in Rawalpindi with Robin Curling and his wife. The main event of this visit was to go to Peshawar and thence up the Khyber Pass to look over the border into Afghanistan. A Pakistani major was my escort, together with a whole platoon of infantry. It was interesting also to visit a tribal arms 'factory'. In a small 2-man workshop were being made perfect copies of the .303 Lee Enfield rifle. On the frontier, my platoon deployed in the most warlike manner but I presume that this was just showmanship.

Whilst staying overnight with a Pakistani regiment, an elderly bearer looked after me. When he brought me a cup of tea in the morning, he stayed for a chat: he wanted to know when the British would be coming back. Thirteen years after partition he could not believe that we had really gone for good. I broke the news to him as gently as I could but I don't think that he really believed me.

I was taken to see their system of locust control. Whilst waiting to take off in England at the start of this trip, I had used a machine that was commonplace in departure lounges at that time: a dispenser of life insurance for the limited period of one's absence. As I was going to take about 25 air journeys in 7 weeks, I thought it worthwhile, although one of the conditions was that one was not covered for flight in a single-engined machine. To get to the locust area we were to travel by a single-engined Oxford. Worse still, as we went to climb aboard, the pilot pointed out a similar machine on the ground which had had to do a forced landing due to flying through a cloud of locusts. Having reached the locust control centre and had the system of control explained with many apologies for the lack of locusts that day, we set off home. The pilot, ever obliging, spotted a cloud of locusts below us and immediately dived into them. Fortunately we got home unscathed!

Before I got back to London, the news flashed round the world that India had invaded the Portuguese colony of Goa and, against negligible resistance, had completed the take-over in a day or 2. The leading troops in this operation were the 1st Parachute Brigade from Agra: so this was the reason for trying to prevent my visit and, when I did go, for taking such elaborate steps to prevent my seeing anything which might have suggested an imminent operation. I wrote a letter to the DMI, apologising for being so insistent and with thanks for the stole.

In late 1961 the Secretary of State for War, Mr John Profumo, decided to do a tour of army establishments in the Far East, including a visit to Kathmandu, where he could check on the arrangements for the Queen's state visit due some weeks later. Mrs Profumo, Valerie Hobson, star of the stage version of *The King and I*, was to accompany him, except for the first few days when she had domestic commitments, their son's half-term holiday, I think. He also planned to take his private secretary, his ADC and me. As Mrs Profumo would be the only woman in the party, Gerry and I thought that it would be a good idea if Gerry went too, the private secretary and ADC being unmarried. So I tried to see Profumo in the office and failed: I strongly suspect that the private secretary did not want another woman added and deliberately foiled my attempts to suggest it!

We set off in our own RAF aircraft, a Viscount, and arrived to refuel in the Maldive Islands at 7.30 am one morning. We were due to be there for only an hour and a half and Profumo had particularly asked that arrangements should be made for us to borrow goggles and snorkels to swim and that otherwise we should not be greeted at all. However, it was an important RAF transport station with about 300 men (and one WVS lady) and they were not prepared to forgo a small break in the monotony. As we circled before landing we saw the station commander and a considerable entourage ready to greet us: we were all in our bathing trunks and nothing more. Grabbing the nearest garments available, Profumo, wearing his own shirt and a pair of my shorts, led us down the gangway. Swimming out to the coral reef, and cruising up and down it, was a delightful experience, the water being clear to a great depth and filled with myriads of wonderfully coloured fishes.

Whilst in Singapore, Mrs Profumo joined us and we then flew on to Jesselton in North Borneo, accompanied by the Army Commander-in-Chief in the Far East, Dick Hull. I had imagined Borneo as being nothing but jungle and so was surprised to find some large open rolling hills, reminiscent of the Wiltshire Downs, parts of which were used as an army training area. After we had taken off for Hong Kong, it was discovered that Mrs Profumo's hats had all been packed in luggage in the hold of the aircraft and were therefore inaccessible. She had a personal rule that she would never appear in public in the same hat twice: what was she to wear to land in Hong Kong, where the press would be in force to greet her as much as her husband? Such few materials as the warrant officer steward could produce were assembled and we all took part in the design and construction, under Dick Hull's guidance, of a hat. It was a success.

The whole party stayed with the Commander British Forces, Roddy McLeod, and his wife, Molly. On one evening, the Governor had invited the Profumos, Dick Hull and the McLeods to dinner to meet many of the more prominent citizens, mainly Chinese. He said that he would like military officers to wear mess kit and expected civilians to wear dinner jackets. Profumo sent back a message to the effect that 'if my officers are to wear mess kit, I shall wear a white tie and tails'. which is, or was then, quite correct. The Governor had to accept this and sent new guidance urgently to all the other guests. Hong Kong tailors are renowned for their speed but they must have broken all records that day.

Our next destination was Kathmandu, where the airport was too small to accept an aircraft our size and so we had to change to a smaller one at Calcutta. Although we were stopping only to change planes, the Indian authorities insisted that the 5 passengers should immigrate and then emigrate, meaning that 2 forms had to be completed for each person. I undertook this task for the whole party, walking across the airfield to do so. Having completed the forms, I found that they had to be signed by each person. The pointlessness of such bureaucracy was then apparent: the clerk happily agreed that I could forge the signatures of the other passengers to save a long walk! Did we teach the Indians bureaucracy, or they us?

Arrived in Kathmandu, I again took charge of the passports and was amused to note that the passport inspector opened each carefully and gave the impression of reading it with care until he reached the photograph and then, if necessary, was able to turn it the right way up.

The best hotel was rather full because a delegation from Britain was there, arranging the details of the forthcoming Royal visit. I was in an adequate room in a lesser hotel but with no heating and December in Kathmandu is cold. I asked at the desk for some form of heat and very soon a workman appeared, took out his tools and proceeded to remove one of the rectangular panes of glass from my bedroom window. It seemed that my plea for heat had been misunderstood, but soon the workman left and returned with a wood-burning stove, its chimney and a rectangle of metal with a hole in it. This last replaced the pane-of-glass and the chimney was fed through it. Within half an hour of my request I had a pleasantly warm room.

On the first evening there, we were asked to drinks with the First Secretary of our Embassy. His house, like all others there at that time, suffered from low and variable voltage electricity. The nominal voltage was 220 but my electric razor would not work in the hotel even when adjusted to 110. Our host, however, had a well-lit room, having installed a variable transformer so that whenever required he could raise or lower the voltage: no doubt to the detriment of other users. Next day we were invited, in faint print on a brown card, to a reception at 'the Ministery of Foreing Affairs'.

There had been a motorable road in the Kathmandu valley for a number of years but it was not yet connected with the outside world. Cars had to be flown in. The airport, however, was fairly new and before that cars had been carried in over the mountain tracks. The wheels were taken separately, the rest of the car being slung on 2 long bamboo poles carried by some 40 porters in front and another 40 behind.

From there we flew to the Gurkha recruit training depot near the Indian border at the bottom of the Himalayan foothills. The British Colonel commanding it arranged a special guest night to welcome us. Chatting before dinner, I found that he made a habit of walking up the 3,500-foot hill behind the camp for exercise. From the top one could see Everest. He, fit and practised, said that he took about an hour and so it seemed to me that ordinary mortals might expect to do it in 2 hours. Several of us agreed to set off at 4.30 am, having failed to foresee that, after a good dinner party, we should not get to bed until about 2 am. It was just getting light as we staggered to the top at 6.30, only to find a bank of low cloud completely obscured the view.

Going down in daylight, we discovered that the track was narrow, with frequent precipices, of which we had been blissfully ignorant on the way up. We had to hurry in order to change, snatch some breakfast and take off at 8.30. The next stop was Bombay and, during refuelling there, the Profumos wanted a guided tour of the city. I had been there in 1945-6 for a couple of days and was therefore elected as guide. By the time we got to Aden at 7.30 pm local time, 10.30 pm by our starting time, all I wanted was bed. But my hospitable hosts had arranged a dinner party.

I had taken quite a lot of photographs, colour slides, on the way round and, a week or 2 after our return, I invited Jack Profumo to see them one evening in the War Office. I concluded the series with temples in Kathmandu: one distant view, one close and finally a real close-up of the sexual activities of their gods. Profumo asked for a copy of the last for his Christmas cards but I declined, fearing prosecution for obscene pictures!

In early 1962 Major-General Desmond Fitzpatrick took over DMO. We had not met before. For the first few weeks all the written work from my section seemed to be wrong; we were not speaking the same language. But, late one evening, when Fitzpatrick had finally accepted my section's briefs for the Chiefs of Staff meeting next day, we somehow started talking about other things and I learnt that he was building a sailing dinghy. He was puzzled about something and, as I too was boat-building, I was able to help. Thereafter we got on well. He trusted my paperwork and I thoroughly enjoyed working for him.

In November 1962 I arranged to attend a weekend Royal Signals conference in Germany, starting on a Friday. Unfortunately it turned out to be the Friday that the Indonesians chose for their incursion into other parts of the island of Borneo: British North Borneo, Brunei and Sarawak. I heard about it on the news on the Saturday and rang the War Office, speaking to my GSO2, Martin Farndale. He assured me that he had everything in hand. As I knew him to be highly competent, I completed my weekend as planned, returning to the office on the Tuesday morning.

We had been taken by surprise by the strength of the Indonesian operation, the approved plans in the event of trouble being to reinforce the existing garrisons by up to one battalion in, I think, about 48 hours. On the Saturday morning, the Chief of Defence Staff, Admiral of the Fleet Lord Mountbatten, and others wanted immediate and secure conversation with Singapore and, at that date, this could be done only by teleprinter from a special installation in the bowels of the War Office. The arrangements were made by Farndale and, when the necessary decisions had been taken, he played a large part in seeing to their implementation. I was very lucky to be served by such a chap: he ended his service as General Sir Martin Farndale, Deputy SACEUR.

Only a week before these events, a long-mooted reorganization of the higher command in the Far East had been implemented. Prior to this there had been 3 single service Commanders-in-Chief, each a 4-star officer, who met regularly under the chairmanship of the political representative of HMG (called, I think, the Political Resident), who for many years had been Malcolm Macdonald. This group, entitled the British Defence Co-ordination Committee Far East, were responsible to the Minister of Defence and the Chiefs of Staff.

Mountbatten was the prime mover, against considerable opposition, in making the change in Singapore to a single Commander-in-Chief, 4-star, and 3 single service commanders, 3-star, with a political adviser. This meant that a fourth headquarters had to be created for the C-in-C, but Mountbatten argued that every extra officer on the C-in-C's Headquarters would replace one officer in each of the single service Headquarters. There was, of course, the danger that an extra officer on the C-in-C's staff would result in an extra officer for each of the single service commanders to answer his questions! Because of the Indonesian operations, considerable extra staffs were justified for the next few years and so the validity of Mountbatten's argument could not be determined.

The change did, however, have one immediate and invaluable result. The newly appointed C-in-C, a sailor, immediately ordered the Army to bring to instant readiness some 4 or 5 battalions and the RAF to move a transport squadron from Burma to Singapore. These orders were given immediate effect by the respective single service Chiefs of Staff in Singapore, their masters, the recently downgraded single service commanders, being away at an American demonstration in the Philippines. The result was that, although the plans were for only one battalion to be sent, no less than 5 arrived there in about 4 days.

Three or 4 weeks later, the Chiefs of Staff decided that someone should go to Singapore to see how the new unified command arrangement was working, having particular regard to operations in Borneo. Neither the Admiralty nor the Air Ministry had its operations directorate organized on a geographical basis and so they had no one staff officer who dealt with the Far East as a whole. The War Office had MO2 specializing in the Far East and so I was told to go, to spend a week or 10 days there and to report back to the Chiefs of Staff.

The new C-in-C was most welcoming; he invited me to attend all his meetings with the Service Commanders and to consult him at any other time. It was soon obvious that he had difficult problems with one or more of his service commanders who had not taken kindly to the downgrading of their posts.

This situation was aggravated by at least one of them being allowed to hold the 4-star rank he had been promised on appointment. It seemed to me clear that, if the 3 had been required to take joint operational decisions without a C-in-C above them, there would have been unacceptable delays and unnecessary references back to London. For the

Borneo operations the new system had been introduced in the nick of time.

As result of my visit, I had found that, not surprisingly, there were a number of teething troubles with which Whitehall could help. I wrote most of my report for the Chiefs of Staff in the plane on my way home. A few days later I was required to attend a Chiefs of Staff meeting for them to discuss my report and make decisions on it. The CDS, Mountbatten, sent for me 20 minutes before the meeting, I presume so that he could be one jump ahead of the others. After a brief discussion, he asked for my general impressions about the conduct of the Borneo operations. I concluded by telling him how a lieutenant-commander in a small ship had been in doubt about opening fire near an international border and had had to seek authority from Singapore, whilst a major in the jungle not far away was expected to make such decisions himself. Mountbatten said that he had too often found that the navy would not decentralize: when commanding a destroyer squadron in the Mediterranean, he had received a signal from the Admiralty, 'Turn north'!

My report consisted of 16 serious points and a seventeenth with my tongue in my cheek. After about 2 hours we came to number 17: I had noticed that the Chief of Staff to each single service commander, a 2-star officer, was entitled by his own service regulations to fly an appropriate flag on his staff car, but the Chief of Staff to the C-in-C, also a 2-star officer, was entitled to no such flag, there being no equivalent inter-service rule. I recommended that this anomaly should be sorted out. Dick Hull was now the CGS and he had always had an interest in such details. He and Mountbatten discussed this at length and it was then decided to appoint a working party to arrange for suitable rules and for the design of an appropriate flag. I was amused to find that, when I was posted to Singapore some 5 years later, the Chief of Staff to the C-in-C flew an inter-service flag on his car.

25

BIELEFELD: 1963–66

In January 1963 we set off for Bielefeld, where I was to take over the job of Commander Corps Royal Signals (CCR Signals), 1st Corps, as a brigadier. Having a few days in hand, we decided to drive there via Paris, where we stayed for a couple of nights in the French officers' club, called, if I remember right, the Cercle Militaire, which they generously made available to all NATO officers. It was bitterly cold at the time, being the start of the great freeze over most of northern Europe from January to March 1963. One night we went to a meal and night-club in Montmartre and were returning around 1 am in a taxi. We were stuck in a traffic jam when a girl in a long black cloak came running out to get into another taxi. A flurry of wind and snow opened her cloak wide and inevitably our driver exclaimed 'O! La la!' as she had nothing underneath.

In Bielefeld we had to stay in an army hostel for a week or so before our predecessors, Max and Phillippa Charlton, left their house. It was a very small house, a relic of the time when the job had been designated as Chief Signal Officer, a staff officer. As it was now a command appointment, the incumbent was entitled to a larger house but none was to be had. After some time there, we found that the brigadier doctor was in a larger house and, being a staff officer, was not entitled to it. It was agreed that when the present doctor left we could have his house. After more than a year we moved and this was much more comfortable and made our considerable entertainment duties easier.

1st British Corps was spread over most of the British Zone of West Germany, as it then was. There were 3 divisions, each of which had 2 brigades, and there was an anti-aircraft brigade. Each division had its signal regiment and each brigade its signal squadron; every major unit, battalion or equivalent, more than 40 of them, had a Royal Signals detachment under a warrant officer.

Whilst all these elements of Royal Signals were under command of the appropriate formation or unit commander, I was responsible, through the signals chain, for their technical efficiency and, particularly as I was required to comment on the annual confidential reports of all warrant officers, I had to visit the lot. To serve the Corps Headquarters, I had 2 signal regiments directly under my command. Like the heads of the other supporting arms, armour, gunners and sappers, I was, of course, adviser to the Corps Commander in my own sphere.

As an example, within 2 or 3 weeks of taking over, I got a telephone call from Ken Darling, the Corps Commander, one morning to ask what I thought of one of the brigade signal squadrons. Fortunately I had visited that brigade a few days earlier and had found that the brigade commander was satisfied with them and particularly commended their marching ability! I was not at all content with their standard of signalling. I had found that their warrant officer seemed ineffective and I had doubts about the squadron commander. The former I had insisted should leave at once because, on medical grounds, he was excused wearing boots: in action he might have had to be a passenger. A few weeks later I decided that the squadron would never be much good until it had a new commander. This, however, was a decision for the brigade commander and I tried to persuade him of the need for a change. Because the major in question was a very nice chap, his brigade commander insisted on keeping him for the remaining 2 or 3 months of his normal tour of duty. I reluctantly accepted this and hoped that a good successor would be appointed.

Unfortunately the new chap was useless. Again, I could

not persuade the brigade commander of this and I considered having a showdown with the divisional or even the corps commander. I found, however, that the brigade commander was, himself, moving in the near future and so I decided to wait for his successor. The latter rang me up only 2 or 3 weeks after his arrival and asked my views on his signal squadron. I told him, and the new squadron commander left at very short notice. I went to great trouble to make sure that there was a really good successor this time. Within weeks there was an efficient and happy squadron.

I had plenty to do and much travelling. I always took a Dictaphone with me in the car and managed to do a good deal of my paperwork whilst in transit, particularly writing notes for confidential reports on the officers or warrant officers I had just visited: I trusted the discretion of my driver! I was lucky to have inherited a very good staff, headed for the first 2 years by an excellent GSO1, Tony Fearfield, and so I had no qualms about leaving them to mind the shop during my travels.

A system for the re-employment of retired officers had been introduced a few years earlier, with the result that I had Brigadier Bill Bradford in a captain's job, responsible for personnel. I have been asked whether this was satisfactory, particularly as Bill had been my boss only 4 years earlier. Bill being the delightful, competent and utterly loyal chap that he was, it could not have worked better. He was always ready to give me the benefit of his considerable experience but never thrust it at me unasked. His wisdom and tact solved many problems.

My relations with Brigadier Norman Wheeler, the Chief of Staff, were at first less than happy and I could not make out why. Eventually it appeared that he had not got on with my predecessor and was prepared to let a cool relationship continue. A few months after my arrival I stupidly made matters worse, although with the best intentions.

Hitherto a divisional signal regiment had been a separate administrative entity from its divisional headquarters.

Although the total numbers at divisional HQ were no more than 600–700, there were 2 of everything that a normal battalion would have: 2 commanding officers, 2 cookhouses, etc. Moreover, for defence of the HQ in the field, separate sectors had to be agreed every time. Obviously it would be more efficient if the 2 were combined but this came up against the hurdle of cap badges: Royal Signals, RASC for clerks and drivers, REME and a large variety of all arms for general duty jobs.

At the time I arrived, trials of a proposed new system were in progress at 4th Division HQ and one of its brigades was trying a similar system at that level. In each case the senior signal officer, CR Signals at division and OC Brigade Signal Squadron at brigade, was given command of the whole of the headquarters and its signals, a considerable administrative task to add to his signalling duties. Assuming that 4th Division would recommend the new system, there were many points of detail and some significant issues to be resolved. After preliminary discussions in the Corps HQ, it was decided that a long meeting of all concerned would be held under the chairmanship of the Chief of Staff to resolve all outstanding matters and to agree what proposals the Corps Commander should be recommended to send through HQ BAOR to the War Office.

This meeting was first scheduled for a date in July (1963) and then postponed to August or September. Based on the July date, I had planned 3 weeks' leave in August in the children's summer holidays, camping in Denmark, Sweden and Norway. I consulted the Chief of Staff, who assured me that there would now be no question of holding this meeting before September and so I need not alter my leave dates.

Having driven up the Baltic coast of Sweden to Sundsvail and then across to Trondheim in Norway, we came south to Oslo, where I got a message from Tony Fearfield that the meeting was to be held a few days before I was due back. I arranged to leave Gerry and the children in Copenhagen and to fly to Bielefeld for the meeting and then back. Owing to bad weather I could not fly and so we all drove through the night to Bielefeld.

In fact the meeting did not reach any earth-shattering conclusions but I had felt that I ought not risk any proposal being put forward which could have had a seriously adverse effect on Royal Signals. It seemed that I had been badly let down by the Chief of Staff and considered going to have it out with him. After some deliberation I reckoned that it would be better if I took advice from the corps commander. I was wrong: I misjudged him. I think that either of the next 2 Commanders would have quite civilly sorted out the matter or told me how to do so. But this Commander, Ken Darling, had a tendency, of which I was not then aware, to take his decisions without listening to the facts properly. He became extremely angry and told me that I was trying to sabotage the headquarters by questioning the authority of his Chief of Staff.

What was more important to me, he got on to Whitehall and tried to get me sacked. Fortunately those concerned pacified him but his efforts did have unfortunate results: I did not get a vacancy at the IDC (Imperial Defence College) which might otherwise have come my way and I was required to serve for 3 years in my present appointment as opposed to the normal 2. Moreover, Darling was not honest enough to tell me what he had done and I only learnt of it through his successor.

The effect of staying an extra year was not only that I would be a year older before being considered for any future appointment but, more important, the best command appointment for a brigadier in Royal Signals was not available for anyone else for another year. I had let the Corps down by taking an action which I had thought was a necessary part of my duty to the Corps.

There were, of course, lots of episodes on the lighter side: for example, the Irish soldier who played an instrument in the Herford town band. The civil authorities responsible for the band were so impressed with his playing that they offered him full-time employment if he left the army. He said that he would have to pay the army £200 to buy himself out. They gave it to him and that was the last that anyone saw of the soldier or the £200!

A soldier who had committed some offence was under open arrest and was required to report to the Regimental Guard Commander at certain hours. When he failed to do so, the NCO informed the Orderly Sergeant, who searched the barracks and then reported to the Orderly Officer. The Sergeant, having finished his duty, went home to his married quarter, where he found the missing soldier in bed with his, the Sergeant's, wife!

For part of a major exercise, we had taken over as our headquarters the grounds of a large castle with a moat. During a lull in the exercise activity, I called in one of my commanding officers in order to ask him some questions about the annual confidential reports that he had written on his officers. I asked what he meant when he had described Captain X as remarkably accident-prone. At that moment there was a knock on the door and this CO's adjutant came in to say, 'I thought that you should know at once, sir, that Captain X has fallen in the moat!'

Sometime during the 1950's, a small team had been set up at Catterick to plan what communications the army ought to have by 1970. They came up with a system which was first class by the technical possibilities of that time. During development it was found that it would cost about £100 million, an enormous sum at that time. So it was suggested to the United States Army that they might like to develop it with us, sharing the cost. They were then badly in need of a modern system and gladly agreed but soon found that our proposals were too modest and they proposed a more luxurious version. After a few years of joint work it became clear that, if we went further, we should be stuck with a Rolls-Royce system at greater cost than if we had gone on alone with our own version. So we had wasted a few years to little purpose. We reverted to our own plans, recognizing that they now would not come to fruition until 1975 or 1980.

So, in 1965, I was asked whether I advised continuing to use our present antiquated methods until, at least, 1975 and then getting the complete new equipment, or whether we ought to have an interim system starting to come in in 1967–8, to be followed by the full new system in or after 1980. Although our present equipment gave adequate communication for exercises, it would not, in my view, survive 24 hours of conventional war, let alone nuclear. The interim system would be likely to provide essential communications for a reasonable period. Moreover, it was a good halfway house towards the final answer, making it easier for both staffs and signals to learn the new way. I therefore had no doubt that the bird offered in the hand was worth more than the 2 in the bush.

This was agreed and so I decided that we ought straightaway to tell commanders and staffs what they would be getting. They would have a lot to learn if they were to make good use of the new facilities which would be at their disposal. Dick Goodwin, the Corps Commander, agreed that a presentation should be made to him and to all divisional and brigade commanders and their senior staff officers. He put out a '3-line whip' and I required all officers of Royal Signals down to major to attend.

Peter Hutchins, commanding 4th Divisional Signal Regiment was largely responsible for preparing a whole morning's presentation. In addition to having a full understanding of the technical changes planned, he had a remarkable and invaluable theatrical flair. We had many rehearsals during which I represented the least technically minded commander or staff officer and continually interrupted to say, 'What does that word mean? Explain it or use a word everyone knows'.

The work that went into this paid off. They really did go away with a reasonable understanding of what was coming. Desmond Fitzpatrick, for whom I had worked when he was DMO, was now Chief of Staff, BAOR, and he attended, having spent the previous day at an Army Air Corps presentation. He pleased me greatly by saying that, whilst much of the latter was, to him, incomprehensible, he had found my day clear and straightforward.

In my closing remarks I took advantage of this mixed audience to ride a hobby horse. I told them that, having had considerable experience both as the senior signal officer and as a staff officer at various levels of headquarters, I had no doubt that not only was the closest liaison between the 2 essential, which was obvious, but it was better still if the signal officer had the experience necessary to do the staff officer's job. For example, a brigade signal officer should, as far as possible, be qualified to be a brigade major. I think this shocked a few people on both sides!

I was due to leave this job at the beginning of 1966 and it seemed likely that I would get another job in the War Office, or rather the Ministry of Defence (Army) as it had now become. My previous Whitehall jobs I had done from our house in Mytchett, near Frimley, Surrey, but in the summer of 1965 we sold this because our immediate neighbours had had to sell (3 old ladies who could no longer manage on their own). The land of the 2 houses was building land of much more value as one estate than in 2 separate parcels. So we were now contemplating buying another house or perhaps investing the proceeds with a view to buying on retirement. Having lunch one day with Miles Fitzalan Howard, then GOC 1st Division, the subject cropped up and he advised us most strongly to buy now: property was much the soundest investment. As the future Duke of Norfolk it seemed probable that he knew what he was talking about. We bought and he has proved right.

Brakey Hill, Godstone, was built in 1931 to 1933 by Colonel R S McClintock, a retired sapper who did his own architecting and built a very sound house, bigger than we wanted but in a most exceptional position with a very fine view. His wife had died in January 1965 and in April he, then 90, married again and went to live in Ireland. With our 2 children we were going to Donegal to stay with

Gerry's family in August and were invited to go to see the McClintocks. We were apparently approved.

The house needed a great deal of internal work before we moved in and we planned to do this ourselves. This meant that, instead of taking the children skiing after Christmas as we had intended, we all worked very hard on the house to make it reasonably habitable. But what was disappointing was that by that time we had learned that my next job was to be in Paris. However on 1 January, 1966 we celebrated our silver wedding in our new house.

26

NATO IN PARIS: 1966–67

We made a preliminary visit to Paris and agreed to take over our predecessor's flat in Meudon, a convenient suburb about halfway between the centre of Paris and SHAPE, Supreme Headquarters Allied Powers Europe, in Versailles, where I would be working. We left Bielefeld at the end of January, 1966, and had a couple of weeks' leave in Beaulieu on the Côte d'Azur.

On the day in February that we finally arrived in Paris, General de Gaulle announced the withdrawal of all French forces from NATO control. To the best of my knowledge these 2 events were not connected! There was great sadness in SHAPE because this meant the withdrawal of all French staff officers and the breaking up of friendships and happy relationships. As far as I could discover, the only French officer in SHAPE who wholeheartedly supported de Gaulle's decision was my new boss, a French Air Force general.

My job was described as 'Chief of Current Plans' and I had a staff of 16 officers of all 3 services and about 10 of the NATO nations. I was immediately impressed with how well they worked together and how well they worked in a language other than their own. Nominally all work was done in both French and English, but in practice 99 per cent was done in English and French translations were only made when required for some specific reason. For all military personnel working in a NATO headquarters the official requirement was that everyone must be proficient in either French or English, which could easily have led to chaos if, for example, an English-speaking Turk tried to work with a French-speaking Greek.

My French Air Force master had an American rear-admiral as his immediate deputy. This produced an interesting anomaly, which only came to light because protocol was deemed of high importance. This Admiral, an American Air Force Brigadier-General and I were required to attend a presentation at which we were expected to sit in strict order of seniority. This Rear-Admiral, by some quirk of the American rules, rated as junior to the Brigadier-General; but the latter was junior to me by virtue of dates of promotion; and I was certainly junior to the Admiral as I was working for him. Fortunately it mattered not the least to any of us but certain senior officers took these matters desperately seriously.

A large proportion of the documents we handled were in high security categories. As every file had to be classified in accordance with the most secret document in it, most files became TOP SECRET. To try to keep track of such files, they were supposed to be passed from one office to another via a central security office which registered them in and out, normally a 24-hour job. Urgent work was unacceptably delayed by this means and so most officers broke the rules and trusted the officers they were dealing with. My office quite commonly had to write papers which would have to be considered by SACEUR (Supreme Allied Commander Europe), General Lemnitzer, and they ought to have gone from me to my French (later American) General, sometimes via the Admiral, from him to the Deputy Chief of Staff, a German Lieutenant-General, then to the Chief of Staff, an American 4-star General, Parker, and finally to Lemnitzer. I soon found that, when something was really urgent, I could walk it into the German General and he would take it straight to Lemnitzer.

There were widely different attitudes amongst the nations as regards each individual's national and international status. In theory each person's first loyalty was to NATO and his own country came second. The most extreme versions of the reverse attitudes appeared to be typified by the Germans who held a briefing of all their officers on alternate Thursday afternoons and one was expected to make any Germans on one's staff free to attend. The Americans did the same thing but were less obvious about it, as they met after normal working hours.

The American General, who had taken over our Division when the Frenchman left, was pleasantly relaxed about national foibles. One evening when we were working later than usual, I went into his office to discuss 1 or 2 things and found him with an in-tray piled high. I said, 'Are you really aiming to get through that lot tonight?' He replied, 'Please look through it, while I finish what I'm doing, and sort out what must be done now.' I did this and said, 'There's only this one thing which is at all urgent and then there are 2 files marked US EYES ONLY.' 'Well, look through them for me too, please.'

I was never given any official British guidance. However, soon after I arrived, a problem reached my desk with apparently 2 solutions of equal merit. So I rang up the British Liaison Office and asked what the British view was. The answer was a stuffy, 'I am not going to tell you. You're international.' I then realized that this was a very healthy attitude.

Only in one respect did I deliberately cheat and that was to counter the cheating of others. I found that important documents were going up and down the chain which I described above and copies were not reaching Deputy SACEUR, Marshal of the Royal Air Force Sir Thomas Pike. So we made an arrangement that, whenever such a document came my way, I would walk it along to his office, where it would be copied for him. He would then, if he saw fit, walk into the Chief of Staff and say, 'Isn't it about time we had that report on so and so?', Parker would apologize and send Pike a copy, which he could then comment on without my part becoming known.

It was the custom in SHAPE that a different division of the staff would organize some kind of entertainment for the whole Headquarters each month. It was our division's turn in April, just before our French General left. He had influence in the right place and managed to persuade Maurice Chevalier to entertain us for a fraction of his normal fee, to be paid to his favourite charity. We were all looking forward to this event, and it was indeed a great success, but unfortunately it coincided with the wedding of Gerry's only niece, who is also my god-daughter, in Donegal and we had to give that priority.

The repercussions of the French opting out of the military organization of NATO were far-reaching. The principal nations remaining, the United Kingdom, the United States and West Germany, had much to discuss before putting their views to the other nations, the Group of Fourteen as they came to be known. A meeting was convened in the Bonn Foreign Office and they asked SACEUR for military advice on several problems. As result my office was required to produce briefs on 4 subjects for SACEUR. A few days after they had been sent up the chain to Parker, the Chief of Staff, I was called to his office in a hurry one afternoon and told that the meeting in Bonn urgently wanted SACEUR to be represented and I was to travel overnight to attend their meeting at 10 next morning. Parker then handed me the 4 briefing files as though I had never seen them, telling me that they would be useful background but that, as SACEUR had not yet seen them, I was not to speak on his behalf. It seemed to me strange that a 4-star general, the same rank as SACEUR himself, was prepared to take no personal responsibility at all.

Perhaps it was not so strange, bearing in mind the recent saga of the good, thick NAAFI cream. NAAFI was established to serve the whole HQ, all nations, and it used to get a delivery of this cream every Thursday morning, cream of a quality not obtainable on the French market. Supplies did not meet the demand and some equitable form of rationing had to be devised. Parker took it on himself to organize this!

I arrived at the station in Bonn about 8 am and was met by our most helpful Military Attaché. He told me at once that the meeting was waiting eagerly to hear SACEUR's views, having expected his representative to have come 2 days earlier. When I mentioned my instructions from Parker, he said, 'You're a brave man if you go into that meeting and decline to speak.' So we went to his office and rang up Parker, who, after some hesitation, reluctantly agreed that I could speak from my briefs, provided that I made clear that I was giving a personal view and not that of SACEUR. This was obviously an impracticable instruction and I ignored the proviso. I had every confidence that, if it had come to the crunch, Lemnitzer would have backed me.

A few weeks later I had to attend another such meeting and, having had more notice, Gerry was able to come with me. There was one day when I was not required and we had a delightful cruise up the Rhine, returning by train.

On a hot summer's day in Paris the NATO Council met as the Group of Fourteen, that is to say without the French. They had discussed for 2 or 3 hours the effects of the French saying that they wished to opt out of this subject but to remain in for that. It was irritating and tempers were rising. A remark by the Turkish Ambassador produced laughter and calm, 'We must remember that the French always prefer to eat à la carte.'

My predecessor had committed me to give a lecture at the Greek Defence College in Athens. I planned this journey so as to call on the NATO HQ in Naples on the way. Gerry came too and we combined it with brief stays in Naples, Rome and Athens.

I had had to submit my text in advance so that an interpreter was forewarned. I said a paragraph in English and he repeated it in Greek. I found this most unsatisfactory because it meant that I could not depart from my script and could pay no attention to audience reaction. I had included 2 funny but relevant stories. At the first, those who understood English tittered and, when it came out in Greek, there was stony silence. On the second occasion, there was tittering again at the English version but the Greek version was greeted with uproarious laughter. I can only suppose that the interpreter said, 'You did not laugh at his last joke. For Heaven's sake laugh now.'

My job seemed to be an extraordinary mixture of high responsibility and farcical lack of trust. For example, no officer below the rank of major-general or equivalent was allowed to authorize a signal from SHAPE. On the other hand, with minimal guidance from above, I was told to head a team to discuss with the French War Office the plans which would have to be agreed as regards the position of the 2 French divisions stationed in West Germany if there should be war between the USSR and NATO in which France was not involved.

The first meeting between the French and my SHAPE team was held in the French War Office in a long room with big windows down one side. SHAPE were invited to sit on the windows side, with the light behind them, which I thought was a generous gesture until I sat down and realized that the whole of the long wall opposite was occupied with large oil paintings of nudes: most distracting!

After 2 or 3 meetings we were nearing an agreed draft on the policy to be adopted and I undertook to send our latest version to my opposite number, a French major-general, for him to look at before we met again. In the preamble I had described the French divisions in Germany as being 'in an anomalous position'. The French general rang me up and asked me to come over to discuss my draft before it was put to the full meeting. He asked me what the word 'anomalous' meant. His interpreter suggested *'anormale'* but I said that I thought that this was not quite right and then said, in French, 'If, General, you found that, by mistake, you had entered the ladies' lavatory, you would be in an anomalous position.' The General was so scandalized at the thought that French soldiers could thus lose face that final agreement on the text was seriously delayed.

SHAPE was naturally run on American lines. In particular it was considered that every officer should be at his desk for set hours, regardless of whether he had work to do or not. The only recognized exception was that Wednesday afternoon could be taken off to play golf, but any other activity was frowned upon.

Although my golf was always very low grade, I played nearly every Wednesday. This was at a time when relations with the French were somewhat strained: in fact, SACEUR, not wishing to risk a snub, had not asked de Gaulle for the usual annual permission to hold a SHAPE ball in the Hall of Mirrors in Versailles in aid of French charities. One Wednesday, coming into the clubhouse after a round of golf, I happened to meet Lemnitzer, who civilly asked how I had got on that day. I replied that I had 'only hit one Frenchman' and got more than the rise I expected. I then explained that a Frenchman in front of us had driven into a wood at about 200 yards and, while looking for his ball, had waved us through. I then managed to drive into the same wood and my warning cry did not register. I hit the Frenchman on the shoulder, which must have been painful at the end of a long shot. He was, however, very civil and said that it had been entirely his fault for not watching.

On one of the few occasions when I had to go to see Lemnitzer personally in his office, we were in the middle of doing whatever business it was, when Signor Brosio, the Italian Secretary-General of NATO, came in unexpectedly. I indicated to Lemnitzer that I had better leave and come back later but he told me to sit down and wait. This was at the time when it had been decided that the political head of NATO, that is the NATO Council, ie the ambassadors, now in Paris, and the military head, the Military Committee, now in Washington, would be co-located in Brussels. SACEUR, being now in Versailles, used commonly, as a matter of geographical convenience, to give military advice direct to the NATO Council, advice which should correctly have come from, or through, the Military Committee. Not surprisingly, SACEUR wanted to retain his influential position and therefore wanted to move to Brussels also.

Brosio, on the other hand, wanted to use the opportunity of the proposed general post to establish the channels of communication as they had originally been planned. To this end he wanted SHAPE to be well away from Brussels and there was a possible site near Mons, some 40 miles from Brussels. I was fascinated by the discussion that ensued that afternoon. The decision would have to be taken by the Council and, as was inevitable, Brosio got his way: in my opinion rightly so.

It was the American custom to mark the promotion or retirement of an officer with much more ceremony than is normal in British service. When my number 2, an American colonel, was promoted to brigadier-general, Gerry and I were both invited into my American boss's office at 6 pm one evening, to find that there was a party consisting of those 2 and the American Admiral and their wives. We assumed that this was just for us all to mark the occasion with a drink. But there was much more to it than that. The American General had to make a formal speech first and then, with due ceremony, to pin on to one shoulder the star of the new rank. The new general's wife was then invited to pin on the star on the other shoulder and this was followed by a formal speech by the victim.

When it came to the retirement of SACEUR's American Deputy, an Air Force General, all general officers (ie brigadiers and upwards), about 28 of them, were instructed to parade on the steps of the headquarters. Our names were sellotaped to the spot where we should stand: in strict order of seniority. I found that I was to stand immediately in front of a French general, a liaison officer attached to SHAPE. As he was about 5 feet 6 inches and I about 6 feet 6 inches, he was plainly going to have a very dull morning, and I suggested to him that we should change places. He said that he was afraid that General Parker, the Chief of Staff, would not like it. At that moment it happened that Parker came by and so I asked him whether he would mind if we exchanged places, 'No. We must stick to protocol.'

27

CAREER PROSPECTS IN ROYAL SIGNALS: 1966

In early September I was considering my own future. At that time NATO appointments were not commonly stepping stones to further advancement, if only because an annual confidential report was initiated by one's immediate superior and, as he was normally of another nation, his views would carry little weight. I was only 49 and had already done three and a half years in my present rank. I was not keen to do 2 more appointments at the same level before being retired at 55.

When the representative of the Military Secretary came on a routine visit to SHAPE, I asked to see him. It was Brigadier Ian Gill, whom I had known in Germany when he was commanding a brigade. I asked him directly what were the chances of my being promoted further when I left SHAPE. He gave me a straight and honest answer: none, short of quite unexpected casualties. I said that I thought that, in that case, I would probably prefer to retire now whilst young enough to try to make a success in some other field. I would think it over for a week or 2.

Having discussed it with Gerry and given it much thought, I decided to retire as soon as practicable. I consulted with the British representative at SHAPE on how to 'send in my papers' and in due course had completed the necessary application. I decided that I would go to London with the documents in my hand, for 2 reasons. First, it would be civil to go to see the present Signal Officer-in-Chief, Peter Bradley, to explain in person why I was doing this. Second, ever since I had written the report on signal officers' careers in 1960, I had been concerned at the raw deal signal officers were getting in relation to their fellows in other arms. Now that I had no longer any personal interest, it seemed that I had an opportunity to bring this to the attention of those at the top – and, in particular, to that of the CGS, Jim Cassels, as I happened to know him personally from when I had last been working for Dick Hull and Cassels was DGMT (Director-General of Military Training) in the next office.

So, from Paris, I rang the office shared between the MA's of the CGS and the VCGS, his deputy. I asked for the CGS but, owing to some error, was put through to the VCGS. This proved, I suspect, a very lucky mistake because the VCGS was Desmond Fitzpatrick, for whom I had worked in MO2 a few years earlier. I apologized for the mistake but, full of curiosity, he wanted to know why I wanted to speak to the CGS. I told him and he politely indicated that he was very sorry to hear that I was intending to retire. He then got the call transferred and I asked Cassels to give me 10 minutes to grind an axe, one which I thought was worth grinding as I was retiring. We made an appointment.

My date with Peter Bradley was at 10 am and that with Jim Cassels at midday. Peter said, 'Before you go any further, let me tell you that you have an appointment with the Military Secretary at 5 pm and you are not to take any steps towards retirement until you have seen him. That is an order. I don't know the reasons but I am passing on what I have been told by MS.'

I said, 'That puts me in a rather awkward position because I have a date with the CGS this morning on the basis that I shall have already committed myself to retiring.'

We agreed that I would have to explain the situation to the CGS and be guided by him. I was careful at this stage not to tell Peter, or anyone else, what the axe was that I wanted to grind, as it might have put him in an awkward position if it were thought that he as SO-in-C had put me up to this.

It was only the second time in my life that I had entered the CGS's office. The first had been when I was in MO2 and was supposed to know something about Gurkhas. I had been sent for and, discovering that Gurkha detail was required, I took with me a Gurkha major. Arriving in the office, we found that the CGS, Frankie Festing, was holding a meeting of about 6 or 7 generals. I introduced my Gurkha friend and he answered the questions competently. Festing then looked round the room with a beaming smile and said, 'It is *very* refreshing to have someone in here who really knows what he's talking about!'

On the present occasion I explained my predicament to Cassels and suggested that it might be better if I came back when my retirement was firm because it was not appropriate that I should say what I wanted to say as a serving officer. He told me to go ahead nevertheless.

I said that I assumed that he would agree that officers of Royal Signals should have career prospects comparable with those of the other arms with which they had to work so closely. Royal Signals was attracting its fair share of good officers into the Corps: in years to come it would do the Army no good if the senior officers of the Corps felt that they were not getting a fair share of the senior appointments for which they were qualified.

I went on to give details to show that, up to the rank of brigadier, Signals got their fair share in the rank structure but that, in colonels' and particularly in brigadiers' appointments, Signals were given far more than their share of dead-end jobs. As result it could fairly be said that Signals had not got enough officers with the right experience for further promotion. On average Signals should expect to get a vacancy on nearly every annual course at the Imperial Defence College: we had had only 3 vacancies between 1945 and 1966. With an army of the present (1966) size, Signals should expect to average between 8 and 9 general officers' appointments at one time: in the last 15 years we had averaged less than one and a half major-generals and had had no officer above that rank.

Cassels said that he was most interested and that, as I had an appointment with the Military Secretary that afternoon, would I please tell him what I had just said.

Dick Goodwin, who had been Corps Commander in Germany after Ken Darling, and whom I therefore knew well, was now Military Secretary, another happy coincidence from my point of view. I said my piece and gave him an aide-mémoire with the details. He then said that the reason that he had sent for me was to say that there had been certain changes since I had seen Ian Gill and that, if I would be patient for up to 3 months, he might have good news for me. He added that, if by that time nothing had turned up, he would ensure that I was allowed to retire as quickly as I liked. Naturally I accepted his offer. It seemed clear to me that this change of face resulted from the kindly intervention of Fitzpatrick and, through him, of Cassels. I was very lucky that they happened to be able to help at that moment.

It is of interest that about 3 years later there was a moment when there were 7 major-generals late Royal Signals serving at one time.

28

NATO IN WASHINGTON: 1967

In early December, 1966, I was rung up by Ian Gill from the Military Secretary's Department to ask whether I would accept a job as Secretary of the NATO Military Committee, in Washington initially but moving to Brussels later. He explained that the chap that they had proposed for the job was going to retire instead and, if I would accept it, it would get MS out of a hole. Whilst this was another brigadier's job and he could not make any promise as to the future, he made clear that MS would then look after my interests. Another problem was that this was one of the jobs that the NATO nations would be voting on and there was no certainty that I would get enough votes. I agreed that I would accept the job if elected.

We had leave from SHAPE over Christmas and the New Year, which we spent at Brakey Hill. Two days before going back to Paris, MS, Dick Goodwin, rang up himself to say that I had got this job and that I had to be in Washington by 1 February. My successor in SHAPE would be an RAF officer but they did not yet know his name.

So, in less than 4 weeks we had to pack up at Brakey and try to let it for an indefinite period, to pack up our flat in Paris, to hand over the Paris job to an unknown successor and to get to Washington ready for work. MS were kind enough to tell those concerned that it was probable that I would be in Washington for more than 9 months, the minimum period for which one could take a family. We decided that we were going to have an exhausting rush, even if we travelled by air at the last moment, and that it would therefore be better to go a little earlier by sea and make sure of a few days to recover.

In Paris I now gave closer study to documents describing the higher organization of NATO. The controlling body was the NATO Council, which met about every 6 months with Foreign Ministers representing their countries. Sometimes they met as the Defence Committee with Defence Ministers. Each member country had an ambassador to NATO who lived with a small staff in Paris, and these ambassadors, representing their Foreign Ministers, also constituted the NATO Council which met weekly under the chairmanship of the Secretary-General, at that time Signor Brosio. The NATO Military Committee similarly consisted of the Chiefs of Defence Staff of each country, who met normally every 6 months but were represented for weekly meetings by Military Representatives, who met in their own small section of the Pentagon in Washington. In each case the Military Committee met under its chairman, who was then Lieutenant-General de Cumont of the Belgian Army.

It had been found that the Military Committee was a rather cumbersome organization for giving advice to the Council 3,000 miles away. So the Standing Group, consisting of the Military Representatives (Mil-Reps) of France, the United Kingdom, and the United States only, had been set up to deal with all normal business. Major issues were referred to the whole Committee and any member could ask for an item to be considered by them. When France opted out of the military side of NATO, members decided that it would not be satisfactory to have the committee represented by only 2 members and it was agreed that, in future, the whole Committee would meet regularly every week and would have a larger staff to support it.

The International Military Staff (IMS) was to consist of a Director and a Vice-Director, both 3-star officers, and 5 divisions (Operations, Intelligence, Organization, Communications and Logistics), each headed at 1- or 2-star level.

There would also be a small Secretariat to serve both the Director of the IMS and the Chairman of the Military Committee. The UK and US considered that the head of the Secretariat would be comparable with that of a national Chiefs of Staff Committee and should therefore be a 2-star officer, a major-general or equivalent. Most of the smaller countries said that he would only be a secretary and should be a lieutenant-colonel or possibly colonel. They reached the inevitable compromise on a brigadier: me.

When I first arrived I naturally took the view that the job should have been for a 2-star officer but after a few months' experience I concluded that brigadier was the right answer. Mil-Reps were 4-, 3- or 2-star according to the size of the country but all had equal status; the Chairman was 3- or 4-star and the Director 3-star; heads of divisions were in practice nearly all 2-star; and all other officers were colonels or below. The Secretary was thus normally in a unique rank and therefore, to the extent that rank mattered at all, he had the entrée to all offices.

We embarked at Southampton in the *Queen Elizabeth*, the pre-war liner, towards the end of January. She called in at Cherbourg, where our heavy baggage from Paris was loaded, and then went to New York. There was a tug strike there and so our captain, the Commodore of the line, had to berth her unaided. This meant going up the Hudson River so as to reach a point a little more than the ship's length above our dock, exactly at the top of the tide, and then letting the ship reverse with just sufficient steerage way, turning a right angle to get alongside the dock. To help with the turn a very large hawser linked the ship to the corner of the dock. All this was being watched by many pressmen on our bridge, with others in helicopters, publicity which we gathered Commodore Last enjoyed. The difficulty of the manoeuvre was demonstrated by the hawser breaking with a thunderous crash when halfway round the corner. In spite of this we came alongside perfectly.

When I reported in the Pentagon, I first had to see

Admiral Sir Nigel Henderson, the British Military Representative. He explained to me that the voting for the new Secretary had been close: 7 votes to 6. He had only secured the Portuguese vote by assuring their Mil-Rep that I spoke French fluently. When I said that I could get by in French but was by no means fluent, he told me to keep clear of the Portuguese until I was fluent.

Next I went to see General de Cumont, the Chairman of the Military Committee. He explained that I would have a dual allegiance, first to him and second to the Director of the IMS, General Pistotti. My prime job was to ensure the clarity of all documents issuing from the Committee: they were to go out in good, concise English and, by English, he meant English and not American.

When I called on General Pistotti, he indicated that my allegiance would be to him and through him to the Chairman. I never tried to resolve this difference of priorities but, with care, managed to avoid the conflict which might have arisen.

The Pentagon is not only a building with 5 equal outer sides: it is also 5 storeys high, with a pentagon of open space in the middle. Each of the 5 sides is broad and has on every floor 5 parallel corridors with rooms on either side. Thus only the rooms facing into the central space and those on the outside of the building have windows, 1 in 5 of the total. I was lucky enough to have one of the offices facing outwards. It was a fairly large room but, with its air-conditioning, seemed to me stuffy. So one morning I tried to open the window. This set off the burglar alarms and I had to desist. Apparently the stuffiness had worsened in recent times because, as result of the Vietnam operations, the numbers working there had risen from about 25,000 to around 32,000 and they had to make do with the same amount of air. The vast car parks around the building were adequate in total space but the more junior staff were allocated the more distant spaces with anything up to a mile to walk.

I had 4 assistant secretaries, British, American, Belgian

and German, of whom the one who wrote the clearest and most accurate English was undoubtedly the German, Hans von Joeden. The British one, Harry Boswell, was a Canadian in the British Army, Royal Engineers, with an American wife. Gerry and I had known them slightly before as they had rented Mytchett Heath from us for a short time before we sold it. On our arrival in Washington they were most kind and helpful to us with all the problems of setting up home in a strange place.

Since the IMS was now much larger than it had been, it was necessary to establish new procedures and to lay down administrative rules. For example, a considerable number of air journeys had to be made, particularly by the more senior officers, to Paris to do business with the NATO Council staff or with SHAPE. Should officers travel first class or economy? (There was no intermediate class in those days.) I asked each nation what their policy was. Germany said that all officers should travel first class; the United States that only generals and lieutenant-generals should go first class; the United Kingdom that major-generals and above went first, brigadiers also first if the journey were more than 4 hours; and there were other variations. Perhaps I was not unbiased in laying down that, in the IMS, brigadiers and above would travel first!

At the end of March I had occasion to go to Paris for one of the 6-monthly meetings of the Military Committee in Chiefs of Staff session. So I took the opportunity to go also to Brussels to see the site which was being cleared for the construction of the new building which was to house both the NATO Council and the Military Committee and their staffs, both national and international. Then no more than a large flat, muddy area, not even marked out for the construction to come, it was due to be completed and occupied by 1 October.

Much time was being devoted in Washington to the allocation of offices in the new building. To make sure of completion by the required date and for reasons of economy, all offices were to be in multiples of one standard unit. For example I was entitled to a 2-unit office and my 4 assistant secretaries had, I think, a 4-unit office between them.

In the Pentagon, partly because the room in which the Military Committee met was small and partly because most countries regarded the Secretary as a mere minute-taker, the Secretary did not get a seat at the main table. He had a small table some 6 feet behind the Chairman. I was determined to ensure that in Brussels I would get a seat at the table. So, at one of our weekly meetings, when some point arose on which I could make a useful contribution, I wrote a brief note, thrust it into the split end of a long bamboo stick, which I had ready on the floor beside me, and put my note under the Chairman's nose. There was a second or 2 of stunned silence round the table and then they all dissolved in laughter. In Brussels I got my seat at the table next to the Chairman.

The first car we bought on arrival was an elderly Ford, a very faded metallic blue. One morning in March I was trying to get to work after about a foot of snow had fallen in the night. Whilst the main roads had been cleared, nearly all traffic was confined to them and the rush hour was clearly going to be very much worse than usual. I tried to take an uncleared road which had almost no traffic and was amply wide but included an uphill stretch. With a bit of a run at the hill, I got nearly to the top but then started to skid and could go no further. So I allowed the car to go gently back and then guided it backwards half into an entrance, with a view to turning to go down the hill again. Whilst I was stationary and at right angles to the road, a car came over the top of the hill at about 40 mph, in this 30 mph limit. The driver saw my car and decided to brake, with the result that he continued down the hill about the same speed but sideways. The left-hand side of his car hit the right-hand side of mine, which was driven sideways against a metal pole with a sign on the top, 'NO PARKING ANY TIME'.

Fortunately for me the incident had been seen by a

Virginia state trooper – ie a policeman – who was parked at the bottom of the hill. He invited me to sit in his warm car whilst he took particulars and, having assured me that he would arrange for my car to be taken to an appropriate repair garage, directed me to a bus which would take me to the Pentagon. It happened that this was a Thursday, the one day in the week when the Military Committee met, and so I was in uniform. A senior British officer in uniform was an unusual bus passenger and caused some surprise.

When the car had been repaired, at the expense of the other chap's insurance, I went to collect it and found that they had repaired the right half of the car well and had repainted it the colour that it had originally been, a bright metallic blue, whilst the left side was the very faded pale blue which I had bought. My American assistant secretary advised me to consult the Pentagon's legal department before complaining to the insurance company. Their lawyer was most helpful. On his advice I rang the insurance company and told them that I had 2 problems: one, I had had a headache and a painful thumb as result of the accident (truthful) and two, I was dissatisfied with being invited to drive a car resembling a zebra. I accepted, with an appropriate degree of reluctance, their suggestion that they would have the whole car painted as new if I would agree that I had no further claim against them. I gathered that, if I had chosen to go to a doctor with my ailments, it could easily have landed them with a very large bill.

Between May and September Washington can be very unpleasantly hot and humid. So we bought a 'camper', a caravan with canvas sides folding down to the height of a motor car. About 7 am each Saturday morning we used to drive this about 90 miles west up to the Skyline Drive, some 3,000 feet up, where we could camp in delightful woodland out of sight or sound of any human being. One morning I heard a scratching at the door: a racoon was wanting to come in.

At the end of July, with Margaret and Hugh, we set off for the west with the camper, taking a slightly northern route to the Pacific coast in Oregon, then south to San Francisco. We came back further south through the north of Texas. The whole trip was 8,000 miles, a lot in 23 days, but it gave us a good idea of much of a very large country.

The Military Committee was invited by the United States to make a tour of the space travel facilities. This also included a visit to a US Navy aircraft carrier off the coast of Alabama. We were then catapulted from the deck in 2 aircraft and landed in New Orleans. There we were given a civic dinner. My neighbour told me that, when he and his wife were changing for dinner, she had asked what this dinner was for and he had said, 'It's for NATO'. She had replied, 'I didn't know that you were interested in football.'

Later my neighbour discovered that we had an afternoon free the next day and insisted on lending me a car for a long as I might want it. The keys were left for me at my hotel desk and I then found my way to a very large limousine in metallic gold, which had done less than 2,000 miles. Very generous and thoughtful.

Another Military Committee trip was to Iceland, primarily to have a meeting with their Prime Minister, who was having difficulty with a large and vociferous Communist minority and wanted to learn all the arguments for Iceland remaining in NATO. Whilst there we were taken to see a large natural amphitheatre which had been the site of the first Icelandic parliament set up in 936 AD. The site had been chosen as convenient for the annual 6-week meeting of delegates from all over the island. They came on horseback and so good grazing was essential, as well as a good water supply.

The proceedings opened each year with the secretary reciting from memory all the laws that had been passed in previous years. One of our Mil-Reps immediately turned to me and said, 'That's your job!' In addition to law-making, the gathering also acted as a court of law to try major offenders. It was therefore convenient to have a high, steep cliff nearby to throw down women convicted of adultery. Apparently men got away with it.

At one Military Committee meeting it was agreed in principle that, for the move to Brussels, the Committee, with the International Military Staff and all the national staffs, with all their families, should travel in one ship. General de Cumont threw in the idea that it would be good for the public image of NATO if we held a formal Committee meeting in mid-Atlantic. I was deputed to find out about chartering a ship, costs, etc. It would clearly be the most economical way of moving and I duly reported the possibilities. All nations agreed in principle. Unfortunately 6 of them made the proviso that the ship chosen must be one provided by their own country. This, of course, killed the project: a sad and expensive decision.

Each country then had to arrange the movement of its own national staff and their dependants. My secretariat had to plan the move of the IMS, which was complicated because the new HQ in Brussels had to open on the same day as the one in Washington closed and nearly all the staff wanted leave in their own countries on the way. A major expense was the transport of classified documents, which had to go in sealed packages by air at a cost of £1,000 a ton, and there was a very large tonnage as we included not only the IMS papers but also national packages. Roughly half such documents then held in Washington were burned before we went (but this left more than 30 tons) and it was interesting to note the variation between nations. One country had almost no such papers, having apparently burned them all soon after receipt, whilst another had not destroyed any paper since arrival in Washington 17 years earlier.

Gerry and I planned to leave about 2 weeks before 1 October, the day of opening in Brussels, so that we could go by sea and take a week's holiday in Donegal on the way. However, the week before that there was to be a Military Committee meeting in Oslo which finished on a Saturday about midday. So I flew back overnight to Washington and, on Sunday morning, whilst Gerry completed our packing, briefed General Pistotti on the Oslo meeting, as he had not been able to attend due to ’flu. That evening we took a train to Montreal, arriving around midday on Monday. We spent Monday afternoon at Expo 67 and then embarked for a cruise down the St Lawrence and on to Southampton.

29

NATO IN BRUSSELS: 1967–68

On 1 October 1967, when I went to the new NATO Headquarters on the north side of Brussels near the airport, it was astonishing to see what had been achieved in 6 months. Here was a 3-storey, flat-roofed building ready to house a staff of 2,000 with 12 conference rooms, with heating, telephones, simultaneous translation equipment etc, completed on the planned date. Later I happened to be talking to the Dutchman responsible for its finance. He said that the NATO building in Paris, built in the 1950s, had overrun its date by years and had cost vastly more than the estimate. This new building cost less than the estimate and was on time because there had been rigid control over what could be asked for and no mind-changing was allowed.

The teething troubles were not serious. General Pistotti was very upset to find that, as a lieutenant-general, he was not entitled to a carpet in his office whilst his civilian equivalent was. Some masterly compromise was reached and NATO continued to function.

Another problem was that, in order to house secret papers, all the staffs, national and international had been issued with metal filing cabinets whose locks were easily opened without using the key. One day I went to see the Turkish Mil-Rep, a 4-star General, to try to persuade him to agree to something. He was hesitating over his answer when I changed the subject by asking him whether he was satisfied with the administrative arrangements in his offices.

In particular I hoped that he was aware of the security risks of these cabinets: did he know that they could be opened with a paperknife? He was horrified. We went immediately to his outer office. A paperknife was produced. I demonstrated and then left him happily practising opening the locks. As I left, I reverted to the question I had come to discuss. He now accepted my view without hesitation: lock-picking was much more fun.

Shortly after arrival there was a formal opening ceremony attended by the Belgian Prime Minister and many senior NATO figures, including the 3 Supreme Commanders, SACEUR, SACLANT and CINCCHAN, and, of course, the Chairman of the Military Committee, General de Cumont. Lemnitzer, who until now had normally given military advice direct to the NATO Council, short-circuiting those in Washington, was keen that the seating on this formal occasion should demonstrate to the world that he retained his pre-eminent role. De Cumont, on the other hand, wished to make clear that the Military Committee was now going to take its proper place between the Council on the one hand and the Supreme Commanders on the other. Who should sit where was still being argued about less than an hour before the speech-making was due to start. I had a small army of chaps with place cards waiting to be told where to put them. Signor Brosio was then called on to make a decision and, as usual, managed to find a masterly compromise by which both parties thought that they had won.

I had occasion to go to see de Cumont that afternoon. He immediately said, 'I suppose you thought we were being a bit childish about the seating this morning?' I didn't disagree and he followed it with, 'You are wrong. The whole future relationship of the Military Committee to the Council and to SHAPE would have been prejudiced if SACEUR had had his way.' He was probably right.

Each nation was responsible for the housing of its own nationals, including those on the international staff. The British had had a small military organization in some rural area of Belgium for some time and their financial authorities knew the rents there. So they authorized the same scale for all the new staff in Brussels, where, of course, the same standard of house or flat commanded a far higher rent. The result was that it took many weeks of pressure to get reasonable rents approved on a case-by-case basis.

For ourselves, we eventually found a possible house in a reasonable area and persuaded those concerned to pay for it. A German colonel was also trying to rent this house but was firmly turned down. He was perhaps not aware that the street in question, Avenue Colonel Daumerie, had been named after a popular local figure who had been hanged by the Germans in the 1939 war.

Our landlord, a retired Belgian general who had been ADC to a British general in the 1914 war, and his wife lived in a large, rambling house nearby and employed a Spanish couple to look after them. Whilst they spoke no Spanish, one of their 12 children was married to a Spanish woman and they lived opposite. Unfortunately it was the wrong sort of Spanish and misunderstandings occurred. One evening we were dining with them and 12 of us assembled for drinks. When we went into the dining room, the table was laid for only 7. However, the mistake was quickly rectified and there seemed to be plenty of food.

Eleven of the senior appointments in NATO were not tied to any one nation, as was, for example, that of SACEUR, who was always American. Incumbents for these 11 posts were selected by voting in the Military Committee and no one nation was allowed to hold more than 2 of the 11 simultaneously. In, I think, January (1968) the Committee was due to choose a new Commandant for the NATO Defence College in Rome, to take effect in a few months' time. I called for nominations and found that the UK wished to put forward a candidate. I went to see the acting UK Mil-Rep, Air-Vice-Marshal Tony Dudgeon, because the Mil-Rep, Admiral Nigel Henderson, was on leave, and I pointed out that the UK had recently accepted the appointment of Henderson to be Chairman in succession to de Cumont; my appointment was also one of the 11 and I did not know that I was being sacked! He rang up the Military Secretary's Department and said, 'What's happening to Hancock?' Answer: 'It's secret and you must not tell him.' 'But I must tell him something because, in his NATO capacity, he cannot allow the UK to put forward someone for the Rome job if he, Hancock, is still going to be here.'

There was then some consultation and my old friend Ian Gill came on the phone to me to explain that I was to be promoted but that this had not yet had the Sovereign's approval. On no account must the individual be told until it was approved. Dudgeon would be given an innocuous explanation for the committee and I must not question it. Meanwhile, if I breathed a word of it, I would probably lose the job.

As it happened, the UK did not get the Rome job and so, on my departure, the UK might have only one of the 11. The next problem, in this context, was to invite the nations to put forward candidates to replace me. Germany and the UK indicated that they had starters. Each had to let me have summary histories of their candidates a week before election day. The job was, of course, open to 14 nations and all 3 services and so it was surprising to find that the UK candidate was a soldier, that he had been in Royal Signals, that we had been at school together where I had taught him Morse in the OTC Signal Section: Charles Page.

The Germans were late putting in details of their candidate and I went round to their office to hurry them up. They assured me that they expected the information within a day or 2; and then, as I was leaving the office, they asked whether I knew anything about the British starter. I explained that I happened to know him well and added as an afterthought that he had commanded a regiment in Burma at the age of 24. Next day the German candidate was withdrawn!

My next job was to be Chief of Staff of Far East Land Forces (FARELF) in Singapore, starting in early June. At the end of March I handed over the NATO job to Charles Page and the Pages took on our house too. With Margaret and Hugh, we went off the ski near Salzburg in Austria, choosing a spot high enough to have a prospect of adequate snow so late in the season. Even there we got only one week before the snow disappeared and so we decided to drive south for about 200 miles to have a week in Venice, which was not too crowded at that time of year.

We then drove home to Brakey Hill. Although this was let at the time, the tenants were old friends, Eric and Mary Bardell, and they very kindly allowed us to use what had been the servants' wing. Gerry's mother, then 87, flew over from Ireland to be with us for 3 or 4 weeks before we left for Singapore.

We flew first to Teheran, where our Military Attaché and his wife had invited us to stay. They took us by jeep one day for a 3- or 4-hour journey over the mountains to the shore of the Caspian Sea, where we all stayed with a retired Iranian General of their acquaintance. He had been a very considerable landowner and, when the Shah decided on land reform and invited those with large estates to offer their land for splitting up, he was one of the first 3 to offer his. He proudly showed us a photograph of himself formally handing over the deeds to the Shah.

He had, at the same time, acquired a half-mile stretch of the Caspian shoreline about a quarter-mile deep, which, when he got it, was wasteland with 5 small streams running north into the sea. A few years later, at the time we went there, this was highly productive land, with oranges, tea and much else. Swimming that evening in a warm, calm sea was delightful.

We also flew to Isfahan for one night: a fabulous city.

The journey on to Singapore was not so good. BOAC had gone on strike but we managed to transfer to JAP Airlines. Their midnight flight, after much hesitation, took off at 4 am and we missed our connection in Bangkok.

After a miserable day in an overcrowded airport with negligible facilities, we flew in the evening to Singapore by Malaysian Airways who could not have looked after us better.

30

SINGAPORE AGAIN: 1968–70

The command organization in Singapore was now as had been arranged at the end of 1962 (Chapter 24): that is to say there were 3 single service Commanders under one Commander-in-Chief. Each of these 4 had a Chief of Staff at 2-star level and I was to be Chief of Staff to the Army Commander. Mountbatten had argued (Chapter 24) that this new organization would save manpower. My impression was otherwise but this was not a fair judgement because of the necessary extra staffs to deal with the Indonesian war, which had only finished recently.

The Army Commander had 3 principal subordinates: Commander British Forces (CBF) Hong Kong, GOC Malaya and GOC Singapore. CBF Hong Kong was responsible to the Army Commander for the Army in Hong Kong and to C-in-C Far East for all 3 Services in Hong Kong. The RN and RAF units in Hong Kong were relatively small and their commanders were responsible both to CBF and to their single service commanders in Singapore. It sounds complicated but worked quite well in practice.

When I arrived, the C-in-C was Michael Carver. The Army Commander was Tom Pearson, an old friend from the days of Norway in 1945, and I could not have had a happier start.

Carver was widely known in the army and it was generally accepted that he was on his way to being CGS. I had never met him before. On my first visit to his office, he greeted me with the words, 'I suppose you've been brainwashed in London about the families in Hong Kong?' and I agreed that I had.

I had had various briefings in London and the most significant was from the CGS, George Baker. He told me that, due to the serious riots in Hong Kong in 1967, Carver had recommended that all service families should be withdrawn and that it should become a non-family station because, as 1997, the year of handing back Hong Kong to China, approached, it would get more and more difficult to ensure their safety. I had been told that the Chiefs of Staff in London and the Army Commander in Singapore vehemently disagreed. The peace of Hong Kong for the next 30 years would continue to depend on the confidence of the majority of the population in British rule. If service families, who were no more than a fraction of the British families there, were withdrawn, it would show to all that we had no confidence ourselves in our ability to maintain law and order. Moreover, the stationing of thousands of British troops in Hong Kong in a relatively peacetime role, without their own families but with lots of civilian families, would inevitably have seriously adverse social consequences. Not only was it my duty to support my Army Commander but, fortunately, my own view was the same as his. At my first interview with Carver there was no need to argue the point.

A few months later the Chiefs of Staff discussed the proposal formally. Carver went to London for the meeting. Pearson happened to be in London already on some other business and, as it seemed to me likely that he would be consulted by the CGS, I signalled him a full brief on the subject as an aide mémoire. Carver was in a minority of one and was overruled: rightly so, with hindsight!

The C-in-C's HQ was located in Phoenix Park on the north side of Singapore city, a mile or so to the west of Tanglin barracks, where the army's GHQ was. The naval HQ was near the northern corner of the island and the RAF HQ at the eastern corner. As the C-in-C had assumed control of the operations in Indonesia, my predecessor had set up his own main office in Phoenix Park, with a smaller office in Tanglin, which he visited as necessary.

After a few days' trial, I found that this was most unsatisfactory because there was now little operational reason for my being in Phoenix Park; my prime job was to serve the Army Commander in Tanglin and to run the very large HQ there. I moved as soon as the office changes could be made, leaving only my Colonel Operations, Dick Randall, in Phoenix Park and I required him to come to Tanglin for a short daily meeting with the BGS, TIG Gray (late Royal Signals), the Brigadier AQ, Dick Worsley, and the Command Secretary, Jolyon Dromgoole.

We took over from our predecessor a pleasant house in Alexandra Park with 4 living-in servants, Chinese, and a gardener and 2 army drivers, Malays. I soon found that one driver was quite enough. This was a pleasant contrast to staff appointments at home. It was commonly said that one moved from sink to mink and back.

There had been some unwelcome publicity for the services generally about serving officers supposedly getting free air transport for wives and children to which they were not entitled. New strict rules had been issued by Whitehall and, as borderline cases in FARELF had to have my approval, I had to be particularly careful to conform to the rules myself. I consulted the appropriate colonel in Movements in the Ministry of Defence about Margaret coming to Singapore. Because she had left school she was not entitled to a free passage but, provided she went at bottom priority for a seat, I would have to pay only about a quarter of the normal cost. Hugh, being still at school, was entitled to 2 free journeys a year.

The new restrictions aimed to prevent newspaper reporters jumping to wrong conclusions. If, for example, an officer was travelling by civil aircraft on a duty journey, his wife must not travel on the same plane even though she was paying her own fare. This was often very tiresome.

When there were spare spaces in RAF transport aircraft,

they were offered to all 3 services, being allotted to the most junior first: a very reasonable arrangement. Gerry and I wanted to go to Hong Kong on leave once and were lucky enough to get such seats. There was, by the rules, no objection to this, provided that we were strictly on leave and I was not on duty. On the other hand it was ridiculous that, if I were in Hong Kong, I should not deal with current business with their HQ. I did: but strictly in civilian clothes!

Tom Pearson left FARELF towards the end of 1968 to become Military Secretary and was replaced by Peter Hunt, who had been commanding the Royal Military Academy. This posting was known before we left England and Peter had invited Gerry and me to lunch at Sandhurst then as we had not met before. It makes all the difference to the life of a chief of staff to work for a general whom one likes and respects. With both Pearson and Hunt I could not have been luckier. Both had the great merit, from a subordinate's point of view, of making their views and policies clear and then trusting one to get on with the job.

Both Army Commanders toured their theatre freely, as was necessary, and, as far a possible, I had to be in Singapore when they were away. Nevertheless I did manage to get around a lot. I started naturally enough with all the branches of GHQ. Although I had no hope of knowing every one of the 600 to 700 there personally, it seemed to me important that I should learn something of what every section did and that at least they should know me. So I spent about 2 or 3 hours every day on such visits. Having completed the military branches, I asked the Command Secretary if I might make similar visits to the civilian branches. He agreed and I found this equally interesting and worthwhile. Word got back to me that the civilian element were delighted to find a senior officer taking an interest in their work: but they would like to have met the Command Secretary! My impression is that lack of interest by the top echelons in their subordinates is a general weakness in the Civil Service.

Having never had a Q (ie logistic) job and being ignorant of the running of a vast base such as Singapore had become, I decided that this must be my next priority. It was all within easy reach of GHQ and so I could continue to work for half the day in the office, learning what went on there, whilst visiting ordnance depots, REME workshops, hospital, schools etc. in the other half. I did not get around to visiting operational units in Malaya and elsewhere in my first 2 or 3 months but there were no significant operations in progress. This gave people the impression that my prime interest was in logistics, which was indeed far from the case.

One of my more distant visits was a courtesy call at the SEATO (South-East Asia Treaty Organization) HQ in Bangkok. Whilst there, our Military Attaché, Peter Body, took me also to make the required courtesy calls on our Ambassador and on the Thai Director of Intelligence. Arriving at our Embassy, he pointed out the enormously high flagpole, telling me that, sometime in the 19th century, our ambassador's coachman had been murdered but the culprit had not been found. By way of compensation, the King allowed the British Embassy to fly a flag higher than any other flag in Bangkok. And so it still flew.

Peter Body also pointed out the very large statue of Queen Victoria. When the Japanese occupied Thailand in 1941–2, they realized how much Queen Victoria was venerated there and decided that it would be impolitic to destroy the statue, and so instead they boarded it up completely. Not long after that some Thais decided that the Queen would be unable to breathe and they cut a hole in the wooden screening. The Japanese were wise enough to accept this compromise.

Arriving in the Thai Director of Intelligence's office, we all sat in comfortable armchairs at one end of a long room. An orderly brought in a tray with coffee and put it on a table at the other end. He then brought each of us a cup of coffee, progressing the length of the room at full knees bend, a skilled operation with a full cup! The others evidently regarded this peculiar operation as normal. After we left, Peter explained that our host was a prince, that is to say he was a descendant of one of the wives of a king. It would have been wrong for the orderly to come near him with his, the orderly's, head higher than the prince's.

Michael Carver handed over as C-in-C in early 1969 to Peter Hill-Norton, an admiral, who had the reputation in the navy of being difficult to work for. I was quite often standing in for Peter Hunt and so I saw a fair amount of him. I enjoyed working for him because he was prepared to listen to arguments and to give clear direction provided one had done one's homework, but, rather like Roddy McLeod, anyone who tried to bluff got short shrift.

In late 1969, Hill-Norton decided to visit his American opposite number in Hawaii, who commanded the forces operating in Vietnam. He was travelling in an RAF plane and so there was room for several hangers-on with wives, as well as his personal staff. The Army Commander could not go if the C-in-C were away and so I was able to go instead and to bring Gerry too. The Army Chief of Staff in Hawaii had made a courtesy call in Singapore and so it was logical that I should return it: not that our jobs were parallel since he was concerned with 10 or 15 times the number of soldiers that I was.

We stopped for a night in Manila and then went to Hawaii for 3 nights. I spent an hour or so with the American Chief of Staff. His most serious problem was lack of leadership amongst junior officers. As their whole structure for the selection and training of officers was different from ours and they had had conscription on a vast scale, I could not give him any useful advice. He had been kind enough to arrange for us to stay in the Army's VIP bungalow on Waikiki beach, which could not have been more delightful.

Our plane-load returned via Fiji, Brisbane, Adelaide and Perth. Our daughter, Margaret, had spent the last 6 months working in Western Australia and we were able to pick her up in Perth. Finally we had a night in Bali on the way back to Singapore.

During 1969 we were told to plan for the withdrawal of all forces from Singapore and Malaya, starting in mid-1970 and completing by mid-1973. Sad though it was, Singapore and Malaya were independent and Britain could no longer justify the vast expense of maintaining a presence in the Far East on that scale.

Planning the run-down was a very interesting and complicated exercise, particularly in the base in Singapore. All the different elements of the base were interdependent and the head of each made clear that, his being the most essential, everyone else had to leave first. I found that the key to this problem was to start at the top. I picked 2 dates spaced by 15 months, say D1 and D2, and laid down that, on D1, the rank of the head of every unit and of every staff branch would be lowered by one. The individual did not suffer this ignominy but was replaced by a more junior officer. All lower jobs would be similarly downgraded. Peter Hunt agreed that he would leave and be replaced by me or my successor. The Brigadier General Staff would become Chief of Staff and so on. Once the head of each arm and service knew that he had to leave, his opposition to the reduction of his organization was minimal. On D2 the operation was to be repeated so that the Army Commander then would be a brigadier.

D1 was to be about September 1970 and D2 December 1971, if I remember right. This meant, from my own point of view, that either I would have to extend my normal two-and-a-half-year tour of duty to three-and-a-half years, or someone would have to replace me at the halfway point, each of us serving there for 21 months. Not being fond of the Singapore climate, I was not keen to extend a normal tour by a year. Moreover, we were looking forward to the chance of living in the house we had bought in 1965 and to living in England for the first time since the beginning of 1963. We would then have a chance of seeing a little more of Gerry's mother, who in 1969 was already 89. It did not seem to be my duty to stay on since there were obviously others well qualified to do the job; and there was probably a fair chance of my being given one more appointment to last from about May 1970 to my 55th birthday, the normal retiring age, in July 1972.

I indicated my personal preference to Peter Hunt and he was kind enough to arrange matters accordingly. Neither of us would have dreamed of this solution had we known the man who was to succeed me. It was the only occasion in my service when I have had to hand over a job to someone who, in my opinion, was not to be trusted: I will not elaborate.

Directors in the Army Department of the Ministry of Defence were at that time major-generals and I hoped to get such a job. I did not aspire to one of the key appointments which normally led on to further promotion and I was doubly surprised to be told that I was to be VQMG (Vice Quartermaster General). Not only was this one of those key appointments but it was a job for which I felt wholly unqualified, having never held any Q post. I protested to Tom Pearson, now Military Secretary, that I had not got the right experience but he did not agree because I had managed to grip the logistic problems of Singapore. There was a world of difference between the workings of a large static base in peace and the responsibility for the operational logistics of the whole army. My deduction from this, that the powers that be wanted to give me Q experience so that I should become qualified for some further employment was quite wrong wishful thinking.

In February 1970 Gerry and I went on leave to Cambodia to see Angkor Wat and the other temples around it. We were very lucky to have this chance as the Communists moved into the area only 6 weeks later. It meant flying to Phnom Penh and changing to a local plane to fly on to the small airport for Angkor, where there was one, and only one, large hotel. We had booked in before leaving Singapore but were a little uncertain of our reception, having been told by Sir Arthur de la Mare, the British High Commissioner in Singapore, what had happened to him and his wife after they had made a similar reservation only a few months before.

Arriving at the reception desk at about 9 pm, they sought to book in: 'Very sorry, no rooms available.'

'But we have firm reservations for 3 nights.'

'Very sorry, no rooms.'

'Here is the manager's letter, confirming our booking.'

After careful study of the letter, 'Yes, a very good letter. I wrote it myself! But no rooms available. Please wait over there and we will try to arrange something.'

Having waited about 40 minutes, a guide led them to what appeared to be the royal suite and then said that they could stay for one night only. They must come to reception in the morning and book out. They avoided reception and stayed, without further argument, for their 3 nights.

We, however, had no such trouble and, soon after booking in, made our way to Angkor Wat itself, where we were only half an hour late for a performance of Cambodian dancing, floodlit in the forecourt of the temple. We had a fascinating few days amongst these temples, which were being painstakingly restored by French experts. Over the years the jungle had absorbed most of them until early in the 20th century work started on disentangling them. In most cases this meant taking each stone separately, numbering it and laying stones out in rows ready to assemble a vast 3-dimensional jigsaw puzzle.

We were due to leave Singapore in April 1970 but my next job was not to be vacant until September and so for once we had a very unhurried move. We found that the travel rules of the day allowed a major-general to travel first class by sea or air as might be convenient. Moreover, if he wished to travel by anything other than the direct route, he could claim the cost of direct travel and make his own arrangements. So we planned to go by sea to Fremantle, the port for Perth, and to stay a few days with my niece, Rosemary Stevenson, and her family in Kellerberrin, about 130 miles east; then to take the train to Melbourne, staying with friends there; and again by train to Sydney. There we were to pick up a large one-class ship, half passenger and half freight, to Auckland; 3 weeks in New Zealand and then on in the same ship from Wellington across the Pacific and home via the Panama Canal. My naval opposite number was returning home about the same time but found that naval rules did not allow the same flexibility: he had to fly!

We stayed in Perth briefly. We had, on a previous visit, had lunch with the Governor of Western Australia, Sir Douglas (Joe) Kendrew, whom I had first met when he was Director of Infantry in the War Office and thus one of the directors whom I had had to co-ordinate on behalf of the DCIGS; and again when he was British Defence Adviser in Canberra (Chapter 24). On this occasion he and his wife again invited us to lunch but this time we were the only guests. Afterwards his wife, who came from Donegal and had many acquaintances in common with Gerry, took her off to chat elsewhere, leaving him and me on our own.

He then astonished me by saying, 'Have you ever thought of taking on this job?' He explained that he had been there for 7 years and he was now being asked to extend for the second time for another 3 years and he was not keen to do so. Whether he had any authority to make such a proposal I have no idea. I did not think that it was my duty to take on such a job, if offered, because there must have been several willing and suitable people available. It would have been a fascinating job in many ways but I would not have enjoyed the ceremonial side of it and the continual entertaining. Moreover, I was keen to get back to England. I knew that Gerry would prefer not to be away for another 3 years, particularly in view of the age of her mother. So I did not consult her before turning down the idea: I did not want her to feel that I had refused the job for her sake. It would probably not have materialized anyway.

31

MINISTRY OF DEFENCE: 1970–72

My predecessor as VQMG was David Price, an old friend who had been so helpful to me in Colchester (Chapter 23). He had had considerable logistic experience and it was immediately evident to me that he had a far better command of the job than I was ever likely to have. I ought to have realized that, as I had a couple of months in hand after my arrival in England before taking over, I should have spent at least a part of that visiting logistic establishments and reading myself into the job. But I was idle.

I was lucky again in serving a delightful and very tolerant QMG, Tony Read. My job was to be responsible for the operational and planning side of army logistics; and there was a DQMG whose province was the day-to-day provision of material of all kinds. In addition I had to act for the QMG if he was away and I had a number of other jobs: to supervise the small corps with which we were concerned: Royal Army Veterinary Corps, Royal Engineers (Postal) and Army Catering Corps; and to be a member of No. 2 Selection Board, which was responsible for promotions to colonel and to brigadier and for the postings of officers in these ranks. But the most important such job was as a member of a committee called SCAO, the Standing Committee on Army Organization. This was a committee which did a lot of the routine work for the Army Board. Most subjects to be considered by the Board had been thrashed out by SCAO first.

There were 2 jobs which were a particular delight. A committee of 3 (the right size for efficiency!), the Permanent Under-Secretary for the Army, Sir Arthur Drew, the Vice Adjutant General, James Lunt, and I met infrequently to decide how best to spend the welfare funds available to the army, principally derived from a percentage of the profits from NAAFI. The other was a meeting of the Commissioners of Chelsea Hospital, which was held at the hospital at 11 am quarterly. The Governor, always a very senior recently retired officer, explained how things were going and his plans for any changes. The committee then approved his proposals and about noon we adjourned for a glass of sherry.

About the time I started this job, I also became a Colonel Commandant of the Royal Corps of Signals. Most of the Colonels Commandant were retired officers and it was assumed that they had more spare time than those still serving: so, initially, this was not onerous. Later I had to take my turn for a year as Representative Colonel Commandant, whose job was to undertake those duties which the Master of Signals passed on to him. Peter Bradley, as Master, was extremely conscientious and left me little to do. I did, however, on one occasion have to go to Lippstadt to receive the freedom of the town on behalf of 22nd Signal Regiment, which was quartered there and which had been under my command when I was CCR Signals. German and British troops were drawn up in about equal numbers on a public square, with the local civic dignitaries and many others watching. A German General and I inspected the lot and then there were speeches in both languages. My German being quite inadequate, my speech had been written out for me in both languages and I had had a tape of it in German. Having taken some trouble to mimic the tape, it seemed to be clearly understood. That evening there was a reception at which I was approached by several of my hosts in voluble German, which they were sure I would follow. They were wholly wrong.

I made one trip to Germany as VQMG and Gerry came with me; Peter Hunt, now C-in-C BAOR, was kind enough to ask us to stay. Amongst the logistic resources which I visited was a distribution point on the main oil pipeline serving BAOR. Not long before, NATO had built pipelines from the west and south coasts of France, which merged in West Germany to serve all the NATO forces there. When first completed there had been an important hitch: when getting the costs approved by NATO, no one had thought to include the cost of the fuel to fill the line before a drop was available at the front end. This was, of course, a capital cost which could not be recovered. If I remember right the figure was around £6 million.

I was due to retire in September 1972 and, before retirement, one was entitled to attend one of 2 courses: the 'bricks and mortar' course, that is to say, instruction in DIY, or a business course. I chose the latter. This was well worthwhile because, if I learnt nothing else, I learnt that business was not up my street.

I applied for numerous jobs, one of which was running VSO, Voluntary Service Overseas. There was an agency handling the selection for this appointment and I was invited, as one of a short list, for an interview. It happened that the man I had to see had been a cadet at the Royal Signals Officer Cadet Training Unit at the beginning of the war and remembered me as one of his instructors. A couple of days later I received a civil letter regretting that I was not considered suitable because it was thought that my military rank would frighten those volunteering for VSO. Had I frightened him when I was a second-lieutenant?

I was annoyed by this because I felt that this job would have been right up my street. I knew something of Whitehall and of dealing with High Commissions and the like in various parts of the world. It was not a well-paid job but a very worthwhile one. I noticed that one of the Governors of VSO was Field Marshal Sir Gerald Templer, whom I knew slightly because he had been CIGS when I was working for the DCIGS, Dick Hull. I rang him up and told him what had happened. He asked me to let him have the details in writing, saying, 'I'll have that firm out of business!'

Some weeks later, when I was already committed to another job and was on a long holiday in Portugal, I got a civil and apologetic letter from the secretary to the governing body of VSO, saying that they would like to reconsider my application. It was too late.

The job for which I had been accepted was as a Planning Inspector for the Department of the Environment. I became one of about 200 such persons, who had to determine appeals against the planning decisions of local councils, on behalf of the Secretary of State for the Environment. I spent the next 15 years dealing with a wide selection of cases, varying between whether Mrs Smith should be allowed to raise her garden wall by a foot and whether a large warehouse was legally entitled to sell furniture to individuals. The latter was a test case for others around the country with a total turnover of about half a million pounds a week.

When I was 70, the Civil Service decided that I should retire. They were quite right. I had, by then, got myself involved in so many other activities that I had no longer the time or energy for a full-time job as well.

EPILOGUE

It would have been wrong to take an active part in political matters whilst serving in the army or as a civil servant. After finally retiring, it seemed to me, in the mid-1980s, that Margaret Thatcher was really achieving something domestically and I supported the Conservative party.

Since working for NATO, however, I have been particularly interested in Europe and have considered that future peace in Europe depends on a strong NATO and a strong EEC, now European Union. Thatcher became violently anti-Europe and I was delighted when Sir Geoffrey Howe, then our local MP, achieved her downfall.

John Major said that he wanted Britain to be 'at the heart of Europe'. It did not happen. Even worse, whilst still a member of the club, when his proposals on beef were turned down in the summer of 1996, he said that he would obstruct all other club business. It is surprising that Britain was not expelled.

In September 1996 I wrote a letter to *The Times* and it was published on 8 October:

> Mr Tony Marlow writes (letter 26 September) that 'it is impossible for the Conservative party to win the election' without declared opposition to the single currency.
>
> How many are there like me (and other voters in my family) who, after a lifetime of voting Conservative, are going to vote Lib-Dem because they appear to be the only party which wholeheartedly supports the views of Heath who took us into Europe, of Thatcher who signed the declaration in favour of an ever closer Europe, and of Major who promised to put Britain at the heart of Europe?

Finding that I also supported most of their other policies, I joined the Liberal-Democrat party. With the 1997 general election approaching, I wrote again to *The Times* and my letter was published on 17 March:

> The Conservatives are no longer aiming to be 'at the heart of Europe', nor honouring their pledge to work towards 'an ever closer Europe'. Labour appear to be equally in doubt about Britain's future in Europe. Indeed their policies are no longer based on principles but, in many ways, seem to have become similar to those of the Conservatives in the hope of more votes. Liberal Democrats have consistently supported playing our full part in Europe.
>
> Our future in Europe is clearly the most important single issue for the forthcoming election and we have the choice. Let us vote Lib-Dem not Lab-Con.

It seems to me that for many centuries the wars in Europe have occurred because of excessive nationalism. Surely, by now, we should have learned to sublimate our nationalistic feelings in sport and other harmless activities? Let us be governed for the benefit of Europe as a whole.

INDEX

Ranks in this index are the highest of which I am aware.